D1528181

SUMMON the Masters

MADELEINE OH
DOMINIQUE ADAIR
JENNIFER DUNNE

ELLORA'S CAVE
ROMANTICA PUBLISHING

*W*hat the critics are saying...

❦

"I don't think Ellora's Cave could have picked three authors that better complimented each other or are better suited to this genre. […] Summon The Masters is a must read in my opinion and will not disappoint anyone who enjoys Masterful, Alpha men and the women who love them. I can't recommend this book highly enough." ~ *Two Lips Reviews*

INTERLUDE

By Madeleine Oh

"Interlude is a short but sweet, wonderfully erotic, sexy story that includes love, lust, magic, fairytales and floggers." ~ *Two Lips Reviews*

"Madeleine Oh puts the spice in erotic romance." ~ *Fallen Angel Reviews*

THE CAJUN

By Dominique Adair

"Dominique Adair brings the bayou alive in this sexy tale of love, lust, and domination. Her storm scenes will have you feeling the whipping wind and rain. Her sex scenes will leave you breathless and reaching to turn up the air conditioning. The vivid descriptions in this story bring it alive and will have you wanting more." ~ *Two Lips Reviews*

"Dominique Adair has made this reviewer believe in fate and magic once again with this awesome story." ~ *Fallen Angel Reviews*

LIFE SENTENCE

By Jennifer Dunne

"The chemistry is unmatched and explodes off the pages of this short but intense story." ~ *Two Lips Reviews*

"Life Sentence takes the reader thru a gallant of emotions that will have you screaming for more." ~ *Fallen Angel Reviews*

An Ellora's Cave Romantica Publication

www.ellorascave.com

Summon the Masters

ISBN 9781419957222
ALL RIGHTS RESERVED.
Interlude Copyright © 2007 Madeleine Oh
The Cajun Copyright © 2007 Dominique Adair
Life Sentence Copyright © 2007 Jennifer Dunne
Edited by Mary Moran and Sue-Ellen Gower.
Cover art by Syneca.

This book printed in the U.S.A. by Jasmine–Jade Enterprises, LLC.

Electronic book Publication January 2007
Trade paperback Publication March 2008

SUMMON THE MASTERS
ଛୠ

INTERLUDE
By Madeleine Oh
~11~

THE CAJUN
By Dominique Adair
~105~

LIFE SENTENCE
By Jennifer Dunne
~185~

INTERLUDE

Madeleine Oh

ജ

Trademarks Acknowledgement

∞

The author acknowledges the trademarked status and trademark owners of the following wordmarks mentioned in this work of fiction:

Fiat: Fiat S.p.A. Corporation Italy

Magic Wand: Hitachi Sales Corporation

Technicolor: Technicolor Videocassette B.V. Corporation Netherlands

The Chronicles of Narnia: C.S. Lewis (PTE) Ltd. Corporation Singapore

Interlude

Chapter One

෨

"Wales? For six weeks! You're going to miss me."

Alex looked into Tom's blue eyes and barely managed to hold back the laugh. She would not miss Tom's moods, pouts and manipulations. She would miss getting spanked regularly and, she had to acknowledge, his skill with bondage and incredible performance with oral sex, but Tom Hampton was one whiny Dom and she was not going to miss his complaining. "I promised my aunt. I can't let her down." She hadn't shared with Tom that the said aunt would be in Tibet while Alex house sat. If he knew that, he'd want to tag along. "Have to run. It takes ages to get through security. Bye." She kissed him goodbye—they had been lovers after all—and joined the end of the winding line.

She was on her way.

A day and a half and a transatlantic flight later, after a long drive fueled by several cups of coffee, Alex was actually standing in front of Aunt Maria's cottage, assailed by second thoughts…and third ones.

"That's *Dwr ffynnon*," Dai Hughes, her aunt's lawyer, said as they stood in front of a stone cottage built right against the hillside.

"De…what?" she asked, not understanding.

He had a downright sexy smile. Nice eyes too. "*Dwr ffynnon*," he repeated. "Spring Water in the English."

"It's small!" she muttered. Heck, she'd seen bigger garages.

"Not so small really," Dai Hughes replied. She hadn't realized she'd spoken aloud. "You'll find it snug inside. Miss

11

Abbott, well she likes her comfort."

Maybe, but did eccentric Aunt Maria's idea of comfort match Alex's? What the hell, she'd agreed. She couldn't let Aunt Maria down. She'd stay and besides, watching Dai Hughes' nice firm ass as he bent into his car to retrieve a bundle of keys was no hardship. If he was representative of the local talent, things couldn't be too bad.

"Here you are," he said, handing over the keys. "I promised your aunt I'd take care of you. Anything you want, just let me know."

To see you naked. Better restrain herself. "I just need to move my things in and get settled. Thanks a bunch for coming up here. I'd never have found it on my own."

"Let me give you a hand."

He gave more than a hand.

He willingly toted in her two suitcases and the numerous bags of groceries she'd picked up in the village. Unnecessarily as it turned out, he'd already stocked the ancient fridge. He even had the thoughtfulness to strip off his sweater and give her a private viewing of his broad back and strong muscled arms.

Not bad at all.

"That's it then," he said looking around the kitchen. "Not as dreadful as you feared, eh?"

He was right about that. Inside, the cottage was neat, clean and well-furnished. It was a little odd, having no rear windows as the cottage really was built into the hillside, but the kitchen was bright and airy and Dai—or someone—had already lit the vast kitchen stove. With the curtains drawn against the early dusk, it would be downright cozy.

"Can I offer you a cup of tea?" Seemed a little more judicious than asking him to strip for her, and besides, much as her mind might lust after him, her jetlagged tired body just wasn't up to it. Yet.

His downright sexy smile held all sorts of invitations and promises. A smile like his was worth bottling up and keeping for times of abstinence. "Wish I could. I'd better get back down. It's my turn to pick the sprogs up from school."

Great! She'd been lusting after a married man. A cast-iron no-no in her book. Might as well smile graciously as she wondered about the unknown female fortunate enough to have snagged this hunk. "Oh! Thanks for your help and I hope I haven't made you late."

His dark curls ruffled as he shook his head. "Nah! I'll be in plenty of time." He turned toward the door. "You have the office number and my mobile, right? Call if you need anything but I think you're all set."

He was gone, all six-feet, testosterone-laden hunk of him. Off to pick up the offspring and no doubt go home to fuck his wife. Leaving Alex alone in the middle of wild Wales in a house that rather redefined the adjective "quaint". Damn! She should have pumped Dai Hughes for a little more info on Aunt Maria.

The only comment he'd made was, "Always a smiling woman, your aunt." And, Alex had to admit, the cottage did exude an air of peace and contentment.

An hour or so later she'd unpacked and warmed up a can of soup for dinner. Not exactly gourmet fare but with half a bottle of elderflower wine left on the table, it wasn't half bad sitting by the stove, sipping the tart wine, smiling to herself as she leaned back in the chair and listened to the humming.

Humming? Or was it a distant faint roar?

She sat up. No doubt about it. There was a steady noise nearby. Where? The next best thing to antique refrigerator? The stove? The vast copper water heater? It wasn't a mechanical sound but not quite human either. It sounded…magical.

What on earth was she thinking? She had had too much wine. Just as well she'd made up the bed when she unpacked.

Better get upstairs and sleep it off. Except she opened the wrong door. Instead of the door to the narrow stairway to the attic bedroom, Alex opened the basement door.

Stone stairs led down into darkness. She was half inclined to shut the door and head on up to the attic bedroom but the cussed and curious half fumbled around for a light switch. After scraping her knuckles on the rough stone wall, she found a swinging cord with what felt like an empty cotton spool on the end. She pulled and a weak light bulb illuminated the spiral stone stairway. Darn good thing she hadn't tried descending in the dark. The light didn't penetrate much beyond the top of the stairs so Alex grabbed a good-sized flashlight and set off downward and found another light switch at the bottom of the stairs. As she flicked it on, bright fluorescent light lit up the low-ceilinged area. "Area" was the word for it. It had to be twice as big—at least—as the cottage above. Was it built on the ruin of a much larger house? She'd ask Aunt Maria when she got back.

Meanwhile, might as well have a good look-see. The space nearest the stairs was set up as a pantry-wine cellar with enough supplies to outlast a siege or nuclear attack. Alex remembered Aunt Maria saying, "If you need to use any of my supplies, dear, feel free. Just promise to replace what you take." There was also a well-stocked wine rack. Filled with a variety of homemade wine. Not that Alex needed any more to drink tonight.

A large worktable filled the center of the room. Beyond that more shelves and cupboards, and at the far end, where the basement narrowed presumably into the side of the hill, was a heavy, dark, iron-banded door. On closer inspection, it looked like an old church door or something out of a castle, complete with black iron studs, vast hinges and a keyhole two inches high.

And no key in sight.

She was curious, and when she put her ear to the door,

she'd swear the humming, buzz, roar, whatever, was coming from the other side. A generator perhaps? Why lock it up?

Curiosity got the better of Alex. She ran, grabbed the ring of a handle, turned and pulled, but it wouldn't budge. No use trying the modern front door key, it would probably fall right though and get lost in whatever was the other side. Alex looked under a couple of nearby boxes for a hidden key but no luck.

She thumped on the door with her fist. No use of course, but it did make a satisfyingly solid thud. She'd have to go to bed, curiosity unsatisfied.

She'd ask Dai Hughes in the morning.

After she had a good night's sleep.

And the odds of a good night's sleep would be greatly increased after a little self-loving. Thanks to her trusty Magic Wand and the adapter and transformer she'd had the forethought to bring, Alex was all set for a self-induced thrill or two.

It wasn't quite the same as getting chained to the bedpost and spread-eagled but she could spread her own legs and grasping the brass bedhead with her free hand and a little imagination would get her humming.

Literally.

As Alex caressed her breasts with the dildo, the sound echoed in her ears, like the soft, persistent hum of the generator downstairs. She closed her eyes to better concentrate on the sensations in her body. The gentle vibrations rippled through her and her nipples went hard as pleasure flowed from her breasts down to her cunt. Waves of goose bumps skittered over her arms and back as she slowly eased the head of the vibrator over her belly and down toward her clit.

She stopped just above, wanting the pleasure of the diffuse sensation spread all over her pussy. She was wet now, really wet, anticipating the thrill of climax, but wanting to extend the buildup as long as possible.

"You've been bad!" she thought to herself, trying hard to adopt the tone and cadence of Tom's voice when they were playing. *"Very bad. Don't you agree?"*

"Yes," she whispered. "I have. I'm sorry."

"Sorry isn't good enough," the Dom in her head paused, waiting. *"Is it?"*

"No," she whimpered. Her voice faltering as wild thrills poured into her cunt, leaving her wetter and hornier than ever. "It isn't."

She pressed the head of her dildo harder against her flesh, upping the sensation and the anticipation.

"Only one thing for it," her imaginary lover replied. *"Discipline is what you need, my girl. Good, hard discipline you won't ever forget. You agree, don't you?"*

"Yes!" she whispered in her mind.

"Right! Roll over and don't keep me waiting. Your ass needs to feel the flat of my hand."

She flipped onto her belly, letting go of her grasp of the bed and slipping the dildo between her cunt lips. Shutting her eyes to imagine the hand descending, the slap of flesh on flesh and the sting of impact, she counted—one…two…three. She drove her hips into the mattress as if responding to the impact and came in a crashing, blinding climax.

Heart racing, she eased the dildo away and flicked the switch off then indulged herself in lying limp between the sheets as wild sensation washed over her. Slowly she moved, picking up the dildo and slipping it into a drawer in the bedside table then pulling the sheets up to her chin and curling on her side as the slow-fading after-ripples skimmed across her sated body.

She felt incredible—relaxed, stimulated and satisfied. No, she was not going to miss Tom. Not much anyway. Of course if it had been sexy Dai Hughes chastising her or tying her to the bed with soft cords, she wouldn't complain. Or better still, feeling the sting of the wide leather belt that held up his pants. Well damn, she was not going there. That pleasure was no doubt reserved for Mrs. Hughes, lucky woman. Besides, what were the odds he was just a vanilla lover anyway?

Better to imagine him the kinky master of her dreams. Nothing like a wild fantasy sex life to keep her happy and it wouldn't entail poaching in another woman's bed.

Even if she did fancy Dai Hughes naked, hard and in her bed.

And with that thought, she drifted off into a deep, relaxed sleep.

* * * * *

Something woke her. A night sound in an unfamiliar house? A movement in the dark? The moon shining though a gap in the curtains?

A shadow moved in the dark and the mattress shifted as if someone were…

Chapter Two

Ⴀ

"Don't be alarmed, Alex," the lilting voice of Dai Hughes told her. "You wanted me. I'm here."

She tried to sit up but a strong hand on her shoulder held down. "How did you know?"

"Your eyes told me, your face said so and your body begged me to return."

Bullshit, she hadn't been that obvious, had she? Besides this was a dream. Might as well enjoy it. "And what did my body beg you for?"

"This!" A dark hand closed over her wrist and pulled her hand over her head. A deep, very male chuckle greeted her sigh. "Know what I want?" he asked as he reached for her other hand. "You, helpless."

Somehow he'd tied her as he spoke. She hadn't seen him move but when she tugged, her hands were bound fast over her head.

"You love this, don't you?" the dark voice continued. "You like being bound. Yearn to submit to whatever I desire. You want to be caressed, stroked, pinched, licked, slapped, kissed." As he spoke, his hands matched each word.

Her body responded. Heating under his touch. Need building between her legs.

Deep in the recesses of her mind, Alex thought she should be frightened, anxious, terrified even, at a stranger in her bedroom rendering her helpless. But it was only a dream, wasn't it? A wonderful dream. As her shadow lover spoke in the rhythmic cadence of Dai's voice.

"That's how I want you," he went on. "Bound and naked

for my pleasure." He pulled off the bedclothes, exposing her to the night. She was naked. Naked and needy.

"Why are you here? Who are you?" she managed to croak out as his hand cupped her pussy.

"You called me," he replied. "I'm the lover of your dreams."

The last bit might be right but... "I didn't call you."

He replied with a deep chuckle. "Oh yes, you did, and I'm not leaving until you're satisfied."

Didn't sound too bad as dreams went. Much better than finding herself at the bus stop in her pajamas or getting chased by a raging lion. "What are you going to do?"

"Fuck you, Alex. I'll fuck your cunt, fuck your mouth, even..." His hands slipped under to caress her ass cheeks, "Fuck your tight little arsehole. You like that, don't you?"

"Yes." It came out like a sigh. Hard to talk coherently with a strong, male finger pressing into said orifice.

"I thought so, you bad girl!" The finger whisked out, leaving her feeling opened and vulnerable. "You like it too much so I won't bugger you tonight. That can wait for next time. Meanwhile..." His hand eased up her belly and back down. "I can do whatever I want with you and I will. I want your breasts..." His hands stroked up to cup them, hefting them gently before he kissed each nipple, pulling them between his lips and dragging his tongue over them until she sighed. "Your neck." He trailed fingertips up the outside of her neck, over her throat and down the other side. "Your arms." Both hands stroked up and down, pausing only to test the knots.

Satisfied, he held her face in both hands. The room was still too dark to see anything but a shadowy outline that descended until his lips brushed hers. "Open for me," he said. "Your mouth is mine!"

She parted her lips, pressing up to him as he opened her

mouth with his. Wild need flushed through her as the tip of his tongue touched hers. Her gasp was swallowed by his kiss. Fast, hard, demanding, his lips and tongue took over her mouth. He kissed with a force and passion that stirred her need. Alex ground her hips upward, straining to make contact with his body, his cock, the arousal he surely must feel. But she felt nothing. Was as if he were only a mouth and tongue and hands.

It was enough.

As his lips took over her will, his hands stroked the sides of her face and caressed her neck. She wanted, needed, more but when she let out a little groan of pleasure, he lifted his mouth away.

The groan became a moan. "More," she muttered. "I want more."

"You'll get more. Much more," he promised. "When I deem you ready. You must be patient. Wait like a dutiful submissive. Accept my strictures and my demands. You will, won't you?" The last he whispered in her ear, his breath warm against her skin. "Won't you!" he repeated so loudly that she jumped.

Not that she could go far tied up like a bale of hay. "Yes!"

"Good." His hand brushed her nipples then trailed lower, pausing over her belly. "I have you compliant and exactly where I want you. What next?" he mused as if to himself. She was darn sure her input was not being solicited. "Shall I open your lovely legs wide and tie your ankles down so you are spread-eagled for fucking at my convenience? Or should I roll you over onto this delightful belly and slap your luscious arse red? Perhaps squeeze those pert little nipples with nasty, tight clamps?" Alex bit her lip. If she let on how much she hated nipple clamps, he'd use them. Tight as possible.

Better play the good little submissive and lie there and wait.

While her cunt flowed like a river.

He had to notice. Surely? She could smell her arousal. He had to be oblivious not to react. She so wanted to feel his cock. See the proof of her effect on him. But she might as well be blindfolded for the little she could make out in the darkness.

Was she blindfolded? Had he put one on her as she slept? No, she could see a little. Barely. Shapes and shadows as he moved, his weight shifting off the bed. A hand closed over each ankle. Was he making good on his threat? Spreading her wide, pinning her utterly helpless flat on her back? Alex took a deep, contented breath in anticipation.

He grasped her ankles, kissed them, opened her thighs and lifted her legs high. Moments later she was spread but with her ankles tied to the ceiling. How? She hadn't noticed hooks or rings, but it was a dream, wasn't it? Who needed accurate hardware?

And she was helpless, more than she'd ever been, even moving her hips took great effort. He'd tied her ankles so securely she had little room to shift.

It felt wonderful! Her sigh of utter pleasure and delight echoed in the dark room.

"Like that, do you? Have a little pervy soul, do you?"

Before she could reply or even consider if a response was expected. His mouth came down, his warm tongue lapped her cunt lips, opening them as he tasted her arousal.

The groan was totally uncontrollable. So was the loud sigh as the tip of his tongue flicked her clit. She'd have been off the bed if his ropes and hands didn't have her fast.

"Like that, do you?"

She just about managed to gasp out, "Yes!"

"Thought so!" He was back, tongue and lips arousing her mercilessly, pleasuring her wondrously as she shut her eyes, gave up any attempt to restrain her cries and let the wild joy engulf her. She'd be happy to lie here forever as his skilled tongue and lips brought her closer and closer to climax.

Until he moved off her with a last gentle brush of his lips across her clit that almost sent her over the top.

Almost but not quite.

A touch of her thumb, a stroke of her finger, and she'd be soaring. But her hands were tied fast to the damn bedposts.

"Patience, Alex. All in good time," he said from the foot of the bed. "High time you pleasured me a little."

As he spoke, he straddled her chest, his strong thighs encasing her, his hands cradling her head. How had he moved so fast? Impossible! Not in a dream. "Suck my cock, Alex. Swallow me deep. Adore me with your mouth."

The head of a seemingly enormous cock brushed her lips. Just as well it was dark. If she'd seen anything this vast in daylight, she'd have gasped with horror. As it was, she just relaxed as her lips encircled him and he pulled her head closer to press deep in her mouth.

By rights she should be gagging. But it was a dream and she accommodated him with ease, her tongue lapping the smooth round head and tasting the sweet bead of male honey. She suckled him, relishing the hard, warm flesh as she ran her tongue and lips up and down his length. He groaned with appreciation. That spurred Alex on, bursting with the power of what she could do to this phantom lover, she relaxed her throat and swallowed him deep, breathing slowly as he penetrated her deeper than any other lover. Deeper than in her wildest dreams. Still her mouth took him and pleasure all but clouded her brain.

He eased back slowly, but reluctant to lose him, to end this possession, her lips grasped his flesh as her tongue explored the ridges that marked this cock. She teased his frenulum with the tip of her tongue, circled his ridge with her lips and wanted to hold him in her power forever.

What she really wanted was to reach up and pull him deep again, to run her fingers over his cock, to stroke his foreskin and to adore his erection with her fingertips. He wanted her bound.

Bound, she would be content.

He pulled out and moved away.

She couldn't hold back the moan, the utter and engulfing disappointment.

What if he disappeared, leaving her bound and helpless, unable to bring herself off? Stuck on the brink until she awoke.

His pressed her thighs even wider apart and entered her in one hard thrust that made her cry out.

He was enormous, stretching, filling, stuffing, her with his muscle, arrogance and heat.

"Like it, my cock?" he asked. "You've been wanting it all along, haven't you?"

"Yes! Yes! Yes!" she screamed in rhythm to his thrusts. "Oh! Yes!"

Her climax peaked fast. Alex came with a great shout as he took her over the edge. She was panting as her screams quieted to gasps and her shoulders sagged back onto the pillow.

He held her fast, still pistoning in the same hard tempo until with his thumb pressing into her clit she came again and again.

"Enough!" she gasped out. "I can't take any more!"

"You can and will," he replied as another climax smashed into her.

She lost count how many times she came, never noticed when he climaxed, lost in a wild sensual fog until she passed out.

* * * * *

She awoke late. The morning sun beaming through a chink in the curtains and the bedclothes neatly tucked around her.

Impossible after such a wondrously wild dream. But there it was. The bed as neat and straight as when she'd curled under the covers last night.

And she felt wonderful. Relaxed. Her body satisfied. Her mind still replaying the wild erotic dream. Odd that she hadn't woken as she climaxed but she wasn't complaining. Sleeping on, she'd enjoyed an impossible string of climaxes. And what a cock. Talk about the answer to a woman's prayer, and the man attached to it definitely knew what to do with his power. He was damn good at the dominant role too.

Pity it was just a dream.

She'd try some more of that elderflower wine again. Soon.

She was debating whether to ease her sated and loose body out from between the sheets or to doze some more with the hopes of repeating the dream when her cell rang.

Downstairs.

She was tempted to let it ring into voice mail but it might be her mother checking she'd arrived safely.

Snapping her mind back to reality, Alex nipped downstairs, glad of the warmth of her flannel robe in the cold kitchen. The wretched stove had gone out in the night.

And it wasn't her mother.

"Hi, Alex, it's Tom."

Tom who? she thought for a minute. Then remembered. "Oh! Hi."

"Missing me?"

He had to be joking. After last night! He'd never give her six, seven-plus climaxes in an evening. "I'm fine, Tom. Still settling in."

"Is it some awful hovel?"

The nerve of him. "Good grief no! My aunt lives in a lovely cottage halfway up a mountain. A bit remote but the views are fantastic and the village is just a short drive down the mountain." Or a long walk if she really felt energetic, which wasn't likely any time today.

"You really are serious, aren't you?"

At last he was getting it. "Yes, Tom. I am. I'll be here six weeks."

"I miss you."

She didn't miss him but that seemed a particularly nasty thing to say. "You'll be fine, Tom." That she didn't doubt. "I must run. I'll call you." Men told that one often enough. It was her turn.

She snapped her phone shut and looked around for the kettle. She needed coffee.

Chapter Three

๛

After her second cup and her finally successful efforts to relight the stove using Aunt Maria's store of kindling, Alex was sitting back, basking in the warmth and debating the merits of toast or cereal for breakfast when a car engine sounded up the lane, stopping at the end of her path.

She listened as the gate opened and closed and confident footsteps walked up to the front door. He didn't knock. Somehow she just knew it was a "he" but Dai's lilting voice called out, "Miss Carpenter, Alex? It's Dai Hughes," as he rattled the doorknob.

And here she was, lolling about in her robe! After that dream last night, she was most definitely not entertaining Dai Hughes, *déshabille*. "Hang on! The door's locked. *Thank heaven!* Let me run and get the key!"

Upstairs in a trice, she yanked off the robe and pulled on briefs and blue jeans. Tempted to just pull on her sweatshirt, caution prevailed and she paused the few seconds it took to hook up her bra and raced downstairs, stopping only to grab the key off the kitchen mantelpiece.

The door opened to morning sunshine and Dai Hughes' dark eyes. Not forgetting the sexy morning grin. Reminding herself very firmly that she was not going to lust after a married man—dreaming didn't count—Alex returned his smile.

"I was passing and just thought to see if there was anything I could do you for."

She was not going to tell him. Ever. "Lovely of you to drop by." She opened the door and six feet whatever of male presence stepped over the threshold. He wore a dark blue sweater that smelled of fresh air and maleness and no doubt had been knitted by the mother of his children. "As it happens there is something. The door in the basement that's locked and leads to the generator. Where's the key?"

He paused, looking at her intently. "Found it already, did you?"

"It's rather impossible to miss."

"It's not a generator."

"What is it then?"

He paused as if pondering her question then shrugged. "What the heck? Your aunt never said not to show you. If she left the key, it'll be there."

Obviously! And how come he knew all about it? He led the way down the spiral staircase, finding the light switch at the bottom with an ease that showed he knew his way around. Without hesitating, he crossed to the door and reached up to the top corner of the frame and unhooked a large black key from a nail that was high and in shadow, easily missed in the dark last night.

Hand on the iron ring he turned and met her eyes. "This part of the cottage is old. Very old. I think the door must have been put on for safely. It's not a generator." He smiled. "It's a hot spring. Morgaine's spring they call it in these parts." The key turned easily and as he opened the door, he reached to his right and pulled on a cord light switch.

Before she could wonder yet again how he knew his way around so well, Alex's attention was drawn from speculation about Dai Hughes to total fascination with the chamber beyond the door.

It was a cave with a high-domed ceiling and a more or less smooth floor, or at least a wide path was worked or worn smooth, the rest was rough rock. What caught her attention was the spume of white water cascading from a fissure high in one wall and the warmth. She'd been in cooler saunas.

"It's incredible," she said, half to herself. "This is just sitting here behind a door in the basement!"

"It was here long before the cottage," he replied quietly. Seemed the atmosphere inclined one to lower one's voice.

"How long?" As she spoke, she guessed his reply.

"Some claim it's where Morgaine drew her powers and think you on what she was supposed to have done."

"Morgaine le Fay of the Arthur legends? That Morgaine?"

He nodded. "This is Arthur's country. It's not far from here that the supposed fight between the red and white dragons occurred."

"And the locals believe this was her well?"

In the dim light his teeth shone white. "Not just the locals. My gran used to talk how back in her gran's day people came from miles around on the great holidays to dip their hands in Morgaine's well. That was before the inn burned down."

"The inn?"

He nodded. "There was an inn here." He looked up. "Right overhead. It burned down just after the First World War. The reverend of one of the local chapels decided it was a bastion of heathen worship and witchcraft and led a party of his devout followers on an arson raid."

"Destroyed it?"

"Yes. Was years afterward, the hill farmer who owned the land built the cottage for his mother. She died when I was a kid. The cottage was then let to one of the English then empty again until your aunt bought it. She did it up, moved in and gave word out that if anyone wanted to visit the spring, they were welcome."

"And they come?" Alex had a vision of scores of villages tramping though the house while she was working.

"Not many. My gran had me bring her up here a while

before she died. Most people have forgotten what it was. Once in a while a few of the New Age Wiccanny sorts make the trip but not many these days remember Morgaine and her power."

"Magic, wasn't it?"

"So they say. She entrapped and seduced Merlin if the tales are true. Maybe it was magic. Perhaps it was all made up by the storytellers." He shrugged. "Who's to tell?" He looked at her, a glint in his dark eyes. "Going to try bathing in Morgaine's well?"

"It would certainly be warmer than the water in the shower!" Come to think of it, not a bad idea. Not that she was discussing showering with Dai Hughes.

Dai stripped off his sweater to reveal a very flattering and formfitting dark blue shirt. Just imagining the manly chest underneath had sent her nipples hard, and *that* he did not need to know.

He smiled. Almost as if he'd guessed anyway. "I bet it would," he said, stepping to the edge of the stone basin and kneeling. "Natural hot spring. Feel it."

With a smile like that, she bet he got his own way often. It just wasn't going to work on her…but refusing seemed petty. She was curious after all. Nothing quite like having instant hot water spurt out of the wall for you.

She sat on the edge, keeping a safe distance. He'd rolled up his shirtsleeves and even in the dim light, she could make out the muscles under his skin as he moved his hand though the water in a figure eight, sending small ripples against the edge of the pool.

Warm wasn't the word. It felt like bath water. "People came here to bathe and take the waters, like in Bath?" Was she living atop a Neolithic spa?

He nodded. "Some say it was once an ancient water shrine. Could well have been. Who knows?" He grinned, a little dimple forming in his chin. "If you won't bathe with me, at least take the waters. Just like at Bath."

Why not? Couldn't taste worse than the Bath spa water she'd once tried in her student days. He already had his hands cupped and filled with water. The look he gave as good as dared her.

She cupped her hand and raised the warm water to her lips and sipped. If drinking warm water were to her taste, she'd have like it. No trace of sulfur or heavy minerals, just the fresh tang of clean mountain water. Warmed up. Courtesy of Mother Nature and maybe Morgaine le Fay.

Alex turned to Dai and all but scowled at the look of sheer interest, desire and speculation in his dark eyes. Dark eyes that met hers as he raised his cupped hands to his mouth. She watched him, annoyed and mesmerized as his Adam's apple moved as he swallowed. He lowered his hands and smiled.

It was not a friendly, "What can I do to help?" smile. This one emanated sexual interest and excitement, and she was having none of it.

Standing, Alex shook the last drops of water off her fingers and rubbed her hands on her jeans. "Thanks a bunch for showing me this. I need to lock it back up and get on with some work. I bet you need to get to the office too." God! She was babbling.

But he got the message.

"Sure there's nothing I can do you for?" he asked as she led the way out at a very brisk pace.

"Honestly, no. I need to get to work and sometime today I'm going to check with the post office about getting mail delivered."

"No need to. Sid Evans will see it gets up here. When you have any, that is. I told him yesterday you'd moved in."

Thoughtful of him. Perhaps.

"Thanks. That's it then, I've enough groceries to withstand a siege and I have to get to work." Hint, hint, hint.

He got it.

"I'd best be off then. You have my mobile number?" She did. "Good luck with the work. Miss Abbot said you were a writer."

Yes, of fetish and kinky erotica, but that she was not sharing. "That's right and I have a deadline looming."

He paused, hand on the doorknob. "Would you care to come to a local Eisteddfod this a weekend? We've some good singers in these parts and it would be a way to meet some people. Think about it."

"Thanks. Sounds great." It did. She wasn't sure why the hell she'd accepted but it didn't sound like a date. "Are your family going?" Might as well be sure.

"Yes indeed. All of them!" he laughed. "To see if I hit a wrong note. I'm competing," he added with a grin. "So are my niece and nephew."

"I'll look forward to it." And meeting Mrs. Hughes would no doubt settle down her fantasies.

He seemed pleased. Delighted even. "I'll give you a bell Thursday or Friday morning about times."

"Great." Maybe.

Chapter Four

જી

Too late to debate the pros and cons of accepting the invitation. Alex poured another cup of coffee, decided cereal was marginally easier than toast and once she had cleared the dishes, set up her laptop at one end of the vast, scrubbed pine table.

Five hours later she had a kink in her neck and aching shoulders but a—hopefully—saleable story based on her wild dream.

Alex stood, stretched and thought wistfully of the whirlpool at her gym the other side of the Atlantic.

Except…

Didn't she have her own personal heated natural spa? Surely Morgaine le Fay wouldn't begrudge a hardworking woman a dip in her pool?

Gathering up a stack of Aunt Maria's generously sized bath towels and grabbing the broom to test the depth for safety, Alex went down to the basement, unlocked the old door, clicked on the light and stepped into the cave. A cautious test with the broom handle around the sides of the pool showed that the first three feet or so weren't bottomless.

Dropping the towels on the rocks, Alex stripped, stepped in up to her chest and let the warm water flow around her as she moved cautiously away from the edge. A careful walk across showed the deepest part was up to her armpits and the bottom of the pool was surprisingly smooth. She floated on her back, looking up at the curved rock roof overhead then rolled over to let the warm water caress her breasts. A few gentle kicks and her pussy felt the benefit too.

This was the life! No wonder Aunt Maria was always so laid-back and easygoing. A couple of easy strokes brought Alex to the end of the pool, just under the waterfall. Testing the depth, she found it was deeper here, but treading water as the warm cascade poured over her head and the swirling water flowed over her entire body was sheer and utter bliss.

Noticing a wide ledge under the waterfall, she pulled herself out of the pool and perched on the smooth slab of rock. Sitting here, she felt the force of the water pour over her naked body. Alex closed her eyes and turning her face to the cascade, leaned back against the rock wall.

No wonder people once traveled for miles to bathe here. Bless Aunt Maria for sharing. Holding her breasts up to catch the full force of the water and spreading her legs so the water ran between them, Alex vowed to make this sybaritic pleasure a daily ritual.

She sat there until her hands and feet wrinkled like prunes, slipped back into the water for one last dip and swam the two or three strokes necessary to reach the far side and climbed out.

Wrapping one towel around like a sarong, Alex gathered up her shoes and clothes, clicked off the light and locked the door behind her. The kitchen was warmed by the stove. She'd dry off there and indulge in a glass of elderflower wine. She'd skipped lunch so wine and a chunk of cheese would go down nicely.

Emerging from the cellar, she left her clothes in a pile at the top of the stairs and crossed to the fridge. She was reaching in for the bottle and the cheese when the door of the cottage opened.

"Ever heard of knocking?" she snapped as she turned and saw Dai standing in the doorway. "What are you doing here?" Damn the man, he grinned.

"The door was open," he said. "I have your ticket for the Eisteddfod." He crossed the room and put a slip of blue paper on the table. "You'll be sitting with my family. They want to meet you." Damn that smile again. "As are half the town. Some of the old biddies are downright perturbed that I've already seen you and they missed your arrival."

He was seeing far too much! Alex hitched the towel tighter and he had the nerve to take three steps closer. And eye her appreciatively.

"Nice outfit." His breath was warm on her face and damn him, she was getting warm everywhere else. His arm moved. She stepped back, against the cold metal of the fridge door. "Wear only a towel often, do you?"

She was not putting up with this, no matter now sexy, bed-worthy and luscious he was! "Only when I've been enjoying my personal warm spring and am not expecting intruders."

She fancied he hadn't even processed the last bit. "You've been bathing in Morgaine's spring?" He made it sound illegal. Hadn't he clearly told her people used to come from far and wide to dip in the pool?

The smile on his wide mouth became positively lupine. Cold goose bumps skipped down her spine. She was alone, the next best thing to naked with a man who was definitely interested. She would not look down but she could make an educated guess as to his state below the waist. Alex edged sideways, shut the fridge door with a satisfying thud and took a step nearer the sink. If she were fast enough and had to, she could make a dash for the butcher knives. "Yes, I have," she replied. And why shouldn't she?

He didn't move but his eyes gleamed with interest…and mischief. Male mischief. "I never told you precisely why people came to bathe in the spring, did I?"

She couldn't help it. "Why?"

The chuckle was the sort to curl any woman's toes. Even one long cold and dead and six feet down in the rocky ground. "It was said it restored potency, stirred sexual desire and made one irresistible to the opposite sex."

Oh! Please! Spare the subtleties! "It's great for washing hair too."

Was there no squashing him? The glint in his dark eyes seemed to count every damp curl around her face and no doubt was imagining the lower ones. "Look, thank you for bringing the ticket, will you please go? I need to get dressed."

"I'd say you do," he replied, not the least abashed. "You'd better wear more than that Friday night, you don't want to shock the locals."

"If they're like you, they're unshockable!"

A pretty good response but unfortunately, by the time she thought it up, he was halfway down the garden path. What was it about Dai Hughes that he seemed to have an infallible gift for coming to her front door when she was *dishabille*?

She turned the key in the lock before nipping upstairs to find clothes. Dai Hughes wasn't dropping in unannounced twice.

* * * * *

David Lloyd George Hughes, better know to friends and family as Dai, whistled to himself as he drove down the mountain. Nothing like the sight of everything but the best parts of Alex Carpenter to tease and make life—and him— hard. Trouble was, for maybe the first time in is adult life, Dai wasn't sure what to do about a woman. He knew what he wanted to do to Alex—kiss her until she begged for more and then give it to her. Preferably with her tied to the bed or bent over so he gave her a lovely fuck from the rear while he caressed her luscious arse. And if that arse were nice and rosy from a well-administered, over-the-knee spanking so much the better.

Whoa!

He was getting ahead of himself. Still a man could dream,

and fantasies of Alex were no hardship. Apart from the hardship in his pants. Still she hadn't thrown him out. All right, he hadn't given her much chance to. But oh how he'd fancied unwinding that towel and satisfying himself that her breasts were as delicious as his imagination insisted. And what about the soft curls covering her pussy?

A man could think all afternoon on the possibilities. Would be much more interesting than finishing the conveyance on Ted Reese's house. However he did have a job to hold down and he'd taken off enough time picking up and driving around his sister's children the past three days. Yes, he had volunteered to take care of them so Blodwen could go off with Samuel to the undertakers trade show in Blackpool. He'd even suggested they stay a couple of extra days and make a holiday of it. Any other week of the year he'd have been quite content to spend his evenings cooking fish fingers and heating up baked beans for their tea. Now with Alex up the mountain, Dai could name more satisfying ways to spend an evening than helping with homework or supervising teeth cleaning.

Two more days and Blod and Sam would be back, and then it was the Eisteddfod and Alex was coming as his guest.

She'd agreed, hadn't she? And taken the ticket. He was half tempted to drive up that evening and bring her down to make sure she came, but the Wesley Chapel men's choir was opening the competition and he was the lead tenor.

Chapter Five

ဢ

Dai might be gone but he sure as hell wasn't forgotten. Alex couldn't decide whether to run after him, take a cold shower or spend a pleasant interlude with her vibrator. She suspected nothing would make the slightest difference. The man was far, far hotter that Morgaine le Fay's spring.

Better get her thoughts onto other tracks. Working on a sexy story wasn't going to help her state of mind. After pulling on jeans and a sweatshirt, she dug out her half-finished mystery, poured herself a generous glass of Aunt Maria's wine, cut a nice hunk of cheese, propped her feet up on the polished brass fender and settled by the stove for a nice relaxing read.

It worked.

In no time she'd calmed down, relegated Dai Hughes to the furthermost recesses of her mind and was engrossed in the knotty problem confronting Adam Dalgleish. Half an hour and another glass or two later, Alex set the book aside and sat half asleep in the warmth.

She should get up and get moving. She'd intended to explore the village this afternoon. Later. She was quite comfortable enough here for the time being.

She let her eyes drop shut and thought about the sheer sybaritic luxury of her own private hot spring. Small wonder Aunt Maria had buried herself in the vastness of wild Wales and never came home again. Alex was sorely tempted.

"Don't be scared, I won't harm you, *cariad*."

It was the voice from her dream last night. No one could have come in. The door was locked. Alex tried to turn but her head wouldn't move and her arms were fixed to the chair. "What do you want?" she asked.

"You," the voice went on, "helpless." Hands cupped her breasts. "Aroused." The phantom fingers swept lower and found her crotch. "You are, aren't you? I can smell you."

Damn, she was, but it was a dream, wasn't it? "You do it to me."

"I'll do more." She hoped so. "Later."

"Now!"

"Tsk, tsk. Naughty, impatient girl! We can't have that."

"Why not?" asking for trouble, but this was a dream…

"Because I can make you wait, *cariad*. I can keep you on the edge until you beg me to permit you to come."

"I won't ever beg!"

"Never is a very long time and while we're talking about permitting…" Were they talking? He was. She was listening and getting hotter by the minute. "Who gave you permission to bathe in Morgaine's spring?"

"What!" She couldn't move. He had tight hold on her head, bending her forward and brushing the hair off the nape of her neck. "It's my house, I'll…" She broke off with a little gasp as warm lips kissed the base of her neck and nibbled a line to her right ear.

"You'll do as I tell you," the voice went on, "and to make sure you remember…"

At a speed only possible in dreams, Alex was out of the chair and bent over the scrubbed kitchen table. She didn't need to guess what he had in mind. Her jeans dragged down her legs made his intention perfectly clear, and as a warm hand stroked and cupped her ass cheeks, her cunt oozed.

She moaned in anticipation as jeans, panties, sneakers and socks disappeared. She was naked below the waist, bent over, ready.

This was the moment she dreaded and longed for. Waiting for the first slap of hard male hand, the first kiss of the belt, the first warm flush of pain and pleasure and the accompanying rush of heat and wetness between her legs.

Waiting…

Damn, he was taking his time. Dragging it out. Wanting her to beg. She was damn well not begging him to spank her. No matter how much she yearned for it.

He stroked a line down her spine, brushed his hand over her bare ass and whispered, "So smooth, so cool. You need warming up." As he spoke, his hand came down hard, firm and punishing. She gasped as the answering warmth spread across her skin from the hot point of contact.

Before the warmth had a chance to ease, another slap followed and a third, each one fast, hard and stinging. And wonderful.

She squirmed under the barrage of slaps, not to escape his hand, but to ease the need between her legs. She was already close to coming but wanted to last a little longer.

He stopped. Her ass throbbed and burned. "Had enough yet?" he asked.

"No." It came out as a whimper. "I need…"

"I know exactly what you need."

His hand came between her legs, parting her pussy lips and fingers—there were two or three at least—pressed deep into her cunt. The rock of her hips was pure reflex. "Yes," he said as he withdrew, "and now to finish you off."

A pause. Not a sound in the kitchen other than the frantic beating of her heart, the echo of her pulse in her ears, a faint clink of metal and the sound of leather pulled through belt loops. She'd heard that enough times to never be mistaken.

She felt the cool rush of air and the burning flash of leather on sensitized skin. Her scream still echoed in her ears as the belt came down a second time and a third. Gasping and panting to control the pain, she was dimly aware he'd stopped and his hands were parting her ass cheeks, cool on her heated flesh, and pressure against her tight opening.

He'd promised, threatened, this last night but now she wasn't ready, needed lubrication.

She tried to move, to speak, but only gaps came from her lips as he pressed against her muscle. "Open for me," he commanded. "I'm coming in, up to the hilt."

As it was a dream, he entered without difficulty, easing into her body until she gasped with pleasure. She was filled, pinioned, invaded. Her cunt flooded and her clit throbbed with need and arousal.

He started moving. There was no gentleness, no slow reentry, just hard and confident pumping as he held her fast to the table.

She was helpless, exposed, beaten and jubilant. Her arousal peaked, climbed, raced, and as he pistoned deep, she came with a scream and a great rush of pleasure. Her breasts hurting as they pressed against the hard table. Her ass aching as he continued to use her. Her mouth was dry from her gasps and cries as she came again and again and again. She was a mass of pleasure, joy and sensation as she collapsed on the table, limp, stated and satisfied.

She came to in the armchair, legs spread, hand inside her panties and feeling as limp and washed out as if she'd run a marathon.

Her book lay facedown on the rug and she'd knocked over her glass, leaving a stain on the rug.

A wet spot!

Right!

Must be something in Aunt Maria's homemade wine. Or the cottage. Or Morgaine le Fay. Or maybe she just needed some fresh air. She'd planned to explore the village. No time like the present.

* * * * *

Alex parked in the first car park she found, between the Co-op Stores and the library and across from a school. Seemed it was close to dismissal. A line of cars waited alongside the curb. One of them looked like Dai's dark gray Fiat. Curious, Alex sat in her car and watched. A bell sounded and minutes later boys and girls in bottle green uniforms — the girls wearing berets and the boys peaked caps — poured of the doors. Some walked down the street in twos and threes, but a bunch of them headed for the parked cars.

She'd been right. It was Dai. He got out and walked to meet a boy and a girl who greeted him with open arms and hugs.

So these were his "sprogs".

She had been lusting after a father of schoolchildren and the said father of school children had come on to her in no uncertain way.

Enough was enough. She was finding someone else to inhabit her dreams. And she might just skip the damn Eisteddfod. She watched fuming as Dai loaded his sprogs into the back of the car and drove off.

She set off in the opposite direction at a brisk walking pace that soon slowed as her irritation faded. The village was interesting enough to ease anybody's bad mood. It certainly soothed hers. She was glad of her coat against the late afternoon chill, but wandering through the narrow streets, looking into shop windows and visiting a wonderful Victorian chapel did a lot to clear her mind. Finding two secondhand bookstores on the same street almost made her forget the Dai Hughes problem.

She opened the door on the first one and a bell over the door jangled a welcome, a wizen old man behind the counter looked up from his tea, nodded at her and went back to his cup and saucer. Unable to resist the pull of the dark little shop, Alex started browsing and soon realized it wasn't that small, four rooms led off each other and narrow, linoleum-covered stairs went up to another floor.

Forty minutes or so later, she carried a stack of books up to the old man. He looked up, totaled her purchases and after taking her money, carefully placed the books in a recycled grocery bag and handed them to her.

"Just passing though on your way somewhere?" he asked.

"I'm here for a few weeks. Looking after my aunt's house." She reached for the bag.

"You would be Miss Abbot's niece then." Alex agreed she was. "I heard you'd arrived." He reached below the counter. "Would you care for a ticket for our Eisteddfod this Friday. It's not as famous as Llangollen but we are proud of our singers and performers."

"I already have a ticket, thank you." She was not about to admit who had given it to her, particularly since she was of two minds whether to lose the ticket or not. "I'm looking forward to it," she lied. And nipped out just as fast as she decently could.

She must have spent longer than she thought in the bookshop. Dusk had fallen along with a soft rain. She wouldn't get that wet walking back to the car but a lighted tea shop opposite promised a dry place to wait and her stomach was protesting the scratch lunch. Alex crossed the street to *y Troell*, which, looking at the painted sign over the door, she presumed meant the Spinning Wheel.

Inside it was almost empty, too late for afternoon tea apparently. But not too late to order coffee, an omelet and as a concession to the country Welsh cakes. As she waited Alex looked around the cozy tearoom with its polished brass and copper and the antique furniture. On the wall not two feet away was a poster advertising in both English and Welsh the upcoming Eisteddfod.

"Here you are!" The waitress put Alex's coffee in front of

her. "The omelet will be up in a minute." She paused and followed Alex's gaze. "Would you like a ticket for the Eisteddfod? We have them for sale."

By the time Alex replied that she already had one and no, she was not a tourist but staying a few weeks, the waitress's face lit with comprehension.

"You'll be going with Dai Hughes and his family, won't you now?"

Wondering how the hell news like that got around, Alex admitted she was.

The waitress gave her a roughish grin. "Oh that Dai! He's starred in quite a few women's dreams around here."

What the hell do you say to that? Alex would be happy if he got out of hers. Or would she? "Do you know him?"

"Too well! He's my cousin."

Good thing she'd kept her opinions to herself. If she stood him up on Friday, she'd no doubt need to find another teashop. Still… "Does he have a lot of family in town?"

"Heavens yes. Half the population are either Hughes or Morgan, and Dai's mother was a Morgan, my Dad's sister."

Fantastic. Now she was being hit on by a married clan member. A sexy married clan member she really fancied. What the hell was wrong with her? Stifling the urge to ask nosy questions about Dai's wife, Alex opted for a second cup of coffee.

Coffee, omelet and two Welsh cakes—which turned out to be a cross between a scone and a small pancake—later, Alex left for home. Followed by the waitress's assurances that she'd be seeing her Friday no doubt. *y Troell* was closing in honor of the occasion.

* * * * *

Dai ran his hands through his hair. For the nth time he wondered how Blod and Samuel kept sane. Not that Ivor and

43

Gwen had been any trouble, but checking homework, making sure Ivor had his kit for football practice tomorrow and Gwen had her shorts and trainers, doing another load of washing—he couldn't, in all conscience leave an overflowing laundry hamper to greet Blod—and deflecting two unsolicited phone offers to fit double glazing, plus the teeth, bath, pajamas, story routine and he Dai Hughes, one-time star forward on the local football team, was ready for nothing more energetic than a rocking chair in front of the goggle box.

Some day it had been too! Between old Maude Evans insisting he get her new will done before the weekend as the world was going to end on Sunday and Selim Nangee having problems with a tenant, Dai was wondering why he ever took up law and hadn't settled for going down the mines like his grandad.

Nancy Jones cornering him in the car park and offering him supper and herself after the Eisteddfod was just the crowning jewel in his day.

Not that he didn't fully appreciate Nancy's talents, but willing as she always was in many things, she flatly refused to let him tie her to the bedposts and Dai longed for a woman to dominate. A woman he could overcome. Who'd submit and satisfy his wildest dreams.

A woman like Alex Carpenter.

If the ancient gods smiled.

Fantasies were one thing, but he yearned to know for sure. Would she kneel at his feet and worship his cock with her mouth, just like the woman of his dreams? Offer her body up to be spread-eagled on the bed. Lay herself over his lap for chastisement. Take him in her body every which way and let him bring her to climax after climax until they were both sweaty, sated and exhausted?

It was a pleasant thought and on Friday night he'd try his luck. He rather fancied a dip in Morgaine's warm pool with Alex. He'd then find out, once and for all, if what he'd imagined under that towel lived up to his fantasy.

Assuming of course she didn't bin that ticket and stay home for the evening.

In that case, he'd take himself and his desires up the mountain.

Meanwhile...

The thought of a slow, loving tease over every inch of Alex's naked body while she moaned and begged him for release would keep him happy and hard for quite some time.

And this time it would be slow, no fast and furious sweaty fuck. He wanted her warm and pliant until he got her so aroused she was begging him for it.

Chapter Six

&

Forget the vast tub in the bathroom off the kitchen. Alex cleaned her teeth then grabbed towels, nightwear and soap and headed for the basement.

She heard the welcoming roar of the cascade even before she opened the heavy door. Stepping into the cave and turning on the light was like coming home. There was something almost magical about the place. Okay, a lot magical. How many people in the world had a hot spring in their basement? Standing under the domed ceiling, she understood why earlier generations saw something mystical about this place.

The presence of Morgaine's spring beckoned. Dropping her towel and nightshirt on the rocks, Alex jumped in, ducking her head under and pushing the hair off her face as she emerged. It was sheer bliss. Didn't take much to imagine wild pagan lovefests or illicit lovers' meetings. Come to that, she wouldn't mind a few hours here with a lover. Dai's dark eyes and sexy smile came to mind but she pushed them back as far as she could. He was married, dammit! But…

A girl could dream, couldn't she? No way would she actually take her clothes off for him, but what harm was a little fantasy?

She bet he was darn good in bed too. But was he her sort of lover? Would he demand she obey, order her on her knees, tie her so she was helpless, forbid her to climax until he so chose, keep her hanging, aching with need and arousal. Stroke and kiss her until she begged him for release.

In her dreams it could all happen.

If he were just sitting over there on the ledge near the

waterfall. Naked? No, he'd be fully clothed and magically not getting the least damp. While she was totally naked so he could eye and ogle every inch of her.

"You're naked," he'd say. "Good, that's how I want you. Always."

"Always?"

He nodded slowly. "Yes. If you need to go out or we have visitors, I'll give you permission to wear clothes but you will never, ever wear knickers. Understand?"

"Yes." Who in their right mind said "no" to a tone like that?

"Good. You must always be open to me. Available. If I ever find you wearing underwear, I will rip them off, put you over my knee and spank you until you beg me to stop."

She swallowed, her throat tight at the thought. He seemed to expect a reply so she nodded and turned to reach for the soap.

"No!" His voice echoed off the cave walls. "Turn back to face me. I want to see your breasts." She swiveled back and took a step toward him. "Stop." She waited, squaring her shoulders to lift her breasts. He wanted to see them, did he? She'd give him an eyeful.

"Hussy," he said, his voice soft and teasing. "Want to show me what you have, do you? Good. Pick up the soap and go sit on the rock over there." He nodded toward a jutting ledge a few yards from where he sat.

Remembering not to turn her back on him. Alex stepped backward gingerly until her ass hit the edge of the pool. Climbing up on the ledge was easy. It was low enough that her legs dangled in the water and high enough that he could lean back on his rock and get a grandstand view.

"Wash your breasts. Soap them up all over and let me watch."

The water had to be really soft. The soap lathered

abundantly and in no time her breasts were covered with soft bubbles. Making sure she had every inch covered, she looked up for his approval.

She got it.

His eyes all but gleamed as he took in the sight and her nipples hardened even more under his gaze. "Good. You listen well. Now spread your legs. Wide. I want to see the pink of your cunt." She shifted, holding herself steady with her hands as she parted her legs. "Wider!" That she managed. Her thigh muscles pulled but he seemed satisfied. "Wash your belly. Slowly."

Two could play tease.

Looking him in the eyes, she dipped the soap into the water and stroked foam over her belly in slow circles, letting her hands drift up to stroke her breasts then down over her belly, pausing just above her pussy before circling once again.

She let out a little contented sigh. This was no hardship.

"You're exceeding directions!" Her hands froze. What the hell? "I said your belly. Keep your hands off your breast and your crotch. I don't want you aroused. Not yet."

Then he was going the wrong way about it. She was hotter than Morgaine's frigging spring. She grinned at her choice of adjective.

"What," he asked, "is so amusing?"

She was not discussing adjectives right now but… "I was thinking how hot this is. You're turning me on."

"Good. I like a woman hot for me. Now, turn your back on me. Kneel up, bend over and let me see you wash your arse."

Cripes! This was getting a bit much but what the heck? She got on her knees, thinking she'd much rather be sucking his cock than washing her butt cheeks at him, but now she reached back and ran her soapy hand over her ass, it did feel sort of naughty and sexy. Like a prelude to getting fucked in the back door.

She did nicely at first but when she reached to dip the soap again, she lost her balance and fell with a most undignified yelp and a resounding splash. As she surfaced, shaking her head and blinking to clear the water from her eyes, hands caught her around the waist, lifting her. He was behind her and holding her tight against him.

He was definitely interested in the proceedings.

Nice!

She pressed back against him and rubbed her ass against his erection. He was naked. He'd been dressed when she toppled off the edge. No one could strip that fast. "What happened to your clothes?"

"I don't need them."

Good point.

They'd just get in the way as he lifted her so the tip of his cock nudged between her legs before lowering her slowly so his erection eased up her crack, parting her cheeks as he moved higher, pressing into the base of her spine before he lifted her up to run his cock down between her thighs. He set up a rhythm of lifting and lowering her as she pressed into him and his hands cupped her breasts.

Impossible! How could he be lifting her as he stroked and teased her nipples? In her dreams anything was possible and this was a fantasy and a half.

Now he held her steady, rocking his hips so his cock brushed back and forth between her legs, not quite reaching her clit, but stirring enough need and heat to have her moving her hips to his tempo. Her little whimpers became moans.

His response to that was to lift her right out of the water and turn her so he held her facedown over his head. How could he be that strong? As if it mattered one iota as his lips closed over her left nipple then her right one before making a trail of warm kisses down her chest and across her belly to her pussy.

She cried out as his mouth closed on her. The thought that this was physically impossible was lost in a wild fog of sensation and desire. His tongue was magic, his mouth incredible and her body rippled with need.

She cried out with loss and frustration as he took his mouth away and set her on her feet. "Why stop? I want more!"

"*Cariad*, more, much more is coming but not yet. Be patient." As he spoke, he leapt out of the water, landing several yards way by her towel and proceeded to wrap her in it before hoisting her over his shoulder, her face looking down at his remarkable naked arse. Okay, it was a sight to behold but…

"What are you doing?" Undignified wasn't the word for being bent over his shoulder and protesting seemed a matter of principal.

"Taking you upstairs to fuck you silly."

Her giggle was sheer joy and anticipation. "Can't wait!"

His laugh was deep, sexy, and rippled over her like the water from the cascade. "You will, *cariad*. Oh you will."

Pausing only to close the heavy door to the springs, her dream lover took the stairs two at a time, the floor sped in front of her eyes as his trim ass flexed with each step.

At the door of her bedroom—okay Aunt Maria's bedroom—he paused. "Usually sleep here, do you?"

"Yes." It came out a bit muffled from being upside down.

"You won't be sleeping for a while," he promised as he eased her off his shoulder and slid her body down his until her feet touched the ground.

She looked up at a face that was shrouded in shadow. "Why can't I see your face?"

"You will, when you can trust," he replied.

Damn! "Who said I don't trust you?"

"Maybe it's your own judgment you don't trust."

She had her mouth open to argue the point but his kiss swallowed all her objections.

He was no amateur when it came to kissing. She didn't want to think about how much practice he'd had to be this good. Couldn't really think anyway as the pressure of his lips and the touch of his tongue unleashed a spate of sensation and emotion that pretty much precluded any coherent thought. Wild heat curled though her from her lips down to her toes. Every nerve ending tingled, every cell in her body rushed with need and arousal as her cunt ran with wanting. She leaned into him, the towel falling to the floor as she pressed her body skin to skin against his.

Her breath caught as a torrent of need, desire and plain and lovely horniness swept through her, blocking out any thought, any idea but the prospect of his body on her, in her, joined with her.

She pressed into him, rubbing her belly against his erection. And smiled.

"What pleases you so, *cariad*?" he asked.

As if he didn't know! "The thought of your cock deep inside me." Brazen yes, but it was a daydream, wasn't it?

He laughed, throwing back his head and letting out a great peal that echoed off the pitched ceiling. "You want my cock, do you?" His hands eased up from her waist to settle strong and firm on her shoulders. "Show me how much you want me. Prove your devotion." As his hands pressed her shoulders, as if by reflex Alex sank to her knees.

The handmade rug was soft but she barely noticed as her hands stroked his thighs and her eyes feasted on his magnificent cock. She'd never before been much impressed by a lover's cock. The man and mind attached being her focus and priority, but there was no denying this was the cock of her dreams and fantasy. Not prodigiously large but of a generous and enticing proportion, long and firm and a satisfying girth.

Deep-throating him would be a delight, not a fight against her gag reflex.

She licked her lips in anticipation.

"If you dither much longer, I'll put you over my knee!"

It was a tempting offer but…

Smiling, she leaned forward, opening her lips as they brushed the smooth red head of his cock and took the first inch or so into her mouth.

Her heart raced with the familiar thrill of power. She might be on her knees before him but she held his cock between her teeth. He was the vulnerable one—she could bite, injure or maim him.

His hands cupped the back of her head, his fingers tunneling through her hair. She wrapped her arms around his thighs, easing her hands up to his nice firm butt and pulled him closer.

His cock filled her mouth. She relaxed her throat and took him in.

He gave a gasp, muttered, "Alex!" and pressed even deeper.

She had him. She held him. She drew his power and strength into her mouth. Her entire body was alert to the heat, need and arousal all but sparking between them. As he held her head firm and worked his cock back and forth, fucking her willing mouth, her body responded. Her breasts tingled, her heartbeat sped and her cunt throbbed with want as damp seeped down her inner thighs.

She was in such need. She tried to speed up the tempo, wanting to move her lips faster against his cock but he held her firm, setting the pace, controlling the fuck. Her mind all but fogged out in the realization of his power and her need.

As she knelt at his feet, her body hummed with anticipation. This magnificent cock that brushed the back of her throat and forced its path in her mouth would soon drive into her cunt and fuck her.

She whimpered.

He paused a moment then came in deep as if to penetrate the very depth of her need before pulling his cock away, stepping back and leaving her bereft.

She looked up. As always, his face was shrouded in darkness, the features blurry and indistinct.

"I want more," she whispered, her throat dry. "I want to run my tongue over your cock, to taste you, to caress you."

"Oh you will," he replied, a soft chuckle in his voice. "You will, *cariad*. I'm not finished with your lovely mouth, not by any means, but…" He grasped her upper arms, lifted her to standing and covered her mouth with his.

She'd never been kissed like this. Never. Ever. A voice inside her head moaned as her lips parted and his tongue took over, caressing and pressing deep, sending her mind wild and her body into overdrive. She clung to him, pressing close, wrapping a leg over his as he pressed his knee and thigh between hers. She rubbed against him, wanting to feel his erection but his thigh kept her at a distance so she rode that, rocking against it, driving her passion higher and wilder as his lips sent trails of desire down to her cunt.

Chapter Seven

෨

She was close to trembling by the time he pulled his mouth off and smiled down at her. "Ready to obey and submit?" he asked.

Her throat all but closed up as she lowered her head and replied, "Yes." It felt so all-around wonderful. Her heart beat a tattoo behind her ribs as she rubbed her clammy hands on her thighs and prayed she wouldn't wake up.

Not yet at least.

"Listen to me," he said, his voice calm but laden with expectation and promise, "and tell me if you agree to submit." Her heart skipped at the last word, spoken slowly as if to draw out the anticipation. "Alex, *cariad*, I will tie you to the bed with these." He held up a set of red restraints, the ties dangling from his hand as he brushed them down her arm. "I will tie your hands over your head, spread your legs wide and tie down your ankles so you are helpless, immobile, completely at my mercy. Do you agree?"

Heart thumping, she nodded.

"I don't hear you."

The edge in his voice upped her excitement. "Yes, I agree," she whispered.

This was too good, too wonderful, too…

"Pay attention! After I have you helpless, I will use this on you." As if by magic—dreams defied reality after all—he held up a matching red flogger. As she raised her eyes, she noticed the tresses were inch-wide tails of soft fur. Oh! To feel the kiss and sting of that on her skin! "Do you agree?"

She took a deep, calming breath. "Yes."

"And this?" Only in a dream could a flogger with soft tresses, morph into a large butt plug already glistening with lubricant. "This will fill up your arsehole while I whip you."

It would be harder than a cock, firmer, colder, but oh, she longed for the sweet hurt of the intrusion. "Yes!" It came out fast at the end of a deep breath.

"And this." This time a string of anal beads swung from his fingers.

"Please!" She shivered with the anticipation of being stuffed with them one by one and the wild rush of sensation as they were pulled out. Fast.

"Good." Alex smiled at the pleasure and praise in the single word. "Now," he went on. "What about a gag?" A black rubber ball gag appeared in his hand. Her shiver was not of pleasure.

"No." She shook her head. "Not that!"

"You refuse?" He sounded halfway amused. But only halfway, the rest was clear annoyance.

Too bad.

This was her dream, wasn't it? "I hated a gag the only time I had to wear one. I won't do it again. It's one of my limits."

"Hmm." He paused, presumably pondering the situation. "What about a silk blindfold, to enclose you in utter darkness?"

Not her favorite either but... "I could accept that."

"You enjoy the blindfold?"

"No, it scares me, but the gag terrified me."

"I see. The blindfold it will be. A little fear will stimulate you." Somehow his hands were empty and one was between her legs, stroking and penetrating. "Looks as though you're ready for whatever I plan." He held his fingers to her nose. "Aren't you?"

She could smell herself. Not that she needed to. Her clit was throbbing and her cunt flowed with arousal. "Yes, I am."

"Good."

With the impossible power of a dream lover, he lifted her. The covers on the bed were pulled back and she was facedown on Aunt Maria's linen sheets. He pulled her hands over her head and fastened them to the bedhead. The ties were tight and secure but not uncomfortable. She lay unmoving, limp and acquiescent, waiting for her legs to be spread and her ankles restrained. For the wonderful rush that accompanied helplessness.

Instead, a slow trail of warm oil trickled down her spine. As she let out a sigh of hedonistic anticipation, his hands eased up her spine to her shoulders, spreading the scented oil. His touch was confident, practiced and spot on. He found and eased each tight spot, massaging her shoulders until they sagged loose on the pillow.

Then he worked his way down her back, his fingers stroking and kneading her flesh. He found the tight place in her lower back—the legacy of long hours in the plane and the rental car and a morning spent hunched over her computer—and totally obliterated any trace of stiffness, along with just about any strength or ability to move. She was as good as a mass of jelly, limp, close to fluid and soft to her bones.

Until his hands eased up her sides to her breasts.

His touch was soft, just a gentle stroke of the swell at her sides, before his fingers swooped under her, a hand cupped each breast and his fingers tweaked her nipples.

The groan came from somewhere deep inside and he drew out the sensation with deliberate slowness. She wanted, needed, more but knew he would not respond to any request. Except most likely to stop and leave her wanting. So she lay there and let the sighs escape her and pleasure and the sweet ache fill her mind.

"Like that?" he asked, giving each nipple an extra-sharp

tug.

"Yes," she replied, "if it pleases you." Whispering the last four words stirred the old familiar sense of submission.

It didn't please him as she'd expected.

"*Cariad*," he said, a soft note of reproof in his voice. "This is about your pleasure, later we may consider what more you can do to pleasure me but for now... Do you like this?" His fingers closed over her nipples again.

"Yes. Very much."

"More than this?" His hands left her breasts and smoothed down her sides to rub and fondle her butt.

"I like that too," she replied as he parted her cheeks. "But I like you touching my breasts best."

"We'll see if you change mind with a plug or beads up your tight little hole." The promise sent her cunt running. "But meanwhile, how about this?"

He kissed the base of her spine then ran a trail of kisses up to between her shoulder blades.

The sigh was totally involuntary. "Yes!" As she caught her breath, he blew on her skin. Warmth brushed wherever his breath hit. She should have recognized the spicy scent. Other lovers, other dominants, had used this heating oil before, but not with such consummate expertise. His breath came in short, controlled bursts, sending caressing tendrils of heat across her back and down her arms and over her ass.

He hadn't ordered silence so she let herself sigh and moan with pleasure until the sounds echoed in her ears.

"Very nice," he said. Did he mean her bound and naked body or her moans? "Let's move on." His hands did, right down to her ass as he slapped her. The sound loud in the quiet room. Alex held back the yelp. Only just.

"Did you like that?"

"I like the afterglow," she replied. The prospect of the

warmth that followed always gave her courage to endure the pain.

"Here's little more afterglow then." As he spoke, he slapped her other ass cheek. Harder. She yelped. "That's all for now," he said, his hands stroking away the hurt. "I'm not inclined to give you a spanking today. I don't doubt there will be other times when you merit chastisement, maybe even severe discipline." Sheesh, he knew how to up arousal and anxiety! "But tonight is about pleasure. Although…" She imagined him staring as her ass colored up. "You do go a lovely shade of pink. Must be your light skin. I bet I could leave a nice handprint if I tried."

A nice hurty one!

"But I have other plans tonight for your lovely arse." Speaking, he spread her still warm cheeks. She felt slight pressure against her asshole before he squeezed lubricant up her. He was very generous with it, smoothing it in deep with his finger until the lubricant warmed inside her. She remembered the rather large butt plug she'd seen and yelped as he rammed it deep.

"Did that hurt?"

She bit back a smart-ass reply—given her current position, mouthing off was not a good idea. "Yes. I wasn't expecting it to come in so hard."

"You prefer a gentle insertion?"

"Yes."

"All right then." It was yanked, making her gasp but she had no complaints about the reapplication of lubricant. He truly had a lover's touch. The tip of the plug pressed against her tight opening. He waited. Pressed just enough to open her a little and waited. Alex let out her breath and when he pressed deeper, rocked her hips to meet him.

He continued the steady pressure, twisting the plug as it slipped past her ring of muscle, turning the plug slowly as he pushed in deep. He was screwing her! Wonderfully!

She made no effort to hold hack her moans and her sighs. "Thank you!" she managed between sighs.

"My pleasure, *cariad*, as well as yours," he replied. "I think we'll leave it right there for now and get on with something else. Don't go anywhere."

Very funny! As if she would, even if she could. She wanted nothing more than to stay in this bed with him forever. Or at least until she woke up. All this was so real, the sensations so fantastic she had to remind herself she was dreaming.

Why?

Better to lose herself in the sweetness of bondage and the anticipation of his next move.

Which was to kneel on the bed and whisper in her ear, "Are you ready?"

For what? As if it mattered. He hadn't disappointed her so far.

She nodded.

"Smashing." He moved off, saying, "Here, take care of this for me." The tresses of the fur flogger were pushed under her arm. Alex pressed her arm against it, rubbing the soft pile against her skin while noticing the flip side of each tress was smooth, soft leather. A flogging with this would be a very new sensation.

Like having soft kisses rained all over her butt while he tweaked and rocked the plug.

Alex didn't even try to hold back the sighs and moans of pleasure. In fact, if he yanked the plug out and buggered her here and now, she'd come in an instant.

But he had other ideas. "Not yet, *cariad*. Not yet." Damn him! Could he read her mind? Why not? It was a dream, wasn't it? "Hold your horses, I promise it will be worth the wait."

She wasn't about to argue as the flogger came down on her shoulders like a caress and trailed down her back to flick at the sensitive point at the very top of her thighs then sweep down the inside of one leg and back up the other.

Incredible! Marvelous! Every nerve ending tingled with pleasure and anticipation. Pleasure that he seemed intent to prolong with caress after caress of the furry tresses until her entire body sang with sensation and her sighs were one continuous litany of rising desire.

He knew just how to stimulate and keep her on the glorious edge. Not a touch too much, no matter how she shifted to bring her cunt and clit into contact with his flogger.

Her mind almost flipped out imagining coming at a flick of a tress. A sharp flick that would send her off the edge. But it never came and she remained suspended on pleasure, her body awake and alert to every touch and every gentle slap. Seemed he covered every inch of her body with sensation until she was fighting to keep her breathing steady. And failing. Gasps punctuated sighs and groans and she was aware of a soft sheen of sweat gathering on her skin.

Too bad he was just a dream. But why be greedy? Her fantasies had often kept her happy. Just nowhere near as happy as this.

Lost in the fog of sensation, Alex slowly realized he had stopped the loving swatting and was running his lips over her skin, across her back and down her spine.

"I'm not sure I can take much more," she mumbled into the pillow, with supreme effort lifting her head to turn to him and repeat herself.

As if from a distance, he chuckled. "Yes you can. I'll make sure of it!"

That she didn't doubt. Smiling to herself, she relaxed back into the mattress, determined to enjoy the ride. No matter how long it took.

Alex yelped as he flipped her onto her back. Impossible since her hands were still tied fast to opposite ends of the bed head but he'd managed it.

He grinned down at her, his features still shadowed but the grin, as sexy as all get-out, told her he was enjoying this as much as she.

He cupped each breast, stroking and squeezing gently and giving extra-special attention to her nipples. By the time he paused they were hard, tingling and felt twice their normal size. Then he moved down to her belly, his fingers tracing slow circles as they drifted lower until they brushed her bush and dipped between her pussy lips.

His finger barely glanced across her clit but her arousal surged as her head sagged back and a long, slow groan accompanied the rocking of her hips.

"Easy, *cariad*," he said, moving away just enough to have her complaining. How could he get her this close and then…? "Just realized your legs are free. Can't have that! Didn't I promise to tie you hand and foot? Wouldn't want to disappoint you now, would I?"

Not much danger of that!

He pressed her legs apart at the knee then closed a hand over each ankle, spreading her wide. She so loved the sense of exposure and helplessness that accompanied being spread-eagled as she waited, panting with anticipation of his tying her ankles down.

He fastened them up all right! Lifting them high until her feet were suspended from the ceiling. As she moved the few inches permitted by the slack, chains clinked softly.

Definitely a dream. There were no bondage chains in Aunt Maria's bedroom.

At least as far as Alex knew. Which on the whole, perhaps wasn't that much.

She wiggled but the chains left her little slack. She was

truly and utterly helpless, and her pussy flooded with desire.

"What next?" she asked.

Again the chuckle that was beyond sexy. "I arouse you more than ever before in your life and give you multiple climaxes so you scream until you pass out."

Not a man who suffered from ego problems or self-doubt!

How nice.

His hand stroked the inside of her thighs and a shift in the mattress showed he was between her legs. "I love to see you spread like this—open, helpless, completely available." A hand smoothed up and down the back of her thigh. "What a lovely arse you have. I'm sorely tempted to redden it for you." Her breath caught at the prospect. "Or perhaps take my belt and give you a few good hard swats and watch the stripes glow on your fair skin." That got a gasp. "But on reflection, no. Not tonight. I promised this was for your pleasure and so..." He eased the plug out, pressing his finger in deep before her muscles had a chance to close.

How wonderful the intrusion of warm flesh instead of the hard plug. He pumped in and out gently, rubbing around her clit with his finger—no, two fingers. Wondrous! Marvelous! He could do anything he wanted to her if he just kept this up and...

"Hold on a minute," he said, slowing the pressure of his fingers as he slipped out of her. "Time for something special."

A buggering? No, he was opening her cheeks wider, pressing something hard, cool and slick past her muscle. A bead! And another and another. Each feeling larger than the previous one until they were all inside and she felt stuffed and filled. It was two, three times as much as the plug and the pressure sent wild thrills inside, stimulating nerve endings deep in her cunt.

"Like it?" he asked in response to her sighs.

"Yes!" Saying anything more was a waste of breath and

energy. He knew. He knew her thoughts and could read every nuance of her body.

"Thought so!" She'd forgive the smugness. Hadn't much brain space to give it any more consideration as his fingers gently opened her cunt lips wide. His breath came warm where she needed him and then his tongue lapped her, the full flat of his tongue covering her. Slow, teasing all-covering licks from her ass to her clit. Each one took minutes and turned her mind to mush. But who needed to think? All she wanted was to feel. She was covered, consumed, devoured. No wonder men called it eating pussy.

His tongue plunged deep inside her. Slow, stabbing movements that sent her head back and her hips taut in her bondage. In and out he went, mimicking the movement of a cock...his cock.

"Come into me. Fuck me!" It was begging, but who cared? Certainly not Alex.

"Like this?"

His fingers penetrated her. She was filled. Stretched. Alex shuddered with satisfaction as his fingers moved in and out. Sweet friction driving her closer to coming as his thumb worked her clit.

Her mind switched off as her instincts took over. She was nearing the edge, heart and breathing racing. Climbing, spiraling up and up. She screamed. Her mind flipped, her body soared and she came...again and again until she collapsed, a quivering heap on the bed. Her dream lover kissed her and she tasted herself on his lips.

"Now it's my turn."

He entered her fast and hard, drilling her with his power and raw male sex, working his need inside her and pulling her back with him. She was coming again and again and again like short staccato bursts of repeating fire. In the haze of what used to be her brain, Alex was vaguely aware of his groans and the heat inside her as he climaxed.

Then as another ripple of climaxes broke inside her, he tugged the beads. One by one they came, each sending her into another harder and greater climax.

It was too much!

It was wonderful!

She screamed her pleasure. Shouting and yelling until the room filled with the sounds of her satisfaction and the smell of sweaty bodies and sex.

She was worn, sated and utterly, utterly satisfied. Exhausted, she closed her eyes, gasping and panting as she waited for her lover to release her restraints.

Chapter Eight

෨

Dai Hughes woke with a start. At thirty-four he should be far too old for wet dreams. Apparently he wasn't. Not that he was about to complain. It had been a darn good dream but was he glad a hundred times over that Blod and Samuel had come back last night, relieving him of the responsibilities of their brood. At least he was in the privacy of his own home. He could just see himself trying to explain why he needed to wash his sheets to their inquisitive offspring.

Throwing off the rumpled covers, he padded down to the bathroom and dropped his boxers in the hamper.

Alex Carpenter was really getting under his skin if she was having that effect on him. Mind you, a dream like that was worth the effort of changing sheets and throwing them in the washing machine. Trouble was, dreams weren't enough. He wanted her naked in his bed, with him doing everything he dreamed about.

Was there an earthly chance she was as kinky as he hoped, imagined, wished?

Only one way to find out.

After the Eisteddfod, they'd go for a long stroll by the river—or perhaps up *Mynydd Cudyll*—the Hawk Mountain that rose behind her cottage—and talk. He'd learned to listen to women, to drop careful hints and watch reactions. The last thing he ever wanted was to scare the willies out of some vanilla woman, but the pervy ones! He smiled as he stepped into the shower and reached for the soap. He loved the kinky ones and they came thin on the ground. A pervy Alex would be the answer to his prayers—and his dreams, come to that.

Better get Blod to drop a word or two about what a perfect gentleman he was. After five days of cooking and eating fish fingers and baked beans on toast, she owed him that much. Not that he grudged her a few days away with Sam. He was just a little envious of her happiness and contentment.

But Alex Carpenter? He had to be barking! She was here for a few weeks and would be back off to Baltimore or New York or wherever it was she came from. But…a few weeks was plenty of time to find out if she shared his kinky tastes in bed.

Whoa! He was getting a bit ahead here. Why not? Faint heart never won fair lady, and hadn't she dipped her hand in Morgaine's well and tasted? Maybe all those old wives tales had a germ of truth.

Once he was done with his entry at the Eisteddfod, he was trying for all he was worth with Alex and hoping to hell she wasn't cooling toward him. Not that she'd ever exactly been hot, except in his mind.

And if by the wildest chance imaginable she was as submissive as in his randy wet dreams… Heck, if he considered himself dominant, he'd better start acting that way.

Once she gave him the very first signal she was inclined the same way.

* * * * *

Alex awoke early, the after-pleasure of her dream lover's attentions still fluttering deep in her clit and her cunt wet with arousal.

Some dream!

She half expected to find the sheets in a tangle and her duvet on the floor but she was comfortably tucked in and the only thing awry was her pillow that was half off the mattress.

While the kettle was boiling, she gave in to the impulse to peek into the spring room. She half expected to see damp towels strewn over the floor of the cave. But no, the two she'd used were upstairs drying by the stove and the spare ones still in a tidy pile on the shelf by the door.

No wild lover had taken her every which way and more.

It had just been a very hot dream.

And that was probably the best it was going to get. Where in this rustic backwater would she find a kinky lover? She'd had a few hopes of Dai right at first, but she was not going to go there.

Better spend her time here having an affair with her Magic Wand and regular baths in Morgaine's pool. Had to be some mineral in the water was absorbed through her skin and affected her imagination.

She'd never had dreams like these in Ohio and she didn't think it was just the fresh Welsh mountain air.

* * * * *

After a very productive day, Alex was almost tempted to skip the Eisteddfod and stay home with a good book. But it did seem a shame to miss what was obviously the event of the season in these parts. Also, she thought, with just the teeniest spike of maliciousness, it might be a chance to come across Dai's family and let him know oh-so subtly that she didn't play around with married men. True, she didn't have anyone but herself to play with, but she'd manage fine with Morgaine's spring keeping her in happy dreams.

Alex even took advantage of it to wash before she changed. Whatever ancient magic was in it would surely give her confidence to face off Dai even when the temptation to forget the thorny little detail of a wife and family was pricking at her thoughts.

She was not giving into that, and heck, if half the inhabitants were turning out this evening, she might well find a Mister Right Now to help her get over her obsession with

Dai Hughes' compelling dark eyes.

Alex took a ridiculous amount of time deciding what to wear. It wasn't as if she had a wardrobe of "out for the evening" clothes with her but settled for her one pair of black wool pants and a black silk turtleneck. It was, she decided, eyeing herself in Aunt Maria's gilt-framed mirror, perfect garb for a Goth evening or a scene party. Since this was a family occasion, she lightened up the effect with large silver earrings and a bright blue scarf.

Her last, subtle—she hoped—concession to her kink was a silver chain bracelet with a tiny handcuff charm. A present from a former lover, who had more than once earned her very welcome attentions.

* * * * *

The hall was packed when she arrived and handed her ticket to the white-haired attendant. He said something to her in a language she now recognized as Welsh.

"Sorry," she said, "I don't speak Welsh."

He smiled and nodded. "English, are you?"

Not exactly. "American."

Recognition lit his old eyes. "Oh! You must be Miss Abbot's niece come to tend the spring for her." That hadn't been the precise wording of Aunt Maria's invitation but... "Young Dai Hughes said to watch for you. Your seat's up front with the competitors' families."

It most definitely was.

There were two empty seats at the end of the row. A tactful, sensitive woman would no doubt not sit down next to Mrs. Hughes and the two kids Alex recognized from the afternoon by the school. But it was a bit difficult to be thus tactful and sensitive with the old attendant announcing, "Here you are!" and "Evening, Blod, here's the young woman Dai was holding a seat for."

As Blod—could that really be her name?—smiled and held out her hand, Alex got an inkling her assumption regarding Dai might be a bit off target. No husband really talked about his flirts with his wife, did he? And what wife would welcome said flirt with a warm smile and a handshake.

"Hi," Alex said taking her hand. "Thanks for keeping the seat for me."

"My brother would have spiflicated me if I hadn't."

Brother? Alex tried very had not to grin. "He really talked this evening up." A bit of an exaggeration but what the heck?

Blod chuckled. "We're not exactly Llangollen but the winners go on to regional and once we did have a choir go to the National Eisteddfod. It was," she added, dark eyes twinkling—the same eyes as Dai. No doubt that she was his sister. Alleluia! "…in my parents' day but no one has forgotten."

"If it's been done once, why not again?"

"Dai would go along with that line of thinking."

"He's competing, right?"

"As always, with Sam, my husband, and in the second half, my children." She paused to introduce Ivor and Gwen. "I'll be a pretty long evening."

After a few minutes exchanging polite pleasantries, during which Alex decided she really liked Blod but didn't exactly dare ask if that really was her name, the lights dimmed and a panel of judges took their place up front.

Minutes later the curtain came up, someone struck a note on a tuning fork and the male choir burst into song. Goose bumps skittered down Alex's back at the sheer and utter beauty of thirty or so male voices in perfect harmony. She had no idea what the words meant. Didn't need to. The strength and power of the singing filled the room and her mind. Dai was in the second row, almost in the middle. He looked like a dark-haired god spreading music magic.

A very handsome, decidedly sexy sort of god. She'd spent so much effort thinking him sexy but a sleaze that to know he was just plain sexy and definitely on the menu was enough to send her mind racing over possibilities. The accompaniment of a brain-sizzling performance had her breathless.

She darn well hoped she'd convince him to manage the same very, very soon. Blod had been right on the nail, it was going to be a long evening.

A long evening of magnificent singing that alternately gave her goose bumps and caught at her throat. During the interval Dai arrived bearing tiny cardboard tubs of ice cream. After handing them out and accepting thanks, he sat his six-foot male self beside Alex.

She took a deep breath and inhaled his male scent. Not a good move, or was it? Heck, he was fair game now, and so she decided by the look in his eyes, was she.

"What do you think?" he asked.

A very wide-open question. She took a mouthful of really good strawberry ice cream, letting it melt on her tongue before she answered. "Thanks for inviting me. The choirs are fantastic and I was glad to meet your sister." Extremely glad and relieved, but no point in going there right now.

"I'm glad you came too. I wasn't certain you would."

She was saved from replying by Gwen and Ivor squeezing past them on their way backstage. Dai wished them, "*Pob lwc.*" Which by their smiles and the backslapping, Alex took to mean "good luck". The affection between Dai and the children was obvious. They both hugged him before scampering down the aisle and heading for a curtain by the side of the stage.

"They're nervous," Dai said. "I practiced with them every night Blod and Sam were gone but they are terrified they'll miss a note."

"I bet they don't."

"What do you bet?" His voice had gone low, almost husky.

Alex took a deep breath and met his eyes. "How about a drink afterward?"

He was silent a heartbeat or two. "Agreed." And held out his hand.

Previous handshakes hadn't been like this. His fingers lingered against hers, strong and confident and with just enough pressure against her palm to have her wondering if his touch would come close to her dreams.

Hold on a minute! They'd agreed to a drink—sort of— and now she was comparing him to her dream lover. Hell, why not?

And he was fingering the chain bracelet around her wrist and caught the handcuff charm between his thumb and finger. "Interesting." So was the light in his dark eyes. "Into handcuffs are you?"

She looked up at him as she smiled and was saved from replying with words by the sudden dimming of the lights and the start of the second half of the program.

Alex did her level best to concentrate on the teenagers' and children's choirs as well as she had on the lusty male voices but it wasn't easy. Not when she was wondering if Dai was just cracking clever remarks or was he really understanding what she needed. Come to that, what did she need, and was it from him?

Okay, she was being unnecessarily skittish here. She did lust after Dai. He certainly fit her idea of a dominant lover and screw it all—and hopefully herself as well—she wanted more than wild dreams fueled by her imagination and nudged along by obscure minerals in the warm spring.

She returned the pressure of his hand and tried—sort of at least—to concentrate on the choir rather than the hunk of male pressing his leg against hers. After a rousing song that sounded as if it had once accompanied fur-clad warriors into battle, Alex decided to up the mutual distractibility quotient by twisting her ankle around his.

Earning a squeeze to her thigh and a rather delicious pressure behind her knee.

"I really want to know about that tiny silver handcuff," he whispered, his breath warm against her ear.

She grinned. Please, oh please, let him be into handcuffs for real. "Later."

Interlude

Chapter Nine

ॐ

Turned out to be quite bit later.

Judging and awarding prizes to winners took time. Dai's choir lost to the combined police and fireman and little Gwen and Ivor's group were clearly outclassed by the Ebeneezer Free Will chapel choir and quite a few others, but no one appeared too put out. Seemed the sheer joy of singing was the point of the proceedings. Finally everyone left, talking and congratulating each other, and Alex ended up being introduced to half the town—or so it seemed.

She knew darn well she'd never remember all the names but she wouldn't forget the knowing looks. Seemed everyone was curious about Dai Hughes' latest acquisition.

She wasn't too sure how she felt about that. Especially after he refused several invitations to the pub and made it quite clear he was taking her somewhere more enticing than the Turfcutter's Arms. His refusal to join his sister and her brood for ice cream earned a very amused and delighted grin from Blod.

"Watch him," she whispered in Alex's ear as they stood in the car park. "He can be trouble."

No doubt, but Alex rather fancied the sort of trouble he might give her. "Don't worry, I will."

"Pity you had to bring your own car," Dai said as his sister and her family drove away. Alex wasn't too sure about that, having a way home was never a bad idea. "Never mind, follow me back to *Dwr ffynnon*, park and I'll take you somewhere special."

Really?

Like a gentleman, he walked her to her car, fastening her seat belt before kissing her. It wasn't a deep kiss, not a particularly long one, really just a brush of his lips over hers, but Alex felt it right down deep between her legs and when he lifted his face away, she gasped.

And smiled. She had no intention of smiling. Talk about involuntary gestures. But it felt damn good and if that was a sample of what Dai Hughes could do... Her smile became a grin.

He grinned back. Obviously pleased with himself. "Follow me," he repeated as he closed her door.

She gave him enough time to get clear of her car then started her engine and headed out of the car park. He didn't even appear in her rear mirror until she was clear of the village. As the road climbed toward Hawk Mountain he followed at a distance, obviously not in the least worried about losing her and pulled in to park five minutes behind her.

She was leaning against her car, head cocked on one side and trying very hard to suppress a smile as he opened his door and crossed the two or three meters between them to stand well into her personal space. "For that little disobedience, you deserve to be put over my knee and given a good tanning on your naked backside."

It wasn't easy to ignore the instant thrill that zapped her pussy. "Really?" At least her voice held steady.

"Yes, really and truly." His hand stroked her right arm from her shoulder to her elbow.

"Aren't you leaping ahead a bit?"

He raised her hand to his mouth and kissed it as he held her little sliver handcuff between a finger and thumb. "Not at all, unless I'm misreading this signal," he paused. "I'm not, am I?"

"Maybe, I didn't wear it for you?"

Even in the dark she couldn't miss his smirk. "*Cariad*, I've lived here all my life, apart from three years in Aberystwyth for Uni. Trust me, if you are looking for a pervy lover, I'm it for a fifty mile radius."

A mite bit of an exaggeration perhaps. But he'd made his point. "What makes you think I'm looking for a pervy lover?"

"I saw it in your eyes. I can read it in every movement you make. You yearn to be dominated. You dream about it. Right now, your body aches for what I can give you." He rested both hands on her shoulders and lowered his voice. "Let me take care of that throbbing ache between your legs."

No point in denying what was happening in her pussy. She could smell herself and bet he could too. Damn, clear mountain air!

Alex swallowed. He could probably hear her dry throat gulp. Deep breath time. "Dai, I barely know you."

She was right there but he planned to remedy that before morning. He took both her hands in his, holding them loosely. No pinning her hands behind her. Not yet. He wanted, needed her, had been half scared he'd read her wrongly but now he knew for sure, he daren't risk moving too fast. Or too slowly. "And I barely know you, Alex, but I know enough to sense a connection between us. Maybe it's just a mutual need we can satisfy for each other. Maybe more. Only one way to find out. Are you willing to have a go?"

She paused, lowering her eyes in a so beautiful submissive gesture that he suspected was pure instinct and then looked up to meet his gaze. "Maybe."

Three thousand percent better than "no". "How can I help turn that 'maybe' into 'yes'?" His hands were getting sweaty with anxiety. He hoped to hell she couldn't feel them through her sweater.

"What makes you say there's a connection between us?"

Trust a sub to grasp the pertinent point. Time for him to

take a deep breath and admit. "You've invaded my sleep. I've dreamed about nothing but you since I met you. Wild dreams. Sexy dreams. You're naked, willing and submit to whatever I demand," he paused. Might as well admit to the lot. "Dreams that had my body acting as if I were sixteen again."

She went quiet. So quiet in the still of the night around them he was convinced he'd messed up royally. She needed a strong man, not one who admitted to loss of control. "I've had dreams too," she replied, her voice quiet.

"What sort of dreams?" He had her now. As long as he didn't botch this up.

He heard her inhale and let it out slowly. "Sexy dreams. About a lover. A lover who fucked me, tied me up, spanked me and teased me. A lover who had me waking sweating and wet. But I never saw his face. It was always shrouded in shadow."

"Where did he fuck you?" Another hesitation. He brushed his hand over her hair. "Tell me."

"My mouth, my cunt and my ass."

"And that pleased you?"

"Oh! Yes!"

"While you were tied up?" She nodded. He'd let that pass for now. "You like that?" This time he heard her exhale. "Yes." Not much more than a whisper on her breath but it was enough. "I'm not going to tie you immobile tonight," he told her, wrapping his arms around her shoulders. She was shaking. Delicious! "Another time I will. But this evening I want to fuck you until you scream. You agree?"

It took her several endless seconds to reply. "I need a safe word."

He had her! "What's your full name?"

"Alexandra Eleanor Carpenter."

"You have your safe word."

"Yes!" Her smile showed pearly teeth in the dark. To make certain there was no misunderstanding, he pulled her closer, pressing his erection into her belly. She let out a little sigh. Turning a little, but keeping her close, he pointed up to the dark outline of Hawk Mountain. "I'm going to take you up *Mynydd Cudyll*. When we come down, I'll have marked you as mine." Her tremor was nothing short of delicious. "You'll come with me." It wasn't intended as a question.

"I thought you wanted to come in?"

"Oh I'll come in," he said, "repeatedly, and later I'll enter your house and tie you helpless to your bed and have my way with you, but tonight we'll stretch our bodies out on the mountain and you can scream and moan to the stars above."

He'd swear he heard the gulp. "Okay."

It was.

Very.

"First, you must make yourself ready. None of these damn trousers." He gave her rump a friendly slap to make his point. "I want to you go in your house, find a skirt that I can lift easily and get my hands underneath. Something I can throw over your head if I want to. And…" he put a definite edge in his voice, knowing it was just what she'd respond to. "Don't you dare come out wearing a bra or knickers. You leave those and any damn tights behind. I want easy access to every part of you. Understand."

Her racing heartbeat pretty much proved she did. In spades. Her "Yes" was pretty much redundant.

He brushed his lips over her ear. "Go in then. You have ten minutes. Don't make me wait."

"I won't!"

Judging by the way she zipped up the path to the front door. She wasn't going to.

Alex could hear the blood pounding in her ears as she fumbled to unlock the front door. Talk about needy! Not that she had time to mull over the point. She threw her scarf off as she crossed the kitchen and was unzipping her trousers as she ran upstairs, all but tripping in the process. Better take care. Breaking a limb would rather screw up the evening. Or at least her chance of getting screwed "every which way".

Once in her bedroom, she kicked off her shoes and stepped out of her pants. A full skirt? Trust him to want what she didn't have but she did have a flared skirt. Nice easy elastic waist too. Her panties and bra ended up on the bed as she rummaged for a clean sweatshirt. Hardly sexy but mountainsides weren't the coziest of places. Not that her body seemed to object. She was sweating between her breasts and her cunt was all but flowing.

She was trusting him, utterly and implicitly. He might not be tying her up but isolated on a bare mountainside was a restraint in itself. She couldn't wait.

Just to be sure, she put on sneakers. Better than dress shoes if she ended up hiking back down under her own steam.

A glance at her watch. Seven minutes. Good. Later she might want to provoke chastisement but not yet.

She locked the door behind her and tucked the keys into her pocket. Dai was standing where she'd left him, leaning against her car. He stepped away and came toward her.

"Perfect. And on time." He took her hand, meshing fingers with hers, then spun her around pulling her toward the car and pushed her facedown on the hood. Holding her down with a hand between her shoulder blades, he lifted her skirt.

"Not exactly full is it."

"It's the fullest I have."

"Will have to do then, won't it?" His hand stroked her bare ass. "You listen and obey well." He pulled her back to her feet, holding her back to his chest as his hands slipped under her sweatshirt. He cupped both breasts. "Good. Nicely available. Just what I like and so do you, don't you. Lovely to feel the breeze on your pussy, isn't it?"

"Yes!"

"Thought so!" He lifted her, one arm around her shoulders, the other under her knees, and carried her across to his car. Setting her on her feet, he opened the door for her. "Tell me, how do you feel about gags and blindfolds?"

"No gags!" No way! If he wanted that, she'd say goodbye here and now no matter what she passed up. "I don't mind a blindfold."

"Fair enough." He fastened her seat belt and closed the door. Moments later he was snapping his own seat belt. "There's a blindfold in the glove compartment. Put it on."

Chapter Ten

ɞ

Her fingers trembled so much she almost dropped the darn blindfold. It was black leather, lined with silk that caressed her skin as she fastened the ties with shaking hands.

"All set?" He sounded distant. Or maybe she was the one sinking into herself.

"Yeah."

Lost in the dark behind the blindfold, Alex listened as he reversed out onto the road and headed up the mountain. There was no sound other than her breathing and the pulse in her ears and the sound of the engine as he changed gears.

She had a hundred questions and he hadn't forbidden her to speak. "How far is it?"

"Up the *Mynydd Cudyll*?"

"Yeah."

"Fifteen, twenty minutes. We'll walk the last bit."

"Blindfolded?"

"Would that bother you?"

"Depends on the path. Grazed and bloody knees would rather kill the mood."

His chuckle came soft and sexy in the dark. "Good point, *cariad*. Besides, I'll need your help to carry all the paraphernalia." What he hell was he bringing? A portable dungeon? "Let's just leave it on for now to put you a suitably submissive mood and while you're sitting wondering what delicious tortures I have planned, tell me a little more about those dreams of yours."

How much detail did he really want? Most likely every

last little shred. "They were wild, really wild as if everything I'd ever fantasized about and the most extreme things I've ever done all happened in the space of a few hours, maybe even minutes. Every time I dozed off or went to sleep, the dreams came."

"Unwelcomely so?"

"Hell no! They were marvelous. Saved me getting out my trusty Magic Wand."

"That good, eh?"

"You bet!" Just talking about them that much sent her body humming.

"I was thinking about those dreams of yours while you were getting ready. Were they more and better than usual?"

"Lord, yes!"

"Same as mine. More vivid, utterly realistic."

"Odd that. Both of us having them at the same time."

"Perhaps."

"What do you mean?"

He was quiet a few moments as if mulling over his reply. "According to some of the old whispered stories, the spring didn't just renew health and vigor but also stimulated sexual function. Couples used to bathe together to ignite carnal interest in each other."

"Might not have been the water. Taking a bath or shower together is a pretty good prelude to sex. Anyway, we haven't bathed together." They could have if he'd come in but as it was…

"We both dipped our hands in together."

Sheesh! They had. "And that caused us to have kinky dreams? No way! I had them before I discovered the spring." Had for years, come to that.

"But it caused us to share them."

Oh come on! "I wasn't dreaming about you."

81

"Weren't you?"

He obviously didn't have ego problems. Okay, he was a Dom after all. "He had your voice." Damn, what had she admitted to now?

"I think," he said, "that by dipping in the water together, we connected through Morgaine's magic. Maybe we both had similar dreams and fantasies and the magic linked us."

That was one of the best pick-up lines she'd ever encountered. Of course he'd already pretty much taken care of all the preliminaries. "Lucky coincidence we were both kinky or one of us would have had a shock and the other a major disappointment."

"Maybe we instinctively recognized the dominant and submissive in each other. Think on it."

She did, all the way until the car hit a rough patch of uneven road and came to a stop.

Alex stared around her after Dai helped her out of the car and removed the leather blindfold. They really were on the mountainside, not at the summit but on a broad, level shoulder, about nine or ten meters from a stone table.

"Here, help me with these." Dai had the boot open and handed her a rolled up sleeping bag. "Gets chilly up here toward morning and you are going to be naked after all."

Maybe, but her body didn't notice any chill. Heat and need roared though her as their hands touched. "Are we going to the stone table?" Sounded like something out of a *Narnia* book.

"Morgaine's *cromlech*," he replied. "It's said that the spring has its true source up here."

Why not? Somewhere deep under their feet, perhaps a warm trickle rose and seeped through the rocks to gush forth in Aunt Maria's basement.

And right now Alex's pussy was pretty much gushing forth. "Want me to carry this over there?" She angled her head toward the dark shape of Morgaine's *cromlech*.

"Just a few more things." He perched a small bundle on top of the sleeping bag. Picked up another and a couple of pillows and smiled at her. "Follow me."

Here, away from any street or houselights, the stars were like bright lamps overhead and the moonlight reflected off the rocks. She had no trouble following Dai.

If she could just keep up with him all the way…

He spread one of the sleeping bags over the top of the table.

"Handy having a stone table when you need one."

He frowned at her. "You're in Wales now, it's *cromlech, cariad*."

Fair enough but… "What did you just call me?"

"*Cariad*. An endearment. It means 'darling'."

Very, very deep breath needed now. "That's what my dream lover calls me." Freaky was not the word.

"You didn't know what it meant?"

"I pretty much guessed but had never heard it before."

He went very quiet and very thoughtful. "I called you that in my dreams."

This was getting a bit too farfetched and downright spooky. "Were we having the same dreams?"

"Maybe. Old Morgaine was said to work magic after all."

That needed thinking about and right now cognition wasn't on the top of her priorities.

Nor his. Dai took the bundle out of her hands and lifted the hem of her sweatshirt, pulling it over her head. "Let's make our own magic."

Seemed a brilliant idea as he cupped her breasts, rubbing the nipples with his thumbs. "Will you submit, Alex? Give in to me completely? Enjoy wild, safe sex with me?"

It was almost an echo from her dreams.

She lowered her eyes. "If it pleases you." With those four words came the wondrous rush of emotion that always swamped her at the realization of what she was doing—giving herself, her pleasure and her body over to a lover.

"Oh! It will please me." He wrapped his arms around her and drew her to him.

It was going to be like her dreams but so much better. This time a warm, strong man held her in his clasp. She leaned into him, pressing her belly into his erection. His magnificent erection if she was any judge.

"Like that?" he asked, rubbing against her.

Did he really need to ask? "I'd like it better inside me."

He laughed, a great roar of pleasure that resounded across the hills. "You want my cock, do you? You want it in your cunt? You want it fucking you until you scream with pleasure?"

Her breath caught at the prospect. "Yes, please."

"You have to earn it. You know that, don't you?"

"How can I earn it, Master?" The title came to her tongue by instinct.

"You know exactly how, don't you, sweet Alex?"

As she went to kneel, he stopped her, dropping a pillow to the ground. "Gravel and stones are hard on the knees, *cariad*."

Not the only things hard around here. Alex rubbed her hands over the soft twill of his pants and rested a palm over his erection. Not wanting to waste any time, she reached for his zipper at the same time as he unbuckled his belt and unhooked the waist.

Dai went commando! Not mucking around with boxers or tighty-whities. His beautiful, rampant cock sprung free. Her dream lover had been well endowed but Dai's cock was sheer male beauty. She rubbed her face against it, letting the heated flesh stroke her cheek as she rested her head against his thigh. Lovely was not the word. He was long and smooth and so wondrously male. She licked her lips in anticipation as she ran a finger down one side of his length.

No demand she get on with it like before, just a very flattering and appreciative sigh as Dai clasped her head.

Alex brushed her lips over the head of his cock, savoring the sweetness of the tiny bead of moisture before opening her mouth and swallowing him down to the root.

He groaned, grasping her head steady as a wild rush of power roared though her mind and heart. She was on her knees but she held the power and the control, and relished it in her heart. Later, he would dominate and bend her mind and body to his will but for these few minutes, she reigned supreme at his feet.

His fingers tunneled through her hair, keeping her head steady as her mouth eased up the length of his cock before swallowing him deep again. She came back slowly this time, caressing every centimeter of him with her lips as her tongue explored the ridges and roughness and the luscious smoothness.

He gave a little groan. "Alex!" he muttered, and pressed his hips toward her.

He was hers! His power and strength filled her mouth as she breathed slowly, delighting in his need and her power and the sexual heat that united them. He now took over, holding her head as he fucked her mouth. This was more, better than any dream. Her fantasies had been shadows and now she held his reality in her mouth as he drove in and out. Using her, thrilling her, and sending her mind and body into overdrive. She was close to coming when he slowed, easing himself out of her mouth and holding his lovely cock to her face. Alex brushed her lips over the gorgeous head—her salute to his maleness and power and dominance. Then lowered her head to rest on his shoes. She had never made this obeisance to a lover before, but here on the rocky hillside it felt so utterly right.

Was there really some sort of mystical connection between them? Had the long-gone Morgaine le Fay wrought magic through the warm waters? Right at this moment in time, Alex didn't give a rat's ass. Far more important thoughts occupied her. The most pressing being what Dai Hughes had planned for her next.

Seemed he liked her bent at his feet. Not that she minded. Kneeling, savoring the building need in her body as her breasts ached and her cunt throbbed with anticipation was fine by her.

"Look at me, Alex." She looked up. Instead of the dark blurry outlines of her dream lover, she saw Dai's face clear in the moonlight. His smile like a benediction, his eyes bright and twinkling. "This is wonderful but we both need more."

He wasn't kidding. Her body virtually hummed with need. Was it the clean mountain air, the darkness and the quiet, or the need and heat sparking between them as submissive and dominant?

Just like her dream lover, Dai grasped her upper arms and lifted her to her feet before he kissed her.

And all but zapped her brain.

His lips were warm, alive and covering her mouth in an act of possession. Marking her body and mind as his. She parted her lips for him and he took over completely. Pressing deep as his tongue caressed hers, leading, invading, leaving her breathless and expectant.

Forget dream lovers! Dai was as real as the rocks beneath their feet. Her breasts rubbed against the roughness of his sweater, his hands played up and down her back, keeping her warm. Promising more and harsher caresses.

"Alex," he said, his voice taut and urgent. "I wanted to

make this last all night, to watch the sun rise as we come together but, dammit, I want you so much it hurts."

The feeling was mutual.

Alex smiled, watching the pale outline of his mouth as she savored the power she held. Power she would hand over to Dai Hughes. "What should I do?"

"Strip!"

The Dom was right to the fore, certain, confident of her need and willingness to obey. In seconds, her skirt had been pulled down to her knees. She stepped out of it, leaving it in a crumpled circle on the ground. "Should I take off my shoes?" She wasn't too keen on rough gravel on bare feet but…

"After you undress me." She nodded. "Using only your mouth."

Sheesh! She could guess what naughty books he'd been reading in his spare time. No lover had ever demanded that. But why not? His pants already hung open halfway off his hips, it wasn't too hard to push them down to his ankles once she was back on her knees. Of course now his pants bunched around his feet and she hadn't worked on his shoes, which naturally enough had laces. "I could use a little help here."

"Looks like bad planning on your part."

"I've never actually done this before."

She swore he'd chuckled. "Then you may use your hands but only to lift my trouser legs." It might be her first time at this lark but he darn well knew what he was doing. That thought spurred her on. She wanted so much to please him.

Gingerly she lifted one pant leg and eyed those damn shoelaces and hoped he hadn't tied double knots.

He hadn't.

Holding one end in her teeth and tugging, the neat bow gave way and she set to work on the other one. It took a little more pulling but soon he toed off both shoes, pulled of his socks and stepped out of his pants, pausing only to fold them and toss them onto the stone table.

As they landed, his belt buckle made a clink against the stone.

"Stay right as you are," he said, and reached over to pull his belt from the loops.

Chapter Eleven

୫୬

Yikes! Alex didn't move but she'd have to be blind not to catch the swing of the narrow leather from his hand. Swallowing, she remained on her knees, but when he stepped back close, standing on the edge of the pillow, she planted a kiss on the inside of his ankle before kissing a line up the inside of his thigh.

His cock enjoyed that but she sensed tensing in his body that maybe signaled displeasure.

"Alex." His tone left her in no doubt. "That was not part of my command."

She dropped her head, "Apologies."

"Accepted, but remember what I hold in my hand."

As if she were likely to forget! Damn fantasies and dreams, she knew only too well how hard a carefully wielded belt could sting as it kissed bare flesh. The prospect made her shudder and sent a wet memory right to her cunt. "May I stand to take off your sweater and shirt?"

"You may." He even helped her to her feet, steadying her with a strong hand on each arm, and had the consideration to pull off his sweater.

That still left the full complement of tiny pearl buttons. She did everything but slobber over the front placket before she got the last one open. She'd had to stand on tiptoe to reach the top one. Then there were the two at his cuffs, but they soon gave and she pulled it off his arms and back.

It was worth the effort.

Naked he was magnificent. A broad chest with just enough hair to be manly. Dark hair that narrowed at his waist to cluster nicely around his cock. One look at his arse and she clenched her fists to control the urge to cup those lovely firm cheeks and stroke them.

"Stop ogling me, *cariad*, you'll get everything you want. Soon."

"How soon?" She bet he just loved to drag things out.

He ran the back of his hand down the side of her face. "When it suits me. Impatience can be punished, *cariad*." To illustrate his point, Dai cracked his belt on the edge of the *cromlech*. A shudder rippled down her spine to lodge like a cold thrill in her cunt.

Would he? She looked at the belt dangling from his hand and longing and fear warred in her mind.

This was so good and so utterly terrible.

"All in good time." His voice held promise as well as a whisper of threat. "First you'd best unpack our supplies." He handed her the lumpy roll she'd carried earlier.

Spread on the *cromlech* in the light of the moon, they made interesting and titillating viewing—fur-lined leather handcuffs, a soft rabbit fur flogger, a butt plug, a tube of lubricant, a bottle of massage oil and a string of anal beads. "We did share the same dream," she said, half under her breath.

"Want it to come true?" he asked, stepping close and wrapping his arms around her.

"Under the stars wasn't part of it."

"That's my magical extra." He was pretty much right. It was magical here. "Are you ready to obey and submit?"

Was she? Could she even consider refusal? She lowered her head and looked down at his broad chest. "Yes."

The kiss on the back of her neck resounded between her legs. "Sure?"

"Whatever you ask of me, I will do. Whatever you

90

demand, I will obey."

His cock seemed to grow at her words. He rubbed himself against her belly. "What if I bend you over the *cromlech* and flog you?"

"Yes."

"What if I choose to bugger you?"

She shivered. "Yes."

"What if I put those pearls deep up your backside?"

Her muscles clenched at the prospect. "Oh yes!"

"What if..." He slipped his hand between them to close over her breast. "I take my belt to your luscious arse."

No! Yes! How? "Yes!" It came out on the tail of a gasp but she said it.

"And the handcuffs are a given, since you like so much to wear them." His other hand closed over her wrist.

It was so all-around wonderful, she whimpered, "Please."

"Oh Alex..." His lips on her neck sent a lovely shudder down her back. "Cold, *cariad*?"

Impossible. His warmth fired her very core. "No."

"Good, so you won't mind lying facedown on the *cromlech* and keeping utterly still for a little bit of needed preparation."

Her heart skipped at the last word, he darn well knew how to draw out the anticipation. "Whatever pleases you." It came out so easily and sent such a chill over her. They were alone. She was naked. Not a living soul for miles.

He edged her forward several paces. It was inevitable he would bend her forward and her body flowed under his pressure. She was facedown, bent over on the *cromlech*, ass presented for whatever he had in mind.

"Spread your legs." His knee between them made certain of her compliance.

She was in the perfect position for fucking or...she hadn't

forgotten the belt that now lay on the sleeping bag, just inches from her right arm.

But right now, his hands on her waist, smoothing down to her butt, took all her concentration. His touch was sheer magic, setting nerve endings tingling as she relaxed under his hands. He leaned over her, rubbing his erection between her ass cheeks. "Ready?"

Dry mouthed, Alex nodded.

"I can't hear you, *cariad*."

"Yes!" It became a sigh as his hand swept between her legs and his fingers parted her pussy lips before pressing deep.

"Like that?" he asked as his fingers penetrated and twisted until she moaned. "Can't hear you." He pumped her harder.

"Yes."

He was gone. "Nice cunt you have, now let's have a go at your arse." As he spoke, he spread her cheeks and pressed cold lubricant deep. Moments later he rammed the plug in deep, making her cry out. "You didn't like that?"

"It came in too hard."

"Want it gentler?"

"Please. If it pleases you."

He eased it out slowly, added extra lubricant with almost agonizing slowness and pressed the tip of the plug against her tight opening. He waited. Pressed enough to stretch the muscle just a little and waited until she relaxed and he pressed deeper, twisting the plug as it slipped past her ring of muscle and he slowly pushed in deep. He was screwing her with hard silicon.

"That's wonderful," she managed between sighs.

"A pleasure, *cariad*. Better leave it there for now while I…"

He was astride her, his thighs straddling her shoulders as

he pulled her hands over her head and snapped the leather handcuffs over her wrists. "Keep your arms like that. No moving."

She gulped as the familiar and wonderful thrill filled her mind and sent her body afire and then yelped as he yanked out the butt plug.

"That's all right," he said, giving her rump a swat. A not in the least gentle swat that left a definite tingle all over her left cheek. "Felt that?"

"Yes."

"You were meant to. Now for a little more. I want you nicely warmed up. This will probably hurt so I don't want you grumbling and carrying on."

The belt moved, brushing the side of her waist as he pulled it away.

Every muscle in her body clenched. He was damn right, it would hurt. He stroked her ass, caressing the side where the sting from his slap was fading. "I won't be able to see the marks in this light. A pity that but you'll be able to feel them. I do have your permission to continue, don't I?"

Now was a chance to safe word out. To refuse. To escape the coming kiss of his belt.

Dai waited as Alex listened to her racing heart. Desire and need overcame reason. "Yes, I give permission."

"Sure? Don't want to use your safe word?"

"No." She made her body go limp. A tensed butt would hurt many times more. "I'm ready."

"So am I!" As he spoke, the leather slashed though the air and landed right across her butt. Her scream still echoed in her ears as the second blow fell and the third. Three stinging lines of heat and pain that brought tears to the corners of her eyes as she waited for the rest.

That never came.

"Enough," he said stroking her ass cheeks. "For now at least." She should have known better than to think it was over and done with. "You do warm up nicely. Next time we'll do it in daylight so I can really admire my stroke work."

The first edge of pain eased slightly to the beginnings of the familiar warm glow.

"Feel it in your pussy yet?" Dai asked.

"Yes." He didn't just take her word for it but pressed several fingers up her.

"Lovely. Let's see how you handle a different sort of stimulation. This you will like but first..." What now? "Scoot up a bit, there's a love. Get your whole body up there." He gave her a little boost as she wriggled and scrambled as best she could without moving her arms. "Smashing! You kept your hands and arms over your head. For that, you get a reward."

As she waited, forcing herself to breathe, Alex basked in the wonderful rush that accompanied helplessness as a warm oil trickled down her spine and his hands eased over her back and shoulders, spreading the scented oil. He knew exactly what he was doing as his fingers stroked and kneaded, finding the tight places and little knots of tension.

Once she let out a little sigh of pleasure, he stopped. "That's enough, *cariad*. Can't have you too relaxed, can we? Time for a little more stimulation." He kissed the base of her spine before blowing along her back, up to her shoulder blades. It was the same spicy oil as in her dream. She went limp as the warmth spread over her back until she felt aglow with heat and sensation.

Something soft caressed her shoulders and trailed down her back. The fur flogger! How could he know? How could they really have dreamed together? Right now she didn't care one iota. Incredible! Marvelous! Every nerve ending tingled with pleasure and anticipation of the next caress of the furry tresses. Dai was even better in real life than in her dreams, knowing exactly how to stimulate and arouse. He kept mostly to her back and ass, but once in a while, when he treated her with a wide sweep up and down her inner thighs, a stray tress caught her clit and wrung a cry from her but it was never quite enough to take her to the edge.

He stopped, tossing away the flogger with a clatter as it landed on the ground and climbing back on the *cromlech* to cover her back and shoulders with kisses as she slipped into a great gulf of pleasure and sensation.

She was half out of her body when his hands parted her cheeks and she gasped as more lubricant was forced up her butthole. Was it the plug again? His cock? Was he going to bugger her? Her muscles clenched in anticipation and earned her a slap on her already warmed-over butt.

"Relax! Don't you dare tighten up for me. You know better."

She did. With effort Alex forced her muscles to relax against his touch and the gentle pressure...of a bead. The first slipped in easily as her muscle relaxed and closed back.

This was going to be wonderful. She let her entire body sag as she anticipated the next intrusion. He was gentle but firm. Soft as his touch was, she knew a slap would greet the first sign of resistance on her part. As each bead slipped in, he counted. "That's two, Alex. Only six more to go." "Just five more." "Four..." A teasing, endless countdown as he paused between each one to stroke her shoulders or brush his erection against skin. As the last bead slipped in, she let out a sigh of relief even as she felt filled, stuffed. Invaded.

"Keep them there," he warned. "Let any fall out and you'll really feel what my belt can do."

As he spoke, his fingers tested her cunt. No need. She could smell her arousal even here in the open air.

"Tell me," he asked, "do you really enjoy my belt that much?"

She had to think, summoning her mind through the fog of sensation to reply. "I like the threats. They arouse me and I like the afterglow, but I don't like the sting and the pain."

"But you'll accept it. You'll present your body for chastisement whenever I demand it, won't you, Alex?"

"Oh yes!"

"Very good of you, *cariad*. Let's see what else you will accept."

He climbed up beside her and gently turned her onto her back. She shifted her hips to find a more comfortable spot for her still burning bottom but then went still, ache was one thing but if she shifted out one of those beads…

He knelt astride her, seeming oblivious to any discomfort her back and ass might suffer. He cupped each breast, stroking and massaging gently, paying special attention to her nipples until they tingled and ached. Pinching each one tightly before leaving them to throb in the night as his fingers trailed down and played her belly, tracing slow circles as they drifted lower to open her pussy lips.

It felt so all-around wonderful as he flicked her clit, wringing a cry from her and setting off a wild rush of pain and pleasure that almost took her over the edge.

She was so needy. Those wild dreams hadn't sated her need one little bit. Rather, they'd spurred it higher.

"Please," she was begging and didn't care. Whatever he demanded, she would comply. If only he'd give her release.

"Easy, *cariad*," Dai said, "Not yet for a while. Not yet."

"I need it! I need you! I need to be fucked. Hard!"

"Yes, you do, and you'll get it all, *cariad*. Just not yet."

Damn! It was the age-old dominant game of stringing her along, taking her to the edge and denying, making her wait until she was taut and high with need and frustration. And she was prepared to love him for it.

Maybe.

If he delivered.

Something she did not doubt for a second. This was one Dom who knew his job. She wanted to scream with frustration.

Dai's hand stroked the inside of each knee, sending wild tendrils of sensation racing up her legs to inflame her already throbbing clit. He clasped her thighs and gently spread them. Wide.

He bent forward, sliding his hands under her still warm ass cheeks and lifted her hips. The cool night air wafted over her heated cunt and then his mouth covered her.

Just as in her dream, he lapped her, the full flat of his tongue covering her. Slow, teasing all-covering licks from her ass to her clit. He took his sweet time as her mind melted. Conscious thought was beyond her. What the hell? Who needed to think? All that mattered was to feel as he consumed and devoured. His tongue plunged deep inside her. Slow, stabbing movements that set her hips jerking and stretched her arms as she fought to keep them over her head. In and out his tongue went, mimicking the movement of a cock…his cock.

"Come into me. Fuck me!" She wasn't too proud to beg, not with need like this boiling her blood.

He penetrated her. It was only his fingers but he filled her, pressing against the beads as he pistoned in and out and his thumb worked her clit.

Her reason blanked out. She knew nothing but sensation and pleasure. She was nearing the edge, heart and breathing racing. She was climbing, spiraling up and up, screaming. Her mind zapped. Her body roared with sensation and building pleasure as she raced toward the edge. In a wild rush of joy she came. Again and again, shouting, crying aloud with each climax until her muscles gave out and she lay in a shaking, limp heap of thoroughly satisfied woman.

"That was wonderful," she gasped. Just getting out those

three words pretty much took her last effort.

"For the first one," Dai whispered. "We're just starting."

He had to be kidding! Her body couldn't take any more and her mind was certainly beyond it.

But when he entered her fast and hard, filling her with his power and raw male sex, her body responded. As he worked her, invading her with his need and strength, he was pulling her back to the edge with him. It was utterly impossible but she was coming again. Repeatedly. In wild bursts of sexual energy. From the depths of what had once been her reason, Alex sensed his growing arousal, heard his groans and gloried in his power deep inside her as he came.

She matched him and more as wild waves of multiple orgasms roared through her. Just as she felt her sated body could take no more, he pulled at the string on her beads, and as each forced past her muscle, the pressure triggered yet another climax. She screamed until her cries echoed back at her from the arc of the heavens and she saw every star double.

She lay on Morgaine's *cromlech*, a sweaty, gasping heap of satisfied woman and while she fought for breath and her pulse beat a tattoo in her ears, she heard Dai as if from a distance.

"You're mine, *cariad*. What is forged on *Mynydd Cudyll* is forever."

She had to be dreaming. Hallucinating most likely. She was vaguely aware of a cover being thrown over her and her head being lifted and laid back on a pillow, but she was too worn, too happy, too satisfied, with sated lust to care. Alex shut her eyes and curled into Dai's strength and warmth.

Chapter Twelve

ꝏ

It was the ruddy dawn chorus that woke her. Whoever would have dreamt there were so many birds on a bare mountainside? Alex opened bleary eyes and blinked, the wondrous events of the night lighting her memory in glorious Technicolor. Dai was curled asleep beside her, his long legs hanging off the edge of the *cromlech*. The ground around them strewn with clothes and sex toys.

This time she had not been dreaming.

She was however, chilled. Sitting up and exposing bare breasts to the morning air wasn't the best idea. It did harden her nipples but maybe that was left over from the cascade of climaxes that still had her cunt mightily contented.

This was certainly a one-off morning after. What next?

"*Bore da, cariad*?" Dai said, propping himself up on one elbow. "Sleep well, my love?"

Now that he mentioned it, the darn *cromlech* was a trifle hard on the bones. Not that she'd been in any state earlier to bother about such a trifling detail. "Yes, thank you, very much, but it's getting chilly."

He rubbed his leg over hers. "I could take care of that!"

"I don't doubt it for a second, Dai, but I'm not sure I can walk as it is and any more…"

"Are you all right? Did I hurt you?" He sounded half panicked.

"I'm fine. Relaxed. Chilly, but you were magnificent." "Magnificent" was woefully inadequate when she thought about it.

"I can take care of the chilly bit!" And at the same time give her a sight for sleepy eyes as he hopped off the edge of the stone platform and gathered up her sweatshirt and skirt and his own clothes.

They both dressed fast.

"Your place is closest for breakfast," he said as he zipped his pants and sat down on the edge of the *cromlech* to pull on his socks.

It was. Mornings after could be so tricky but with Dai it seemed right somehow. "I've got eggs."

"You have bacon too, unless you've eaten the whole pound I stocked you with."

She hadn't touched it but... "Look, Dai..." They'd made some wild promises but passionate oaths seldom lasted beyond daybreak. "I don't want to hold you to anything."

He paused in gathering up the discarded sex toys and came close. "Don't lie to me, *cariad*, and for the record I never use that endearment loosely. You do want to hold me, every bit as much as I want to hold you. You're mine. Morgaine's magic saw to that. Now you'll stay with me."

A nice dream but... "Dai, I can't just stay here on your say-so. I have a job, a career."

Didn't seem to faze him. "Of course you do. You're a writer. Write here. I'll buy you a computer as a wedding present if you like and I'll even proofread for you."

"What do you know about my writing?"

His grin verged on lascivious. "It's brilliant, sexy. Miss Abbot lent me some to read. Told me she thought we'd get along famously and I was to take care of you. I've taken pretty good care so far, haven't I?"

That, she could not deny but she'd definitely have a thing or two to say to Aunt Maria when she got back from Tibet. And come to that, what was Aunt Maria doing reading naughty stories? Okay, dumb question that.

Dai was obviously not giving her time to raise objections. "Stop fussing and frowning, *cariad*. You can't go anywhere. You know what they say about couples who stay all night on a mountain together?"

"Can't say I do."

"The mountain magic binds them. Between *Mynydd Cudyll* and Morgaine's spring, we're as good as married already."

It was ridiculous! They barely knew each other but who was she to argue with Morgaine? And mountain magic?

"Okay," she replied, standing and rolling up the sleeping bag. They could argue it out later, after breakfast. "How do you like your eggs?" Who knew what Dai might do if she managed to burn the toast?

Also by Madeleine Oh

ഋ

Party Favors (*anthology*)
Power Exchange
R.S.V.P. (*anthology*)
Single White Submissive (*anthology*)
Tied with a Bow (*anthology*)

About the Author

ഋ

Madeleine Oh is an expatriate Brit, retired LD teacher and grandmother now living in Ohio with her husband of thirty-five years. She has published erotic short fiction, novels and novellas in the US, UK and Australia. For information about Madeleine's work visit her web site: www.madeleineoh.com.

Madeleine welcomes comments from readers. You can find her website and email address on her author bio page at www.ellorascave.com.

Tell Us What You Think

We appreciate hearing reader opinions about our books. You can email us at Comments@EllorasCave.com.

THE CAJUN
Dominique Adair

&

Dedication

❧

To the Hurricane Katrina Survivors

Author Note

Dear Readers—this novella was started in August 2005, just days before Hurricane Katrina made landfall on the Gulf coast. Without a second thought I put writing aside to head south and give whatever aid I could. The experiences I had changed my life forever and these brave survivors taught me so much more than I ever imagined.

Thank you for saving my life.

Chapter One

ဢ

When Rachel made the last minute decision to pay her parents a visit, getting caught in a tropical depression wasn't quite what she'd had in mind.

Her grip tightened on the steering wheel until her fingers went numb. Rachel strained to see the marsh road through the blinding rain though her headlights barely made a dent in the storm. Even though she knew the road as well as her own face, the car barely crept along the road. Shrouded in sheets of rain and buffeted by strong southeast winds, what was once familiar was now alien territory. One false move of the wheel could send her little car plummeting into the marsh.

Under normal circumstances she enjoyed a swim on a hot summer day. She'd been born and raised in the heart of bayou country in southern Louisiana and she knew how to handle herself outdoors. Her father was a third-generation shrimp boat captain and her brothers had followed in his footsteps, each of them running his own boat and crew. Their house where she had grown up was less than thirty feet from a large bayou and consequently she felt there wasn't much out here she couldn't handle.

But it didn't mean she wanted to be driving though the marsh in the middle of a fierce storm.

Rachel slowed her rusty compact car, taking a quick moment to rub her tired eyes. She'd worked late and Mama had woken her to make sure she knew about the incoming storm. She hadn't wanted her only daughter to drive out to Dulac in bad weather. But it was her father's fiftieth birthday and she didn't want to miss it. It had never occurred to her that she'd get caught in the storm—she'd thought there was more than enough time to get home.

How wrong she was.

A blast of air slammed into her car causing it to shake. For the first time, fear nipped at her toes. When she got within an arm's reach of her papa, he'd give her an earful then paddle her butt with a quickness.

Anyone who'd grown up on the bayou knew better than to go outside during a big storm. In southern Louisiana the water table was so high it only took a few inches of rain for the area to flood. In a ferocious storm like this, the roads would be flooded out in less than two hours and on the marsh it would take even less time.

When she'd left her apartment in New Orleans, she'd thought the storm was still several hours away. By the time she'd reached Chauvin, darkness had fallen and the steady rain increased enough to slow her progress. It was when she reached the final drawbridge before the marsh road, all hell had broken loose.

The rain diminished visibility to less than fifteen feet, making for a miserable drive. It had been a while since she'd passed anyone on the road. Squinting through the windshield, she tried to get a frame of reference to indicate how much farther she had to go. The unrelieved darkness made every twist and turn a sheer nightmare. Though it had been several years ago that the road had been paved, it was rarely used. It was the only route through the marsh and in good weather it was an easy drive. Roughly nine miles long, some sections of the road weren't even a foot above sea level. No one with any sense could live out here as it flooded with any decent-sized storm.

As kids they'd come out here to fish, raise hell, drink beer and get kinky in the backseat of their cars. It was a beautiful, wild place she loved with all her heart though tonight she wished she were anyplace else but here.

Through the gray veil of rain, her headlights faintly illuminated a wide spot in the road. Each side sported boat docks and she was familiar with this place as it was a great spot for shrimping or fishing. This was also the only area for direct access between the marsh and lake.

"Damn," she muttered. "I'm not even halfway yet."

The wind, as if hearing her curse, slammed into the car and she yelped, quickly counter-steering the wheel to the left. The car shuddered and the engine coughed. For a moment she thought it might die on her.

"Not now," she groaned. "You need to hang in there for a little while longer."

Her car was in dire need of a tune-up and she'd hoped that Jimmy, her younger brother, could oblige her this weekend.

She couldn't see the end of the dock on the lake side as it was already submerged. The gravel lot where they used to park their cars was flooded to within a foot of the road. On the marsh side the water was being blown onto the road to flow in a steady stream into the lake.

This was not good.

Creeping past the docks, they faded quickly in her rearview mirror. Judging from the condition of the gravel lots, the road would be flooded within the next half hour or so. With the water at that level, the lowest points of the road would already be flooded. One of the first lessons she'd learned when her father taught her to drive was to avoid standing or running water.

It only takes two inches of running water to shove a car off the road.

She bit her lower lip. Her car wasn't exactly the sturdiest thing on the road and lately it would act as if it were going to stall every now and then. As long as she could keep it running she should be okay. Turning back was no longer an option, not when she'd come this far. Her parent's house was almost within reach.

You were a damn fool to try this, Rachel girl.

"Thanks, Papa, I realize that now."

A dark lump loomed out of darkness and it was blocking the road. Screaming, she slammed on the brakes and the worn tires slid on the rain-slicked pavement. Her blood ran cold when the rear slid to the right toward the lake. In a desperate attempt to remain on the road, she wrenched the wheel and instead of correcting the skid, she oversteered and flew across the road. Her heart plummeted when she saw the oak trees. Still in a slide, the driver-side rear slammed into one with a jarring crunch. Even with her seat belt engaged, she cracked her head on the driver's window.

For a few moments she sat there stunned, her ears ringing. Her temple hurt from coming in contact with the window. After a few moments the ringing dissipated and she turned her head very slowly, relieved when she didn't feel any pain.

"Well, I think my brain is still intact."

Her voice was shaky and she quickly took an accounting of her body to make sure everything still worked. Other than an ache in her temple, she'd survived without any lasting damage.

Through the rapidly beating wiper blades, the steady rain continued. Her car was resting at a tilt which meant she had one or more wheels off the road. Her lips twisted. If she wasn't in trouble before, she definitely was now.

Slamming the gearshift into park, she strained to peer through the rain, trying to get her bearings. She sucked in a noisy breath when she saw the lump in the road had moved. As if in slow motion, its massive head turned toward her and golden eyes glinted in the murky light from her headlights.

This was one big alligator.

It was hard to judge exactly how large the creature was but it was about ten feet in length. Their gazes met and a shock wave ran through her. If she weren't mistaken, the alligator was smiling at her. She blinked and the creature turned away. With a slow lumbering walk it headed into the marsh. She wasn't fooled by its seemingly lazy movements—alligators could be incredibly fast when they were in pursuit of a meal. When they were kids they'd stand on the bank of the bayou and bark like dogs to see if any of the beasts would make an appearance. Alligators couldn't resist a tasty puppy snack.

The gator vanished into the water just as the back of the car shifted just enough to set her heart pounding. There was no way she could stay here any longer. It was only a matter of time before the water would sweep the car into the marsh and she'd become the catch of the day for all sorts of critters.

Her hands shook as she located a flashlight on the floor of the back seat. Muttering a small prayer that the batteries still worked, she grinned wide when a bright light came on. Reaching for the door handle, she braced herself to face the storm.

First she needed to assess her car. If it was drivable then she needed to figure out how to get it back onto the road. If not, she would have to come up with a Plan B. Unfortunately that would involve walking and she didn't want to consider that possibility quite yet.

One thing at a time, girl.

Pushing hard against the door, Rachel struggled to get out of the car. Gritting her teeth, she stumbled to her feet, dismayed to realize her flashlight was about as useful as high heels on a goat. The wind and rain was fierce and the light was swallowed up less than a foot away.

Clinging to the car, she stumbled forward, shining the light on her rear tires. The wind tore at her clothing and tossed her hair from its usual sloppy twist. Wet strands slapped at her face when she bent to inspect the damage.

Her tire looked okay but somehow she'd managed to get lodged with a large tree limb in front of the wheel. Water lapped at her ankles and she grabbed the branch, the bark digging into her palms when she tried to dislodge it. Grunting and cursing under her breath, she soon realized that her car was immovable.

She was stuck.

Soaked and shaking, Rachel stumbled back into the dubious safety of her car. The wind tore the handle from her hand and she fell into the front seat, face first. She yanked her feet in just before the wind slammed the door.

Huddling against the steering wheel, Rachel's breathing was harsh as she pondered her options. In retrospect, taking this trip in the face of a storm was a stupid move. The worst mistake of all was that she hadn't notified anyone she was headed home and in this case, the consequences could be dire.

Serena, her coworker, would figure it out in the morning as she'd left a note with the opening cash drawer for the store, but that was a few hours away. She glanced at the illuminated clock on her dash. Make that many hours away.

The only reason she hadn't notified her parents was because she didn't want her family to worry about her. As it was, they worried all the time. Her mama believed that a single woman living in New Orleans was fresh meat for the slaughter. Little did her mother guess that she'd find herself in far more danger less than ten miles from home.

Propping the flashlight on the dashboard, she reached for her purse. Maybe, just maybe her cell phone would work. Pulling out a slim silver phone, she flipped it open. Her gaze was glued to the screen and she held her breath as the phone searched for a signal. *Network Unavailable* flashed on the screen and her shoulders sagged.

That was another problem with the bayou area, inconsistent cell service.

She tossed the cell phone onto the passenger seat then propped her elbows on the steering wheel. The rain showed no signs of slowing, and with every minute that passed the water rose. With her car in such a precarious position, she had only one option left.

She'd have to walk and try to find help.

It was suicide and she knew it. Her best bet could be to find a sturdy tree and lash herself to it. The water would rise but she'd never seen the trees be completely swallowed — uprooted yes, swallowed, no. She winced when a pain ran through her head. She touched her temple, surprised when her fingertips were smeared with blood. When she hit the window she must've cut her head without realizing it.

Grabbing a tissue, she wiped her fingers then tossed it onto the passenger seat with the useless cell phone. Just the thought of trying to walk in this storm was enough to make her nauseous. A gust of wind hit her car and she felt the rear of the car rise then sink, coming to rest at a level lower than before. Her heart stuttered and she grabbed her purse and looped the strap over her neck and shoulder. Staying in the car was no longer an option. A few more moves like that and her car would be in the marsh with the fish.

Shoving the phone and keys into her purse, an image of the alligator flashed in her mind. She just couldn't shake the idea that the creature had been smiling at her as if amused at her plight.

"Wish I'd killed the thing. Too damn many alligators 'round here anyway."

Picking up the flashlight, she said a silent prayer then opened the door, allowing the storm to sweep over her.

Staggering against the wind, she gasped when the marsh water reached several inches above her ankles. Holding onto the car, she stumbled around the front end. The lights were still on though they made little difference. Ducking to create a smaller target for the storm, she scrambled over to the tree she'd hit. Now that she was on the other side of the car, she could see the extent of the damage. The rear tire, at least the part that wasn't underwater, was bent at an odd angle and the quarter panel was smashed in. Even if she could've removed the branch, the car wasn't going anywhere soon.

After muttering another small prayer, she faced west and walked into the storm. Rain slashed at her body and the wind and water threatened to sweep her off her feet. Keeping to the marginal shelter of the trees, she made her way along the edge of the road, desperate to keep her footing against the water sucking at her legs.

She'd only walked a few yards when she heard the shriek of tearing metal. The water had lifted the rear end of her car and it almost looked as if it were trying to suck the car into the marsh. Slowly, the back end descended, coming to rest against another tree at a hair-raising angle.

A wave of water crashed against the car and the headlights flickered then dimmed. Panic struck Rachel and she took a step without hanging onto the tree. Water slammed at her legs, knocking her to the road, and the flashlight slipped from her grip. The light went out and she realized that trouble had arrived in spades.

Struggling against the pull of the water, she grabbed at the tree, using it to haul herself onto her feet. Shaking the damp hair from her eyes, she surveyed the hostile, watery world.

If she remembered correctly, there was an old house less than half a mile away on the Marsh side. The great-grandparents of a childhood friend, Etienne Broussard, had lived there for many years. His great-grandmother was a healer or *traiteuse*, who lived in an elevated house in the heart of the marsh. The house had been built in the 1920s and it had survived many storms much worse than this. If she were lucky, it would still be standing.

Her knees felt wobbly and the water sucked at her legs. Judging from her current circumstances, luck was in short supply.

Pushing all thoughts of fear or discomfort from her mind, she set herself to the task of walking through the storm. The strain of the storm was taking its toll and very quickly her senses went dead. The fight to walk was taking all of her resources and nothing else existed around her.

She had no idea how long she'd walked, the steady rain and growing darkness had served to confuse her already muddied senses. Her cheap watch wasn't waterproof and it had stopped the moment it had gotten damp. Weary to the bone, she felt as if she'd been walking for days though in reality it hadn't been even an hour. The urge to grab onto a tree and sit for a few minutes was strong but that wasn't an option. Rachel was afraid that if she sat down she'd never get up again.

Dreaming of warm blankets and steaming hot chicory coffee that her papa made, she stumbled and almost fell down. An unfamiliar noise sounded and she snapped to attention.

Was that an engine?

She spun around and the storm seemed just a shade lighter. Six high-powered lights were mounted on the roll bar of a pickup truck and it was moving toward her. She gave a wild shout of joy.

"I'm saved!"

Moving to the edge of the road so as not to be run over, she raised her arms and began screaming at the top of her lungs. If this person tried to drive past her, she'd throw herself into the back if she had to—she'd do anything to get out of this storm.

The engine grew louder and she began to jump up and down to gain the driver's attention. When the lights grew closer and she could make out the grill of the truck. Rachel leapt and came down hard on the edge of the road. The water-damaged asphalt gave way beneath her feet and she fell.

Her scream was cut off in mid-note as she was catapulted into the marsh. Water filled her nose and mouth and she was pulled under by the strength of the current. Her exhausted mind didn't know which way was up and she clawed at anything within reach. Images of bodies floating in the water flashed before her eyes.

She was not going to die like this.

* * * * *

Etienne Broussard drove slowly along the marsh road with heavy metal music blaring from the stereo speakers. For the thousandth time he asked himself what the hell he was doing. He was supposed to be in New Orleans with his twin brother to celebrate the opening of Jacques' art gallery, instead he was headed back home for no good reason whatsoever.

He'd left the house well over two hours ago and he'd have been in New Orleans if he hadn't been forced to turn around. Just before he reached Petit Calliou he'd had a flat tire. That in itself was puzzling enough as his tires were new and there'd been nothing in the road that he'd seen. After changing the tire he'd headed north when an obstacle prevented him from going any further.

A large alligator had climbed out of the bayou and was stretched across the road blocking both lanes. Having grown up on the bayou, Etienne didn't worry about the alligators. They were basically lazy when it was warm and they came out to play in the early evenings. In a storm they liked to lie on the road as the cement would still be warm from the sun.

But this creature had been different.

From nose to tail it had almost covered the road from shoulder to shoulder. The most interesting quirk was that when Etienne had tried to drive around it, the old rascal had moved, preventing him from going any further. As he contemplated his next move. It was as though he'd been struck with an overwhelming urge to return home.

Now, he wasn't a superstitious man, but having been raised in a Cajun community and he'd been surrounded by superstition all of his life. Even he had to admit that something otherworldly seemed to be at work with this animal. The alligator had kept his eye on the truck and when Etienne decided to turn back, he could've sworn the animal winked.

But why in the hell was he driving through a storm to get back to an empty house?

It was only by sheer luck that he was driving the truck today or he'd be unable to get back to the house at all. His work truck was two feet off the ground and he could drive through a lot of water before it would have any effect on it mechanically. His personal car was a sports car, and while it was a great machine, in a big storm it was like driving a toaster on a patch of ice.

One of his favorite songs came on and he increased the volume. He loved his great-grandparent's home, and when Ms. Emma had passed away she'd left the property to him. Soon he'd graduated college with a degree in nature conservation then took a job with the state monitoring the effects of weather and pollution on the Gulf Coast. After spending months remodeling the house, it was now his favorite place in the world.

It didn't get any better than this.

Reaching a dip in the road, he wasn't surprised to see the water level had risen enough to create a runoff from the marsh into the lake. Coming to a stop, he shifted into the lowest gear and the big engine dropped to a deep growl. Carefully he maneuvered through the newly created river where a road had been only hours before.

Rain slashed at the windows and he continued at a slow speed as he sang along to the thundering music. The wipers were making very little dent in the deluge but he wasn't terribly concerned as he knew this road with his eyes closed.

Etienne glanced at the dashboard clock. It was only nine p.m. and if the storm hadn't ruined the evening the sun would be setting soon. This weather would probably ruin his brother's opening so the possibility of Jacques coming out in the morning for a fishing trip as they'd originally planned was slim to none. He grinned. Then again, with all this rain they just might be able to fish from his front porch.

Rounding a bend, he touched the brakes when his headlights illuminated a small car half on and half off the road. His lip curled. Obviously some fool had thought they could navigate the marsh road in that little tin can and survive.

Idiot…

Etienne maneuvered his vehicle as close as possible to the other. Grabbing the handle of the spotlight mounted on his truck, he flicked it on and pointed at the car. It was empty. The car hadn't been there when he'd left so chances were whoever owned this car was out wandering around in the storm…which meant he'd have to go looking for them.

"Fuck."

After turning the spotlight to illuminate the road ahead, he took his foot off the brake. So much for stretching out on the couch and listening to the rain fall. He scowled. It seemed like lately something was always happening to destroy his plans. If another alligator appeared on the road, he was going to give up and visit the voodoo priestess who lived in Cocodrie.

"Fuck," he muttered again.

When he got his hands on the driver, he would give them a right hook that guaranteed they'd be unconscious for at least a week.

The road was narrow and twisty though the parish had paved it several years ago. He guessed they got tired of dumping gravel after every major storm only for it to be washed away with the next.

Straining to see the road, Etienne carefully guided the truck along the road. Of course it would be a major problem if the driver had left the road and wandered into the marsh. If that were the case the authorities might find their clothing next week as they'd be crab bait already. It would be easy to get lost out here if one didn't know the area.

Every year at least one or two people made the mistake of thinking the beautiful marsh was good walking and they'd have to be rescued. More often than not the ground beneath their feet was a flottant, an island of grass and dirt that floated on the marsh water. It looked solid but it really wasn't. He'd lost count of the times he'd fallen through while surveying the marsh, but he always carried equipment to rescue himself.

It was only a few years ago a man had lost his life when he'd been swimming in the marsh. A cranky gator had caught the man and stowed his body under a flottant to keep him fresh. Several weeks later all that had been found was his shredded swim trunks.

Such was the life on the bayou.

A movement on the side of the road caught his attention and he slowed. Turning down the radio, he cracked his window just in case someone was out there screaming for help. Using his spotlight, he checked the area. Other than raging water and sodden marsh grass, there appeared to be nothing amiss.

Closing the window, he turned off the spotlight and continued on his way, humming along with the music.

Chapter Two

ॐ

Clawing her way through the marsh grass, she began to cry when the red taillights vanished into the storm. Rachel propped her forehead on her arm, her breathing reduced to gasping sobs. The scent of marsh mud and rain was strong in her nose but she lacked the energy to move. She felt utterly defeated.

A few minutes passed and her breathing calmed. Though she felt shaky, she had to get up whether she wanted to or not. How many times had her parents pounded that into the heads of their offspring.

Life doesn't always hand you a fishing pole and bait, sometimes you just have to do things the hard way, on your hands and knees.

They were certainly right about that. Rachel struggled to her knees and climbed onto the roadway. Luckily it was still warm from the day's sun and she lay down to soak some of that heat into her body.

For the first time ever, she knew her life was in serious danger.

The temperature was in the low eighties but her body didn't realize that. She was chilled due to her prolonged exposure to the elements and her thinking wasn't exactly clear. On top of that her body was on the verge of total collapse. Her swim in the marsh had cost her a great deal of strength—fighting the water filled with mud that had been stirred up by the storm was no easy feat. After lying on the road for just a few moments she already felt better and soon she might even be able to get up.

In that moment, she knew only one thing, there was no way she was going to lie down on this road and die.

Several years ago when her great-grandmother had passed away, she'd decided that was the way she wanted to go, at ninety-two in her bed surrounded by family and friends. There was no way in hell dying on a roadway in a storm figured into her death plans.

Gritting her teeth, she forced herself to her knees then to her feet. Her head swam and she staggered to a road sign, clinging to the metal post for balance. Counting under her breath, she'd reached thirteen before realizing she wasn't going to go headfirst onto the pavement. With clenched fists and jaw locked, she released the pole and began to walk.

Left foot, right foot, left foot, right foot, one step at a time.

Time faded to a blur and she paid little attention to her surroundings. The water was getting deeper with every twist and turn she walked. When she reached a dry section, she counted herself lucky as this signaled she'd reached the highest section of the marsh and she was close to Ms. Emma's old house.

Buoyed by the knowledge, her step picked up and she was just off power walking by the time she reached the muddy drive. Leaving the road to walk in the grass, her feet sunk into the mud. The ground was saturated to the point her feet sunk into the grass making walking all that more difficult. Swearing at Mother Nature, she struggled up a slight incline until she reached the top, then her heart sank.

The sound of rushing water told her everything she needed to know. The drive descended into a little gully and the house sat on the other side. Sliding down the hill, she heaved a sigh of relief. The gully was full but there was maybe only a foot of water. She should be able to traverse this obstacle as long as she was careful.

When she looked up, a flickering light caught her eye.

The house!

Even from this distance she could tell it was still standing. Never in her life had she seen anything quite so welcome. With her gaze locked on that small beacon, she crawled through the water on her hands and knees, trying not to grimace when confused fish bumped into legs.

By the time she reached the other half of the drive, the light in the window of the cabin was more distinct. Still crawling, she reached the porch steps with a sob. Grabbing the handrail, she hauled herself to her feet then staggered up the steps only to fall at the top. She barely noticed the pain when her shin connected hard with the edge of the step. Three words kept repeating in her mind.

Safety.

Security.

Rest.

She crawled to the door and wished she had the energy to leap with joy but she didn't. Leaning her cheek against the wooden door she heaved a sigh of relief. Just being out of the driving rain was a slice of heaven. If she wasn't so cold she could fall asleep here. Instead she knocked on the door.

"Is anyone home?" When there was no answer, she pounded harder. "Hello, I need help please."

Without even thinking she dropped into the language of the bayou.

"*Donne moi voir de aider.*"

Nothing moved inside the cabin.

"This cannot be happening," she muttered. "Only I would make it to the house and it would be empty."

Sheer determination got her to her feet. She grabbed the doorknob and wrenched, surprised when it opened easily. Stepping through the doorway, she paused to listen. With the exception of the storm, the house was quiet.

"Hello? Is anyone at home?"

A gust of wind whipped in the doorway, bringing with it the rain. She shut the door and her hands shook when she reached for the light switch, not surprised when nothing happened. At the best of times electricity would be sketchy out here, if it was even available at all. Hurrying over to the window, she picked up the battery-powered lantern. Judging from the light sensor on the top it probably came on when the sun went down.

At first glance it was obvious that someone lived here. In the center of the large room was a double-sided fireplace and a fire had been laid on the grate complete with tinder. In a flash she was across the room searching for matches. Unfortunately she'd lost her purse in the water—she'd had a lighter in there. Finally she located them on the mantel and lit one with shaking hands. After applying the flame to the tinder, within moments a low fire was eating the dried twigs and marsh grass, gradually gaining in strength.

Satisfied the logs would catch, she went in search of a bathroom. When she was a child she'd been in this house on several occasions. Etienne's great-grandmother baked fresh cookies every Tuesday and Friday afternoons. In the summertime she and her siblings along with the Broussard kids could be found on Ms. Emma's porch drinking ice-cold colas and munching on the batch of the day. Ms. Emma had been a lovely lady.

The floors gleamed with a high shine and she was surprised to see the kitchen had been totally refurbished. The ancient woodstove was gone, replaced with sleek silver appliances, though she was pleased to see the handmade kitchen table and chairs remained.

Maybe one of the Broussard's lived here now?

The wide window that looked out over the marsh was shuttered and a cooking island had been added near the stove. The counters were clean save for an alligator-shaped cookie jar.

Two doors opened off the kitchen, one the pantry and the other was the bathroom. Ms. Emma had grudgingly sacrificed a large portion of her pantry to have the washroom added on when Rachel was a child and she'd carried on like a cranky old thing. Secretly Rachel knew she'd been pleased as she was always asking the kids if they had to go to the restroom just so she could show it off.

After making quick work of the facilities, she removed her sodden clothing then grabbed a thick towel. She was so cold her skin felt like raw chicken and she rubbed hard in an attempt to bring the circulation back. Binding her hair in the towel, she found a large man's flannel shirt behind the door.

Even though it felt very odd to wear a stranger's clothing, she donned the soft shirt, shivering when the owner's scent wrapped itself around her along with the flannel. A mixture of male skin and the outdoors caused a spark of arousal to flare in her breasts. Stunned, she clutched at the neckline.

Down, girl. That's what got you in trouble the last time.

Still shivering, she hurried out to the living room relieved to see the fire was gaining in strength. Grabbing an afghan from the couch, she sank onto a lush flokati rug with a happy sigh. The lantern flickered out and she put it to the side.

Her last relationship had been a disaster even though Peter had been a nice guy in the beginning. They'd met at college and had a great deal in common. They both loved music, art and the nightlife of New Orleans. They were in many of the same classes and he'd never failed to make her laugh.

The only major drawback had been that he was, at best, mediocre in bed though his lack of experience was supplemented by his enthusiasm. The relationship had lasted about six months then he broke up with her because he'd decided she was a pervert for wanting to be tied up.

How in the world did he ever figure that out if he didn't experiment?

Rachel had made it a policy to never lie about her sexual needs. She was an experienced woman who enjoyed sex and needed plenty of it. Her favorite indulgence was bondage and role-playing, both of which Peter had absolutely no clue. Whenever she brought it up his canned response was that she should be turned on by him, not by the game playing.

Poor boy, he never really did understand what made her tick.

She reached for the towel and began to dry her hair. It didn't take a great deal to turn her on. A little soap, a shower and bam, she was so there. Her sexual hobbies weren't about the inability to be turned on; it was about a change of pace, a giving over of her mind, body and soul.

Both activities were about the fantasy, an escape from reality. The role-playing fed her creative side and allowed her to explore her sexuality in ways that both frightened and fascinated her. Bondage was the sensation of giving up the ultimate control, though it was an utter illusion. The person being bound was the one who held the power, not the other way around.

Rachel began to finger-comb her damp hair. She was pretty sure he'd taken her to his bed only because she was a slightly older, more experienced woman. She snorted. The reality of dating a serious college student who also worked full-time had quickly lost its appeal. On the first day of the summer break she'd awoken to a hastily written good-bye note and that was the last she'd ever seen of him.

Lucky her! It was pretty sad that she considered her vibrator a step up from a living, breathing man. For the past year she'd concentrated on school, she was within nine months of graduation and nothing was going to get in her way. She was about to be the first person in her family to accomplish this feat. No matter how horny she was, she wasn't about to let herself become distracted by wild, adventurous sex, no matter how much she craved it.

A wave of sleepiness washed over her and she gave up on her hair. Curling up on the rug, she pulled the afghan over her exhausted body and the stranger's scent tantalized her nose.

What if it were Etienne who lived here?

She grinned. In high school she'd had the biggest crush on him. He was so good-looking that all the girls wanted him which made him all that much more unattainable. He'd never looked at her, not once. That was the lot of a gangly sixteen-year-old with braces and pimples.

An image of a handsome nineteen-year-old with olive skin and dark brown eyes surfaced. He'd played football in high school then received a scholarship from Louisiana State University. For a Cajun he'd been quite tall, topping out at six feet even. Thanks to his athletic ability he'd been built like a wall and his six-pack had its own six-pack.

He was hot.

The best, or worst part depending on how she wanted to look at it, was Etienne was best friends with her brothers. The Broussard and Thierry boys were the bad boys of the school and all the girls wanted to date them. Etienne and his twin, Jacques, had been linked to more girls than was humanly possible.

She wondered what he was doing now. She'd lost contact with him after he left for college. Matthew had stayed close though he hadn't mentioned Etienne lately. She'd have to remember to mention him when she got home.

The fire wavered before her eyes and sleep staked its claim. Around the house the storm continued while inside, Rachel slept.

* * * * *

Etienne was exhausted by the time he made it home. He'd driven the length of the marsh road and into Dulac in the hopes of finding the owner of the car. The yards were already flooding and the roadsides were crammed with cars in an attempt to avoid the encroaching waters. In the lowest areas the houses were islands surrounded by rainwater moats. The bayous had already flooded onto the roads with a continuous river of water pouring in from the bayous on one side and into the yards of the houses on the opposite. Some would lose everything in their houses tonight.

Pulling into his drive, which resembled a mud pit, the tires slipped and slid in the muddy soup. It was past time to have the drive paved and to build a bridge over the wash. Damn thing flooded any time a decent rain paid a visit and he was tired of ruining a pair of boots every year.

Cresting the tiny hill, he slowed to survey the damage. The wash wasn't running hard, but it was a good two feet deep. The truck would make it but unless the rain stopped soon, he'd be trapped in his house like those in Dulac.

Then again, there were worst places to be trapped.

Putting the truck in gear, he eased down the slope and into the water. Aiming the nose of the vehicle away from the house, he made it through by using the angle to compensate for the pushing of the water against the much lighter back end.

And to think, right now he could be sitting in his brother's gallery with a stupidly sexy woman in his lap, a martini in one hand and a breast in the other, as he contemplated just how to get the woman tied up in his hotel bed.

Some women could be funny about things like spankings and leather restraints.

Reaching the other side without incident, he drove behind the house and straight into the garage. Located near a stand of trees behind the house, his great-grandfather had been a wise man and he'd worked like a dog to bring in enough earth to create the hill for his home. Both structures were on the highest land around for miles and it had never flooded.

Knock on wood.

Exiting the car, out of habit he left the keys in the ignition. If there was any fool moving around in this weather and they wanted to steal his truck, they could have at it. Though chances were he'd end up rescuing them from the wash.

Standing in the open door, Etienne watched the rain slash through air. In the past hour or so it had gotten steadily heavier and with it came stiffer winds. A mighty crash of lightning turned night into day for seconds and he knew it was going to be a very long night.

According to the last weather report, they were facing the remains of a strong tropical storm. It hadn't stayed in the gulf long enough to gain hurricane strength but this was bad enough. The area was in for many hours of wicked weather and damage come daylight. He wasn't overly concerned as he'd grown up in this area and his family had been foolish enough to bed down through Hurricane Betsy in the sixties and Katrina just a few years ago. Cajuns were tough stock.

Another bolt of lightning flashed and the thunder reverberated through the air leaving only a whiff of ozone. Now, if Mother Nature were truly merciful, the driver of the little car would be a plump redhead with skin the color of milk and a mouth made for sucking. He'd walk into his house and find her naked on the rug before the fire with the handcuffs and paddles at the ready.

It was too bad that Mother Nature was a fickle bitch.

Ducking his head he dashed through the storm to the kitchen door. Upon entering the house he realized he wasn't alone. A low fire crackled in the fireplace and the house was overly warm. Without thinking he removed the shotgun from over the door then checked to see if it were loaded. With the gun at the ready, he crept toward the living room and was shocked at what he saw.

A woman lay on the rug by the fire but she was no redhead. Her long dark hair hid her face and she'd kicked off the afghan in her sleep. She wore his shirt and it had ridden up to expose her wide hips and shapely legs. Even though he knew he shouldn't do it, he couldn't help but look at her pretty pussy. The hair was neatly trimmed and sweat broke out on his upper lip.

She looked good enough to eat. His shirt covered her belly but the neck gaped to expose one perfect, ample breast. Her skin was the faint olive color of a Cajun and her nipple was dark, deep rose. Etienne's mouth began to water and he licked his lips. He would've given everything he owned to take that nipple into his mouth and tease it into awareness.

This woman had the body of a siren, lush and curvy with the type figure that never failed to turn his head.

In one word, she was sweet.

Another clap of thunder shook the house and the rain was coming down harder now. The chances of them getting stranded were a given at this point and it looked like he and Sleeping Beauty would have lots of time to get to know each other.

Chapter Three

❧

When Rachel awoke, she wished she hadn't. Every inch of her body ached and her head throbbed in time to her heartbeat. Getting beat up in the storm was bad enough, and sleeping on the floor had not helped the situation.

After taking a mental accounting of her condition, she rolled to her side to hold her head in her hands. The worst of her pain was her head and in her shin. What in the hell had she done to her shin? The last time she'd been hurting this badly was when she'd been playing volleyball—she dove for the ball and all of her brothers landed on top of her. They thought she'd played like a girl and they didn't want to miss the shot.

"I feel like I've been tackled a thousand times," she moaned, "by elephants."

"Aw, can't be that bad."

The deep male voice shocked her out of her fetal position. From her position on the floor, his jeans-clad legs seemed to be at least a mile high. His white T-shirt hugged every inch of his broad chest and wide shoulders. His face was shadowed by dark hair and there was something very familiar about him.

"W-why not?" she asked.

"I played football for ten years and let me tell you, that's pain."

It can't be…

Sitting up, she stared hard into his handsome face. He had coppery skin, high cheekbones and black eyes with a glint of mischief.

It is!

"Etienne Broussard, is dat you?" Without thinking she reverted back to the heavy accent of her childhood. "I'd know that mouth of yours anywhere."

His face went blank and his eyes narrowed. How she loved that slightly confused expression.

"Rachel, Rachel Thierry?"

"That's me."

Without warning her eyes began to sting and her lip trembled. This man was a huge part of her childhood and even though he'd teased her mercilessly, she'd always felt safe with him.

"What's up, girl?"

Etienne sank to the rug and pulled her into his lap. Clutching at his arms, she sobbed into his shirt while he continued to stroke her hair. After what seemed like an eternity, her tears subsided.

"Was that your car on the road?" he asked.

"Yes." She took a deep breath and closed her eyes, comforted by the sound of his heart. "I never thought I would get caught in the storm."

"Yeah, well, the marsh claims its own when we let our guard down." His voice was a soft rumble in her ear. "Remind me later when you're feeling better and I'll kick your ass."

"Be nice, I'm traumatized."

"Yeah, right. You're just plain tired. Them stupid brothers of yours spoiled you to death and made you into a girly girl."

"Hardly," she snorted. "When I was five they tossed me in the bayou and I thought they'd let me drown."

"The water wasn't even two feet deep in that spot."

"Yeah, well, to a five-year-old that was deep."

He chuckled and gave her a squeeze. "Point taken."

He released her to look into her eyes. Her stomach did a flop. What the hell? This was Etienne, her childhood friend, not some man to get all moony over.

"I think you need to take a bath and relax," he said.

Well it wasn't exactly wine and roses…

"Yeah, I probably stink." Self-conscious, she pushed her ratty hair away from her face.

"Marsh mud, smells like home to me." His grin was wide. "Besides woman, you were born beautiful and you know it. A little mud on you would be a new fashion in the city."

She laughed. How little this man knew about her life now.

"Since the electricity is out you'll have to take a bath the old-fashioned way."

"Tin tub?"

"You've got it." He released her and rose, helping her up as well. "I kept all of the contingency supplies Ms. Emma had."

"I remember those days. We would live for months without hot water if Papa had a bad season."

"Been there."

"So how did you end up living in the middle of the marsh?"

"She left me the house when she passed a few years back. She knew I was the only one who would appreciate it for what it is."

"That and no one with any sense would live out here," she retorted.

"That too," he chuckled. "I've always loved the marsh, and I wouldn't want to live anywhere else."

Walking into the kitchen, he opened a cabinet under the sink to pull out two metal buckets.

"You always said you'd never leave the marsh, even when you were a kid."

"I meant it."

Next to the sink was the old hand pump. Setting a bucket in the sink, he began pumping water into it.

"I played football for four years and got my degree in forestry and conservation from LSU, then I took a job with the state. I really lucked out as I'm based out here."

"Was that after you bedded half the women at the college?"

His brows shot up. "Where the hell are you hearing stories, woman? Matt been running his mouth again?"

"Lucky guess. Since you and Jacques were born, your names have been linked to woman after woman."

"Most of which was an out-and-out lie." He grabbed the bucket and headed toward her.

"That you perpetuated. Not once did you step up and say that you hadn't been with so-and-so."

Damn, the man looked hot carrying a bucket of water!

This is Etienne, I cannot be turned on by him…

"Yeah well, back then I felt I had to maintain a certain image." He brought the bucket to the fireplace and hung it on the metal hook Ms. Emma had used for cooking pots.

"You did not need to help. The girls talked about you all the time and they had some pretty serious imaginations."

"Most women do."

Rachel rolled his eyes. "Sexist."

"In your dreams."

"Honey, you don't know anything about my dreams. You aren't nearly old enough and they would corrupt you."

Etienne laughed and it was a full belly, bent-double laugh and she couldn't help but smile. One of the many things she'd loved about him was his ability to throw himself into any situation without restraint. Just the sound of his laugh was enough to awaken the sleeping tiger in her belly.

"Are you through?" she asked.

"Not even close." He was still grinning when he vanished into the pantry and returned with the tub. "Who knew you'd be such a funny woman?"

"All the boys in high school?"

"Did you even date? I don't think I noticed."

"You noticed," she chuckled. "When I went out with, hmm, what was his name, Eldon? I thought you were going to choke to death the night you saw us at the diner."

"I don't remember that—"

"I do. You were there with Crystal what's-her-name but you didn't seem to be paying much attention to her."

"Well it was hard to when Eldon was staring down your shirt," he shot back.

"So you do remember." She sauntered toward him, well aware that her shirt was unbuttoned to her navel. "Well, my breasts are pretty spectacular."

He grunted and her gaze locked on his face. A muscle ticced in his jaw, and was that sweat on his lip?

"Did the boys ever talk about me in the locker room?"

His gaze darted away. "Not that I ever heard." He headed back to the sink.

"Liar." She rose and walked over to him, her hands crossed over her chest. "What did they say about me?"

"Nothing—"

"You never did lie worth a damn, at least not to people who really know you." With her index finger she poked him in the chest, hard. "What did they say?"

"For crying out loud, Rach. The only boy who dared to say anything about you in the locker room got his ass kicked by your brother. After that every guy in school was afraid to ask you out."

"Yeah, Matthew ruined my high-school dating experience. You know he's getting married in the fall, I may have to stuff his suitcase with anal lube."

"You're evil." He chuckled.

"You have no idea."

"Obviously not." He retrieved another bucket and began filling it. "So I hear you're doing well in college."

"I am. I'll graduate early next year."

"Congratulations. What else have you been doing?"

"Learning how to spank very naughty men." If she hadn't been watching him, she never would've seen him fumble the bucket.

"Nasty girl," he said.

"Yeah, well, a girl has to have options, you know."

"And spanking men is one of them?" He poured the bucket of water into the tub.

She shrugged. "Whatever works."

His gaze bore into hers and she didn't have a clue what he must be thinking.

"You've changed, little girl," he murmured.

"Mm, I'm not very little anymore."

His gaze moved over her body coming to linger on her breasts.

"So I noticed. But you're still my best friend's little sister."

"Baby, I'm nobody's little anything."

She propped her hip on the table and reached for her shirt, surprised when he stopped her. Holding her hands, he looked down into her eyes and she was stunned by the naked hunger reflected back to her.

"You're exhausted and it's been a very long time since I've had a woman." His voice was low. "Right now you need to get cleaned up, I'm going to warm up some dirty rice, and after you eat, I think you need to take it easy for a while. You've had quite an adventure—"

"You sound like my father."

"Good, because he'd slap your ass if he heard the things you been saying to me."

She laughed. "Not hardly. How do you think he and Mama hooked up?"

* * * * *

Etienne sat in the living room while Rachel splashed around in the tub. It wasn't that he was trying to watch her as it was only after he sat that he realized he would catch glimpses of her through the fireplace.

Pervert.

Yes I am!

The sound of splashing water and flashes of wet skin were enough to set his body on full alert. There was something undeniably erotic about the sounds of a woman bathing. The scent of soap, the mental image of a soapy cloth over her breasts, over the curve of her belly, down her legs, up her thighs to the slick flesh in between—

"Etienne?"

He had to clear his throat before he could speak. "Yeah?"

"I'm going to need some help rinsing my hair."

Yeah, right. Like I'm going to fall for that.

"Dunk your head in the water and you'll be good to go."

"It's dirty."

"Rachel—"

"Etienne, I cannot go back to bed with my hair still cruddy. All you have to do is bring me a bucket of water," she sighed. "You'd think I was going to jump on your bones."

From the way you were acting earlier…

"Fine, just stay in that tub then."

He walked into the kitchen and he was relieved she had listened to him. The only body parts visible were her knees and soapy head. Still, his body didn't care if she were respectably covered, all his dick knew was that there was a naked woman in the vicinity and his dry spell had been way too long.

Stalking to the sink, he grabbed the bucket and began pumping water into it.

"This won't be very warm," he said.

"That's okay. I can take it."

Bucket in hand he turned and almost swallowed his tongue. Rachel stood nude in the bathtub, her body gleaming with moisture and rivulets of soap. Seeing her fully nude for the first time gave him an appreciation for just how beautiful she was. She had the classic violin shape and her breasts were full and her nipples large. She didn't have the flat belly that most women seemed to think was attractive and her hips were ample just the way he liked them.

With her dark bedroom eyes and a mouth made for sin, Etienne knew he was in serious trouble.

"Hello, Earth to Etienne. What 'cha doing with the water?"

Her breasts jiggled when she waved her hands to gain his attention. His cock threatened to bust out of his jeans and his control was held by the merest of threads. Catching amusement on that angelic face was the final blow. He stomped over to the tub and dumped the water over her head.

"Etienne!"

Ignoring her dismay, he dropped the bucket by the tub and stomped out the kitchen door to cool off.

* * * * *

He wanted her.

Rachel couldn't wipe the grin off her face as she brushed her hair. He was outside in the garage doing anything he could to avoid her. It was rare that she set her sights on a man and tried to seduce him but Etienne would be her exception. There was something forbidden about him. Maybe it was a hangover from her puppy love that she'd felt for him since the time she was nine. It had always seemed like he was open to dating any girl in school except for her.

In retrospect she understood. Her brother would've kicked his ass if he'd dare to lay a finger on his sister. But they were grownups and no one outside of this cabin would ever have to know what happened between them.

In reality, it was the perfect situation. Her life was firmly entrenched in New Orleans while his was here in the marsh. There would be at least sixty miles between them so it wasn't like there was any possibility of a real relationship. Her stomach twisted.

Besides, he was hot and judging from the rumors she'd always heard from her brothers, Etienne Broussard was a man who knew how to pleasure a woman. Right now that was exactly what she was looking for. After Peter, having monkey sex with a big horny man was a pretty hot fantasy—

"Ouch!"

Rachel dropped the brush and touched her forehead. It was damp and her eyes widened when she saw the blood on her fingertips. Vaguely she remembered hitting her head when she wrecked her car and obviously she'd cracked her head but good.

She rose and headed for the bathroom. The electricity was still out and she peered in the mirror, unable to tell how much damage had been done.

"Damn it, where is that lantern?"

After checking the kitchen and living room she had to admit defeat. She'd have to call in Etienne and have him dress her wound.

"You didn't tell me you were hurt."

Etienne dabbed her wound with an alcohol wipe and her swift intake of breath told him it stung. He blew a gentle breath over the wound to soothe the ache.

"I didn't realize I was hurt until I brushed my hair."

"Well…" He alternated dabbing the wound then blowing on it. "You probably should have stitches but there's nothing I can do about it. My sewing skills aren't up to your standards."

She giggled and the lilt of obvious pleasure put a wide smile on his face. Her laughter was infectious.

"Yeah, you'd probably use a shrimp net hook and some baling twine," she sneered.

"Naw, fishing line is all the rage."

Her headshake was minute and for some reason it brought his attention straight to her breasts. She was the only woman he'd ever seen who could make a simple bath towel look like a party dress. Her breasts strained against the cloth and the part had gaped open, exposing a mouth-watering length of her thigh.

Damn, when did she become so uninhibited?

"All I can do is put some bandages on it. When the water recedes you'll need to pay a visit to your doctor. He'll probably have to put you on antibiotics as well."

"Yeah, who knows what diseases are growing out there."

"I do," he chuckled. "That's why you need the antibiotic."

"Ah, I feel so much better now."

"Better safe than sorry."

"Yes, Papa."

Etienne dropped the bandage wrappers and took her chin, tilting her head back. His gaze bore into her surprised one.

"Trust me, I am not your father nor do I have any remotely fatherly feelings toward you."

Her mouth formed an O and her eyes went wide. For the first time she seemed to be speechless. Dropping a hard kiss on her forehead, he grabbed a bucket and dipped it into the tub then carried it outside.

That woman was going to send him over the edge.

Etienne threw the water in the direction of the wash. It was too bad he wasn't a smoker as he needed a smoke very bad. It had been at least seven or eight years since the last time he'd seen her. Then she'd still been thin and a little gawky as if she wasn't quite sure what to do with her arms or legs. He grinned. She'd always been a beautiful girl, even with braces and pimples.

Beautiful wasn't a large enough word to describe her. With her figure, that smile and her wicked sense of humor, the men in New Orleans must love her.

Hell, he didn't even know if she was seeing someone.

He was struck with a sense of discomfort. She'd always been a little sister to him. Someone to tease, put critters down her shirt and he was the first to kick ass if someone had hurt her feelings. In all his years he'd never imagined that he'd be sexually attracted to her. Then again he'd never guessed she'd grow up to be so hot. He could only hope that when she woke up her wicked streak had passed. He'd really hate it if Matthew showed up on his doorstep to kick his ass.

Chapter Four

৵৩

Even when he was asleep she wanted to touch him.

Rachel slipped into bed beside Etienne, taking care to not disturb his sleep. Her gaze slipped over his delicious body. Well, at least one question was answered.

Boxers.

In repose he didn't lose any of his masculinity like some men did. His mouth was softer which only served to increase her desire to kiss him. His hair was tousled, shadowing his eyes, and that made him look all that much more dangerous. One arm lay by his side and the other was over his head.

What was it about the exposed skin of a man's inner arm? It had always turned her on. Maybe it was the vulnerability of that pale skin with no hair? It was the polar opposite of the outside of his arm.

Etienne was the kind of man women easily fell in love with. He was intelligent, attentive and had an innate instinct to protect those who were weaker. Not to mention the fact he was possibly the sexiest man she'd ever seen. What woman wouldn't want Etienne Broussard?

How about you, Rachel?

All of her life she'd loved him with the adoring puppy love of a child, but she was a woman now. Would her adoring love take a more womanly form after she seduced him?

She leaned forward, and her tongue snaked out for a tender taste of his skin. He stirred and she held her breath, thrilled with the game of teasing him in his sleep.

Once he settled, she moved to his shoulder, kissing the warm curve before working her way down to his breast. A simple flick of her tongue over the flat nipple caused him to jerk but not awaken. A silky purr escaped her mouth and she covered him, her tongue teasing him into hardness—

She squealed when a thick male arm caught her around the waist and flipped her onto the bed, flat on her back. Etienne lay on top of her, his eyes blazing with frustration.

"You're playing with fire, little girl," he snarled.

Rachel slid her right leg from under him to wrap it around his hip. "Lead me not into temptation, for I can find it myself."

Grabbing his head she brought it down for a kiss. Their lips met and in barely the blink of an eye she went from the hunter to prey.

Their mouths came together in a kiss that was part need and part frustration. Their tongues dueled while their hands engaged in combat to see who could expose every inch of skin first. Her T-shirt was shredded by the time he broke the kiss.

With urgent, hungry noises he laid claim to her breasts. While he suckled and nipped one, his hand was stroking and teasing the other. Rachel let her eyes drift closed and her fingers tangled in his thick hair. His erection nudged her thigh, sending a shaft of excitement through her. Now this was how a man seduced a woman.

Every inch was warm, heated by his body and the anticipation of what was to come. She shifted her other leg to wrap both around his waist and lock her ankles. The slide of his teeth of her nipple sent a dart of exquisite pleasure pain to her pussy. Tilting her head back, she groaned long and loud.

He soon repeated the movement, from one nipple to another, until her pussy ached and she needed to come hard and fast. She tightened her thighs and tried to urge him into giving her what she craved.

"You're beautiful," Etienne whispered in Cajun French.

"As are you."

"I need you to touch me."

Rachel reached for him, her hands sliding over hot, male flesh. His chest was thickly muscled as was the dense column of his neck. His skin was living silk over firm, thick muscles and she enjoyed the silky steel feel. She enjoyed his scent, a mixture of clean skin and a faintly woodsy fragrance combined with an underlying scent of male arousal.

Sliding her hands up the column of his neck, she twined her fingers in the long locks, trying to urge him back to her mouth but he wouldn't have any of it. He nipped her chin then placed an open-mouthed kiss on her throat. Purring like a cat, she released his hair to tease his flat nipples.

"Your body is like a drug," he hissed. "Heady. I want absorb you into my skin, my body, my soul."

Her head swam with his potent images and damp warmth flooded her pussy, readying for his possession. His leg moved, bringing her pussy into direct contact with his hot, hard thigh.

"Yes," she hissed through clenched teeth. "Please—"

"In time," he chuckled. "We're in no hurry."

His big hand covered her breast, teasing her nipple into a hard point and sending a wave of heat to her belly. His body shifted, bringing her underneath him. The weight of his body sent her arousal into overdrive. His mouth brushed the tip of her breast, the rasp of his faint beard made her tremble.

"I want to taste you." He was kissing his way down her belly. His hand touched her knee, sliding upward toward her weeping pussy.

Her breath was coming in pants and her fingers dug into his resilient flesh. Her head was spinning. Never had she been so utterly and completely aroused from her head to her toes. This man's mouth played a symphony on her body, every nerve tuned to even the slightest touch.

She wanted to scream when he covered her pussy with his palm. Instead, she stifled the noise by clenching her lower lip between her teeth. Her groan was throaty and he chuckled against her lower belly.

"Let it out, *belle chérie*. I need to hear you, how you feel when I touch you."

Parting her pussy lips, he stroked the damp flesh, coming close to the hardened flesh that ached for him, but not quite touching it. Her breathing was harsh and she grabbed his hair with both hands.

"You're making me crazy," she moaned.

"Good."

His tongue licked at her flesh and she felt as if her body had become electrified. Arching, she screamed, her fists holding his hair even tighter. His mouth closed over her clit and he began to hum. The gentle waves of sensation were enough to make her grind her hips into his mouth. Moaning, she struggled for more but the tones were gentle like the licks of a feather against her flesh.

"More, I need…harder."

"Mmm."

She tried to push his head away but he refused to budge. The tickling sensation continued then he gave her the faintest of licks. Her body jerked in response to the painful, sweet touch. Spreading her thighs as wide as possible, she placed her legs over his shoulders.

His hands came up to grasp her hips and he set to work. His tongue moved over her clit in long, firm licks. With each one she whimpered, her hips beginning to move in time to his licks. Lights swirled behind her eyelids and her heart threatened to burst from her chest. Release beckoned, her fingertips tingled with sensation.

Orgasm washed over her at the same moment lightning stuck somewhere close. The wildness of the storm outside combined with the magical touch of this man's tongue made her feel wanton. She was one with the storm, waves of release washing over her again and again. Her sobs were loud and uncontrolled, her muscles turning to liquid.

When he removed his mouth, she couldn't move. Her entire body tingled with relaxation and her mind was on fire. He spread her legs and his big body moved over her. When he lay on top of her, she received him with open arms.

"That was fantastic,' he whispered.

"I'll say."

Her words sounded slurred to her own ears and she couldn't help but giggle. She felt as if she'd been on an all-night drunk, utterly and totally relaxed, but without the headache the next day.

"I can tell you feel good." His mouth touched the rim of her ear. "You're so wet, so soft."

He shifted his hips and brought his erect cock into contact with her pussy and her eyes flew open.

Oh MY.

Shuddering with need at the feel of his long, hot cock against her, Rachel wished with all her heart that she could see his erection. It had been a while since she'd had sex but it felt as if he were a foot long.

"I'm a big man," he said.

She gazed up into Etienne's dark eyes and a sense of unreality washed over her. His features were shadowed by his long hair and the flickering firelight, but his voice was more than enough to coax her into keeping her panties off. Rich with the Cajun accent, it was a rich, deep voice, the kind a woman dreamed of hearing when having wild sex.

"I can imagine," she responded. Without conscious thought her hips moved restlessly.

"I don't know if you can take me." His voice was a strained whisper, firelight gleamed on his sweaty skin. "A lot of women can't—"

"Shh." Her fingers touched his lips, stemming the flow of words. "Slow, just take it slow." She hooked one leg over his hip, bringing them into closer contact. "I want to feel you inside me."

He groaned when her fingers encircled his thick cock. Her eyes slid closed and she began to stroke his massive erection. Pausing only seconds to dip her hand into her wet pussy, she spread the moisture over him.

"I won't be able to take much more of that."

"And that would be a shame," she whispered.

Guiding the head of his cock to her pussy, they both groaned when the head touched her aching slit. Slowly, tentatively his hips pressed forward, spreading her aching flesh, sending a river of desire through her gut.

"Yes," she breathed.

Grasping his shoulders, she held on tight when he entered her just enough to stretch her pussy. Rolling her hips, he slid in a few more centimeters, the sensation part pleasure and pain. Never had she experienced such a sensation and if anything it made her hungry for more.

Capturing his hips with her legs, she pulled him in farther, the movement sending intense sensation dancing along her nerve endings. Her indrawn breath sounded like a hiss.

"I'm hurting you."

"No," she said. "You're not hurting me. I love the feel of you inside me, I'm so…full, stretched…" Her gaze met his. "I want you to fuck me," she panted. "Now."

He needed no further encouragement. His arms braced his upper body, his cheek touched hers and his hips thrust. She wrapped around him like a vine and reveled in the sensation of being filled. Her hips met him thrust for thrust, her body doing anything to ensure her release. All too soon the peak beckoned and with no effort from her, his thrusts pushed her over.

Starlight danced against her closed eyes and he increased his thrusts. Low growls sounded from his throat and she gave herself over to him. She'd ceased to exist, morphing into a vessel for his pleasure. Wave after wave of release broke over her, and she was a mindless creature clawing at his flesh and begging for more.

His body grew taut and the roar of his release echoed through the room. His massive cock jerked and strained in her pussy like a separate living being. After long, drawn out moments of sensual excess, he collapsed over her.

Numb with exhaustion and numerous releases, Rachel closed her eyes and was soon fast asleep.

* * * * *

Etienne stared up at the ceiling. The feeling of unreality had overtaken him and he was numb from head to toe.

What in the hell had just happened?

Beside him Rachel made a soft noise in her sleep. Her backside wiggled until her butt was pressed against his hip.

He should've kicked her out of the bed…

She started it.

He rolled his eyes at the childish response in his head. For crying out loud, he was a mature man who should've had the willpower to refuse a hungry woman's advances—

She tasted of sin.

It didn't matter that it had been five months since he'd broken up with his latest partner. At this time in his life he had no desire for a serious relationship, there simply wasn't time for a woman in his life.

Then your dick should've stayed in your boxers, boy.

Irritated, he rolled onto his side to spoon with Rachel. Even now he could hardly believe she was here, in his bed. When they'd spent a lot of time together in school, he never paid attention to her at all. It wasn't until his senior year when he'd seen her with Eldon that he realized she'd grown from a gawky girl into a lovely young woman.

To this day he couldn't say why he felt the way he did but it had taken all of his willpower to not knock the boy's teeth into the back of his head for being anywhere near Rachel.

His mama, grandmother and great-grandmother had always hoped they'd hook up, but he'd done everything in his power to avoid her. Teasing her unmercifully until she disliked him had been the hardest thing. The summer he'd noticed she'd grown up was when he'd decided to do everything to stay away from her. If that included destroying the look of utter adoration he'd seen in her eyes, then that was that.

He'd been so good at it that when he left for college, she hadn't attended his going away party. He'd never told anyone but he'd spent that entire night waiting for her and she never showed.

That's what he got for being mean.

All of this was in the past and what mattered now was she was in his bed. Of course the next issue was, now that he had her here, what would he do with her? If her father ever got an inkling that they'd been together, Etienne knew he'd find himself standing before a judge with a shotgun pressed into his ribs. Rachel wasn't a virgin but that wouldn't matter to John Paul Thierry, her father.

Etienne winced at the thought. Not to mention the fact that her eldest brother had been his best friend since second grade. Matthew was a hothead and he loved a good fight. He'd take great pleasure in pounding him into the ground for touching his sister, not that he didn't deserve it.

"Fuck," he muttered.

Rachel stirred, her warm flesh against his and his cock took notice. It hardened and he gritted his teeth. There was no way they could do this again. Sliding out of bed, he took great care to not disturb her. Once was bad enough but the images of her tied to his bed wouldn't fade and it just might be enough to send him to confession on Sunday.

* * * * *

Some hours later Rachel woke slowly, feeling toasty warm and incredibly relaxed. Keeping her eyes closed, she stretched, her eyes flying open when a cramp hit her in the leg. Rolling to her side she stumbled to her feet only to stub her toe into the footboard on the bed.

Gasping, she hobbled around the room to realize she was still in Etienne's bedroom. In that moment, everything came back to her in a stomach-wrenching rush.

The alligator.

Her car.

The nightmarish walk on the road.

Falling into the marsh.

Finding Etienne's home.

Safety.

Seducing her brother's best friend.

"Damn."

Rachel sat down hard on the bed, her mind reeling. Had it really happened? Her hands flew to her chest and belly to realize she was naked.

Bedroom.

Naked.

Oh yeah, they'd had sex all right. Wild monkey, hanging from the chandelier sex. The kind of sex that women in romance novels had every day. That thought was enough to

147

send Rachel bolting across the room to dig though his drawers. Locating a pair of running shorts and a T-shirt, she hastily pulled them on.

What had she been thinking?

Of getting laid by a real man.

Her libido had definitely led her astray this time. If anyone in her family ever found out, they'd both be in big, big trouble. Maybe she could get him to agree to a mutual partnership. What happens in the marsh, stays in the marsh.

That would certainly solve a lot of their problems—

"Rachel, are you awake?" Etienne's voice sounded outside the bedroom door.

"Yes."

"Good, dinner is on the table."

Her stomach growled and she couldn't help but laugh. It would appear she was hungry.

"Coming."

By the time she walked into the kitchen she was feeling marginally calmer. Etienne had lit two lanterns, one sitting on the table and the other on the counter. A portable propane stove sat on the counter beside it and a pot bubbled away on top.

"How long will the power stay out?" she asked.

"Hard to tell. This road is down on the totem pole as far as the electric guys are concerned. It could be a week, maybe two. If the state sticks their nose in and asks them to step it up, it could be shorter."

"Why don't you have a generator? Papa has two in the shed."

"Yeah well, I do have one but," he chuckled and if she weren't mistaken, he was blushing. "I used the gasoline last week when I went fishing."

She gave him the look she always gave her brothers when they did something to mess up a situation. "So you used your emergency gasoline to fish in the marsh where the catfish probably have more toxins than the bayous?"

"Hey now. The catfish in the lake here are perfectly safe. The marsh has been scrubbed clean what with the storms we had."

"Hell, Katrina scoured everything down to dirt."

"Amen. Did you stay in the city or come down here for that storm?"

Rachel sat at the table where he'd placed a stack of paper napkins and some plastic silverware.

"I stayed in the city. My apartment is on high ground in the quarter and it never really occurred to me to leave. My family has never left for a hurricane so why should I?"

"I'll bet you will next time."

"Well, if New Orleans is in the path of the hurricane then I will probably come back home. With Katrina it wasn't the storm as much as what happened afterwards."

"I hear you." He retrieved bowls from the cupboard. "This is some of Mama's Gumbo."

"Fab, I haven't had Ms. Mamie's gumbo in ages."

"She does make the best."

"That she does."

"What does your mama and grandmother think of you living out here all by yourself?"

"They've never said anything. I think, deep down, they like knowing someone in the family is keeping the place up. The last three generations of Broussards all played in this house, had seafood boils in the backyard and we all learned to swim in the lake. It is our home."

"Yeah, I hear you. We still own the land my grandfather lived on though now it has turned more into swamp than land.

Papa is thinking about turning it into a fishing camp," she said.

"Sad, isn't it? Every thirty-eight minutes the Louisiana coast loses one football field of land to erosion."

"Yeah. In about ten to fifteen years the marsh might be completely gone." He carried two steaming bowls to the table. "That's what I'm trying to work against."

Rachel picked up her spoon then paused, giving him a smile. "Thank you, for the work you do."

His brow shot up. "You're welcome."

"Most people don't realize how necessary the coastlines of the gulf are and they're too precious to let the sea reclaim them."

"True." He brought two more bowls. "We've reached the point of no return and if the conservationists and government don't step in soon, all of this could be gone in a hundred years."

Rachel stirred her bowl, her throat tight at the thought of the place she loved lost to the gulf.

"But, on a brighter note, I do have some cold potato salad for the gumbo."

Rachel laughed. "How did you keep it cool?"

"I have an emergency propane cooler in the panty. I got damned tired of replacing everything in my refrigerator every other month."

"You're very prepared."

"Do you need some rice?"

"What more could I need?" Rachel inhaled the rich scent of homemade gumbo. Only the people of the bayou could make a proper gumbo.

"A cold beer?" Etienne put a steaming bowl of rice and another of potato salad on the table.

"If you have one."

"That's my girl."

His statement sent a wave of warmth to unfurl in her stomach, surprising her. After Katrina hit the Gulf Coast she'd learned some life-changing lessons. No longer was she squandering her time waiting for the next big thing to happen in her life, now she was out making it happen. When her time came she didn't want to die with regrets and she was determined to wring every ounce of experience from every minute of the day.

It was also very possible that Etienne was to be her next life experience.

He returned with two bottles of cold beer and gave her one before taking his seat.

"So, you found my car on the road?"

"Yes, about a mile from here." He picked up the bowl of potato salad and began spooning it into the gumbo.

"My poor car." She sighed. "Was it submerged?"

"No." He gave her a sympathetic smile. "But it's probably been washed away by now. You went off the road at one of the lowest points in the marsh."

"Well I didn't go off the road willingly."

"What happened?"

"Almost ran over an alligator. I came around that bend and a damned gator was just chilling in the middle of the road."

"No kidding."

She stirred in some hot sauce then took a bite of the gumbo. "This is fantastic."

"Thanks. So when you saw the gator, did he do anything?"

She looked at him and saw he was still stirring his gumbo. "Not really." I tried to avoid hitting him and my rear end hit a tree and got caught up. He just sat there for a few more moments then took off into the marsh."

"Was he a big one?"

"Huge."

Rachel concentrated on her food though after a few moments she realized Etienne seemed preoccupied.

"Why are you so quiet?" she asked.

"Just thinking."

"About what?"

"Superstitions."

Rachel was surprised. As a people, the older Cajuns were superstitious but she never imagined Etienne would be.

"What kind?"

"Animals. Did you know the Native Americans assigned a spiritual sign to each animal? It is said that the one representing you will show itself when it's time."

"I did know that. My grandmother is a big believer in the animals carrying messages, especially the crows. I can't say I know much about it but it did seem to me that the crows did seem attracted to her."

"And you saw an alligator."

"You're being very strange, Etienne. You of all people know that the gators will emerge during storms, they do all the time. Seeing him doesn't mean anything."

"But what if he did, what if the alligator was a sign?"

"Then he needed to speak up because I didn't hear anything," she said dryly.

"Rachel."

"Etienne." She dropped her spoon. "What if he was a message or totem? They've been around for millions of years so they are very intelligent, they stay alone, coming together only to mate, they digest their food very slowly and they eat only when necessary. What message would one get from that?"

"That slow and easy is the way to go." He shook his dark head and grinned. "I was just thinking out loud."

Rachel gave him a look and somehow she didn't think that was the end of the story but she decided to let him have his way.

"So, let's talk about sex," she announced.

Etienne joggled his spoon then glared at her. "I think we have enough problems already, don't you"

"Not hardly. We could be here for a few more days, how do you propose we…amuse ourselves?"

"We could chop wood. I have a ton of things I need to take care of around here."

"Hmm, I'm sure my wood chopping skills are pretty rusty. I'd only hurt myself."

"I don't think you need to be doing much of anything. That's a pretty nasty cut you have on your head."

"I've had worse. Remember when you and John whacked me in the head with that little *Popierre* net? I had a welt for a week."

"Yeah, sorry about that. Your brother and I weren't quite as prepared to shrimp with that thing as we'd thought."

She polished off the rest of her gumbo and pushed away the bowl.

"I used to think you were looking for Lafitte's treasure."

He chuckled and a soft, sticky warmth awoke in her belly. He had the sexiest laugh and it alone was enough to get her all hot and bothered. Now that her belly was full, her mind taking a fast U-turn to another hunger to be appeased.

"We did play pirate quite a bit when we were kids."

"No kidding. Ya'll would tie me to the tree and pretend I was the prisoner and you left me there a few times. If it weren't for Mama coming out ya'll would've found me weeks later after the birds had picked out my eyeballs."

"Trust me, we would've come back for you."

"Only when you remembered me." She rose from her seat and instantly his gaze moved to her tight shorts. "How many times did you forget me, Etienne?"

He didn't speak for a moment, his gaze glued on her thighs. "Um, what?"

She smiled. "I said, how many times did you forget me, Etienne?"

He blinked and she knew he wasn't paying full attention to her words. It wouldn't take much more to get him into bed and deep inside her.

"I'll take that to mean you didn't," her voice dropped. She walked toward him and he pushed away from the table as if he were going to escape her. She perched herself on his knee. His burgeoning erection was heavy and hot against her hip. "I never forgot you, either. I think I fell in love with you my sophomore year. You were so handsome and all the girls wanted you."

"You had a crush on me?" He seemed stunned.

"Why are you so surprised?" She looped her arm around his neck, dipping her head to taste his neck. "I wasn't any different than the girls you dated. I had feelings," her teeth grazed his jaw and he tipped his head in response, "I had urges."

"Urges?"

"Oh, yes." She nipped his earlobe. "Urges. I would lie in my narrow virginal bed at night and think of you. My white cotton panties would get all wet." She breathed into his ear and she felt him tremble. "My pussy would be aching and I didn't know what to do about it then other than yearn for you."

"Rachel—"

"What? Are you going to tell me that my feelings for you were those of a child and I should put them aside and be sensible?" She shook her head. "I stopped being sensible when Katrina destroyed the coast. I stopped being sensible when I realized that one minute you're there and the next, you're gone. Life isn't about being sensible, certainly not for me."

She put her hands on her shoulders. "I want you to love me. To touch me." She caught his hand and placed it over her breast. "I want to feel beautiful, out of control, wild."

Her hand covered his and she pressed it tight against her breast. "Feel me, how my heart beats for you. How my nipple grows hard—"

"I'm going to have to spank you, aren't I?" His voice was husky and in the depths of his eyes there was an answering fire, a hunger that matched hers.

"Yes." She dipped her head and nipped his forefinger. "Spank me, tie me up, fuck me." As she spoke she guided his hand down her belly then between her thighs. "Do you see how hot I am for you?" she murmured.

"You're wet." He slipped his fingers from hers and began stroking her gently. "Are you asking me to make you my submissive?"

The rush of arousal was so strong that she didn't trust herself to speak. Instead she nodded, her breathing slowly turning into pants.

"And you'll do as I command?"

She licked her lips. "Yes."

"No talking back."

"None."

"And no one will ever know of this, especially your family."

"Especially my family," she whispered.

His big hands caught her shoulders and pushed her away. "You will get on your knees and suck me, now."

For a moment Rachel could hardly breathe, her arousal level had reached the point where thought was incredibly difficult. Her gaze locked with his and it was obvious he was highly aroused by the thought of her on her knees. For her it was the thought of his massive cock between her lips that was enough to drive her to her knees.

After grabbing the padded seat cushion from the kitchen table, she dropped it on the floor between his feet. As gracefully as she could manage, she sank to her knees and reached for the straining placket of his taut jeans. The sight caused a deep tingle of arousal deep within her pussy. It may have been a long time since she'd seduced someone but after only one round of sex, she was as hot and damp as a summer day in the bayous.

He lifted his hips to help her remove them. His thick cock sprang forth and her eyes widened at the sight of the thick, heavy member. Never had she seen anything this big on a man before. Easily he was nine inches in length and thick enough around that her fingers didn't touch. Sucking him off would not be easy but she was more than willing to give it her all.

Leaning forward, Rachel inhaled the scent of his cock and the thick hair at the base was enough to cause a wash of arousal through her pussy. Closing her eyes, she sank into the morass of sensuality.

With long strokes, she licked every inch of her master's cock. The musky flavor of his aroused flesh wove a tapestry of sensuality around her mind and body. Wrapping her hands around the thick base, she squeezed him gently in time with her strokes. Her tongue licked across the wide head and his indrawn breath was music to her senses.

She was doing this to him!

Her mouth covered the head and she took him as deeply as she could. Slowly she began to fuck him with her mouth, her hands moving up and down his shaft in time. His hands landed in her hair and he began whispering encouragement, instructing her to touch him here and lick him there.

"Rachel, you will stop."

Ignoring him, she continued her assault on his cock. All too soon his fingers dug into her scalp and he was balanced on a knife's edge. Keeping her mouth over his head, she released one hand to cup his balls.

"Rachel."

The warning in his tone was obvious and she chose to ignore it again, giving them a gentle squeeze. He came with a roar. His cock spasmed, shooting his release deep into her throat. After the tension left his body, she slowed her movements, opting to lick him like an all-day sucker. With great care, she cleaned all evidence of his release before letting go of him.

Sitting back on her heels, she felt a little smug and boldly met his gaze.

"Rachel, I said you could suck me, but I didn't say anything about bringing me to release."

Chapter Five

ℰꙮ

It was hard for him to just sit here doing nothing. Just knowing that Rachel was in the living room, naked and posed on the rug before the fire was enough to make his blood run hot.

Etienne sat in the kitchen listening to the crackle of the fire and the storm outside. Even though he'd had two powerful releases in the past few hours, anticipation hummed in his veins. If he weren't mistaken, the storm was weakening. Probably by morning it would have blown itself out, but for now, the scream of wind and the pounding rain only served to create a cozy little nest for them.

Through the double-sided fireplace he saw that Rachel hadn't moved an inch. He'd created a pallet by the fireplace and she was on her knees upon the comfortable pile of blankets. The firelight gleamed on her olive-tinted skin accentuating her long, toned body.

Rachel was, in four words, a work of art.

Her long dark hair fell to the middle of her back. Her form was womanly, her breasts large and her hips ample. She was built the way he liked his woman. Her laugh set his nerves on fire and when she smiled, it was as if all were right with the world. She was self-confident, at ease with her body and he couldn't wait to touch her again.

Hold on, Broussard, you barely know this girl anymore.

Somehow that didn't bother him. They might not know each other well but there was time. Their bodies recognized each other and they communicated on a level much deeper than mere conversation.

Spiritual?

He shied away from that idea. No, he wasn't ready to investigate that further, not yet anyway. She was but ten feet away, waiting for him to possess her again. His blood quickened at the thought of spanking her plump buttocks.

And there was no time like the present.

* * * * *

As Etienne's footsteps approached, with every second that passed her body grew more aroused. She didn't know how long she'd been kneeling on the pile of blankets, fifteen minutes, maybe twenty. Anticipation was the best way to begin game playing in her opinion. It was the buildup that guaranteed a rocking good time.

The fire was warm on her skin and a light sweat had broken out shortly after he'd positioned her here. Closing her eyes, she could imagine herself in the past, a man and woman living in the marsh at the time of Jean Lafitte, the notorious pirate. It was the late eighteenth century and she was but a slave girl freed by the man who now approached.

Her breath caught.

What would he do with her? He'd fed her and allowed her to warm herself by the fire. Surely he wouldn't just toss her into the elements, would he? Was there something she could do to ensure she would remain in the house for the night?

Rachel touched her chest, allowing her hand to dip to the tip of her breast. Her nipple, already aroused, ached when she gave it a gentle pinch. An answering ache sprang to the fore between her thighs. Would he find her desirable? Men usually did though her previous master had let none touch her, only him.

She shuddered. He'd been a small man with beady eyes. He had been kind to her in bed though he'd had no regard for her pleasure, only his.

"Did I tell you to touch yourself?"

The rough Cajun words came from the darkness. Her hand stilled and she looked in the direction of the voice.

"No."

"Master," he ground out.

"No, master." Her voice was little more than a whisper.

"Remove your hand, I wish to see you naked before me."

Etienne stepped into the firelight, the sharp bones of his face seemed to be etched in wood. His pants clung to strong muscular thighs and his feet were bare. He'd removed his shirt and the golden light kissed the honed muscles and illuminated the sprinkling of dark hair. He had a tattoo of thorns around his upper left arm.

Rachel did as he bid, allowing her hand to drop. Sitting back on her heels fully nude and exposed to his hungry gaze, she tilted her chin up and met his gaze defiantly. This man might possess her body but never her soul.

"You are exquisite," his voice was hushed.

With haste he removed his pants and his massive cock sprang forth and she couldn't help but gulp. He was, in a word, magnificent.

On the pallet in front of her, he sat, his legs straight out in front. "Come, sit on my knees."

A trickle of arousal burned in the back of her throat. Without a word she rose to her knees and came forward. Spreading her thighs to bracket his, she sat back on his knees.

"Closer."

He grabbed her knees and pulled her forward until she was within inches of touching his torso. Their eyes were on the same level and a dark, sensual fire burned in his black gaze. Something tightened in her lower gut.

"Do you know what I will do to you?" his voice was low.

"No, master."

"I want you to touch yourself, pleasure yourself before me."

Hesitant, she reached for her breast.

"No, not like that."

He caught her hand and drew it down to her pussy, plunging her fingers into the damp, needy flesh.

"Stroke yourself and tell me of your pleasure."

Her cheeks burned and her gaze darted away. He was very forward.

"Close your eyes."

She did as he bid and her vision faded to black. Suddenly the world around her emerged. The crackle of the fire and scent of wood burning, the sound of his breathing, the storm outside, the scent of his aroused male flesh.

Without her command her fingers began to move over her puffy, wet pussy. Parting the lips, she stroked the delicate inner lips, centering on her clit. A sigh slipped from between her lips and he made an encouraging sound.

Her mouth parted and her hand continued its dizzying dance. Stroking and teasing her flesh into submission. Her breathing changed to soft pants and her fingers increased their pace. Her hips began to rock and she realized that when she moved forward the back of her hand touched his burning cock. She did it again and his indrawn breath was ample reward.

"I'm so hot," she whispered. "I can't, I don't—"

"You will." His voice was firm. "You want to please your master, do you not?"

Yes, oh yes…

Moving forward, she was shocked out of her rhythm when his tongue came to touch the valley between her breasts. Her eyes flew open and his teasing gaze met hers.

"Nectar. That is the taste of angel sweat," he said.

She moved again and he gave another long, leisurely lick, causing her to shiver. Her eyes closed and she felt her body sinking into the pool of liquid heat. Inexorably she began the climb to the peak, doing anything she could to take him with her. Shivering and on the edge of a blinding release, she paused, her fingers half in and half out of her pussy.

"Master, please."

"Ah, but I have made my wishes clear, slave. I do not wish you to find your release, not just yet. Already you have displeased me this evening and you must receive your punishment. Do you wish to have two spankings instead of one?"

Yes!

Reluctantly she pulled her fingers out of her pussy, the final touch enough to send shivers through her body.

"Good girl," he said. "Now, you will lie across my lap and present me with your buttocks."

For the first time she felt a jolt of apprehension. Talking about it was a very different thing than performing the act itself, and now that the moment was upon her, she was feeling a touch of trepidation.

"Are you having second thoughts?"

Her gaze met his and she was pacified by the tenderness reflected there. She would be fine, this man would never hurt her.

Shaking her head no, she removed herself from his lap and together they shifted so that they were far away enough from the fire to be comfortable. Laying her body across his lap was an odd experience though not unpleasant. He'd gotten her some pillows so that her head was even with the rest of her body. The funny thing was that with her backside exposed like this, she felt even more vulnerable than she was sitting face to face.

How odd was that?

His big hands came down on her buttocks, and he squeezed and plumped the resilient flesh.

"You have the perfect ass. Plump and well rounded. I shall enjoy this very much." He sounded breathless.

Judging from the jut of his cock against her hip, he was more than enjoying himself now and he'd barely laid a hand on her yet. He began to rub her ass with strong, sure strokes then, without warning, he parted her cheeks.

"What a sweet little mouth," he whispered. Gently he pressed his finger against her anus and her hips arched automatically. "I can see you enjoy that, my slave. This pleases me very much. Have you had a man in your ass before?"

"N-no, master."

"Ah, perfect then. I will look forward to plundering this sweet place."

She gulped at the thought of his massive penis trying to enter her rear, though she was strangely turned on at the same time. Would it hurt? Part of her hoped not while another part, the darkest and most secret part hoped it would ever-so sweetly.

Her thoughts were shattered when he reached between her thighs and parted the lips of her pussy. Her hips arched higher and he chuckled and gave her a sharp slap on the buttocks.

Her breath was sharply indrawn and she was shocked at the rush of pleasure she'd received from that sharp pain. Was she sick in wanting this?

"Wanton," he said. "Someone has trained you well. That said, I will have to train you to anticipate my desires."

His hand fell on her buttocks again while his other hand continued the slow finger-fucking. Her butt clenched then relaxed when he began stroking it.

"So, lovely."

His hand fell again and she had to shove her face into the pillow and scream with pleasure. The spanking continued and reality faded for Rachel. Her entire being was focused on her lower torso, the hand tormenting her ravenous pussy and the other spanking her for the impudence earlier. Pleasure numbed her senses and her body became one big nerve, every stroke and spank setting her on fire.

"Master," she panted when she could stand it no more. "May I come?"

"No, not yet. I have one more delight in mind for you."

She groaned when his hands left her though within a second they were back. She heard a squirting sound then her buttocks were parted and cool gel was applied to her anus. The contrast between the gel and the warmth of his finger was welcome. He worked the slick gel into her anus and around the outside until she was slick and every nerve was on edge.

His slick fingers slid inside her anus, stretching her, preparing her for his entry. Her nails dug into the pillows and her breathing was reduced to pants. Straining against his hand, her hips slapped against his, the edge almost within her grasp.

"Master—"

"Come for me."

In that moment, his fingers entered her anus giving her an amazing sensation of fullness that was enough to send her over the edge. She screamed and her body tightened around his fingers. Waves of pleasure rocketed through her, draining, dazzling until all she could do was collapse.

Etienne assisted her off his lap and onto a pile of pillows. Numb to the point of being sluggish, it barely registered when he spread her legs and the hair on his thighs caressed her legs. She heard the crinkle of tearing foil then his hands covered her ass and parted her cheeks. The broad head of his cock rubbed against her anus, eliciting a whine from her mouth. Pressing backward, her breath caught when the tight little mouth opened to take only centimeters of him.

He groaned and began rocking his hips, the slide of his erection against her ass mesmerizing. Arching her back, she adjusted the angle so the next time he pushed forward, the head of his cock entered her anus.

Both were frozen.

"Rachel?" His voice was barely a whisper.

"Slow, easy."

He moved his hips, his cock sliding inside another few centimeters. They were locked in this tentative embrace, their bodies straining and slowly he pushed inside her until Rachel felt full.

"That's enough,' she hissed.

He pulled back then thrust again, the movement bringing a gentle wave of sensation that wasn't unlike vaginal sex. It felt more dangerous, more…forbidden.

Rachel bit her lip and groaned when he pressed forward. She pushed back, allowing him in just a tiny bit more. Her body sang when he reached around her hip to slide his hands into her pussy. The first touch of her clit sent her mind racing. His movements remained slow and controlled while her need for release spiraled higher.

The rhythm of his fingers increased and suddenly she was thrust out into the wilderness. Her body soared and she screamed with her release. Still inside her, he remained still, his grip on her hip harsh as he jetted his release deep inside her anus. Completely spent, Rachel was limp on the pillows.

Now that was what she'd missed!

Chapter Six

ℬ

"I think the storm is moving away,"

Her silky voice roused him from the sated wonderland he'd been floating in. His arm tightened around her waist, his body spooning hers. The feel of her flesh against his, his cock nestled against her buttocks and he didn't want to move.

"Yeah. It isn't the storm you need to worry about, it's the flooding." He nuzzled her shoulder. "The storm may end tonight but you may not get out of here for a day or two. It all depends upon how deep the wash is."

"Do you have a boat?"

He chuckled. "Are you in that much of a hurry to get away from me?"

"No." She relaxed into him. "I didn't want my parents to worry about me."

"If the storm has blown out in the morning, I'm sure we can come up with a plan. I'm very resourceful."

She chuckled and he nipped the curve of her neck and inhaled her intoxicating scent. While he'd always been extremely protective of Rachel, he'd never been sexually attracted to her before now. In his mind she'd always been his little sister, someone to kid around with and tease unmercifully. Now, ten years later, to be lying with her, cuddling her in his arms was surreal.

"I'll bet."

Her body smelled of musky sex and rainwater. Arousal nudged his cock and a slow tingle awoke. Etienne wanted her sprawled on their pallet, her body open and receptive to him, as he pounded into her.

Rachel turned in his arms and their gazes met. Her eyes were so dark and it felt as if he'd fallen into her eyes. Leaning forward, their lips met and she made a hum of pleasure. The kiss was leisurely, a mix of playful and greedy, and he wanted more of her.

Then her kiss changed. She leaned into him, her body curling to embrace his. She made a hungry noise and he thought he'd lose his mind. Her slim hands touched his cock and she stole his breath. Her legs parted and she draped one over his hip, bringing her pussy into contact with his cock.

They fit so well together. He was taller than her but not by much and they were lips to lips, breast to chest. It would take so little to remove her hands and slide inside her sweet body and fuck them both into oblivion.

Instead he slid his hand between her thighs, parting her labia to plunge into the sweetness inside. She felt like oiled silk against his fingers and the soft, gasping noises she made into his mouth were sweeter than pralines. He entered her vagina with his fingers and slowly began finger-fucking her, enjoying the slick feel of her body preparing the way for him.

He circled her clit and she made a keening sound that sent a wave of lust straight to his cock. Her hands were soft and she continued stroking him in a leisurely way that wasn't meant to bring him to a peak, rather to maintain the sensations he already felt. He withdrew his hand from her pussy then added a second finger to the first. She nipped at his lower lip and he growled. Pressing her thighs farther apart, he began finger-fucking her in earnest.

With a noisy gasp she broke the kiss, her sigh deep and earthy, her hands tightening on his cock. He stroked the hard clit and her hips moved in time. Removing his hand, he pushed her onto her back then moved between her thighs.

Her dark eyes watched him, her lips glistened from his mouth. She drew her legs up, bringing him closer. Her hand, still around his cock, led him to her pussy and without hesitation, he thrust into her body and they groaned simultaneously. He braced his arms against the floor and she wrapped around him, like a warm kitten.

Intoxicated with her, he began to thrust, reveling in the feel of her body, the scent of her skin and the taste of her mouth. He nipped at her throat and she cried out, her nails digging into his back. All too soon she came, her body arching into him, the slip and slide of their bodies igniting the slow tingle in the back of his calves. Racing up his legs, the sensation coalesced into his groin and he came with a roar. Each wave was deeper and more intense.

Exhausted and sated, he rolled to his side, bringing her with him. Still buried deep in her sweet flesh, he closed his eyes.

* * * * *

"How long will it take for the water to recede?" Rachel asked.

Etienne dropped into the porch swing next to her. The day was sunny and warm, the first good day since the storm.

"That's hard to tell. See that post in the water there?"

"Yes."

"That's how I measure the water. There are only two lines visible and that means we have six feet of water in the wash. Usually it would take about two days for that to recede."

"Why do I feel a 'but' in there?" Rachel snuggled her head on his shoulder.

"It was a pretty good storm and Chauvin, Dulac, Montague and Houma were flooded in the low-lying areas. The chances are they're pumping their floodwater into the bayou and all that water comes straight down through here."

"Which means the level will stay even for a few more days."

"Exactly. We probably have the better part of a week, four days at the least before we can get the truck through."

"Damn. That means I can't get word to my family for a while yet."

He hugged her. "If the electricity doesn't come on today then we'll see about swimming the wash and walking down to the outpost. They have backup generators and a shortwave radio. We can contact one of the bridge operators or maybe a shrimper and get word to them."

"Okay, if that's the best we can do. I just don't want them to worry."

"Me, either." He kissed her hair. "Besides, if they find out you're missing they will head out here to get my help to look for you."

Rachel laughed. "Yeah, you always did have the knack of finding me when I didn't want to be found."

"You mean like the time you ran away in fifth grade?"

"That would be it."

"Rachel, you only made it down to Tricia Ramos' house—that wasn't too hard to figure out. Her mama made the best chocolate chip cookies in the parish."

"Yeah, I'm still addicted to chocolate chip cookies. Only now I run to the bakery across from work. They aren't quite as good as Ms. Ramos' but they run a close second."

He laughed and began stroking her shoulder. "Do you like living in the big city?"

"I do. There's always something to see and do, always someone to talk to and I have access to some of the best restaurants in the world. What's not to like?"

"Not being close to nature."

"I'm in the quarter, I can walk to Riverwalk."

"No boat, no open water."

"That I do miss."

"No quiet."

"No dancing out here, or jazz bands."

"The crime rate."

"They find bodies out here too," she pointed out.

"But they are rarely ever residents. Most of them are people from the city who are murdered and dumped out here to feed the crabs."

"Point taken. What are you trying to convince me of?"

"That you miss it, this place, your home."

"Well I never said I didn't miss home. I love the bayou and I'll always love it. Chances are once I get my degree and a good job, I'll move back here at some time. I don't like being far from my family." She leaned her head back, their mouths mere inches apart. "What about you, Etienne Broussard, do you miss the city?"

"In some ways." His voice was hushed. "I miss the energy, the nightlife, hot jazz and the beautiful women."

"I'll bet you do. Just how many words does it take you to remove a woman's panties?" she teased.

"I don't know, how many did it take to get yours off?"

"I wasn't wearing any." Her tongue snaked out and licked his jaw.

"Are you now?" He bent his head and gently rubbed his bristly cheek against hers.

Silent, she shook her head.

"Mm, I like the idea of you sitting here beside me, no panties on and I can touch you at any time."

Rachel's cheeks colored and she looked around as if she expected someone to pop out of the bushes at them.

"Here? Now?"

"Why not? The road is probably still flooded on both ends so we're safe enough." He slid his hand down the inside of her left leg, lifting it over his. "Does it bother you that someone could see?"

"I may be uninhibited in bed but I'm not into the public watching me."

He ran his fingers up the pale, silky skin of her thigh. "That's too bad. The possibility of getting caught can be very...stimulating."

Rachel laughed. It was a throaty laugh of arousal. "Naughty boy."

He nibbled the way down her throat, each taste of her flesh inched his arousal higher. Parting the v-neck of her shirt, he released a few buttons until the top gaped wide enough to slide over her shoulders, leaving her breasts bare to the fresh air.

Instead of aiming for her nipples, he kissed her. His mouth covered hers and he was rocked by her taste. With every kiss it was as if it were the first. Warm woman and a hint of gumbo, what more could he want from his woman?

Rachel made a silky sound of acquiescence, her tongue tangled with his, teasing, darting back and forth. Her fingers tangled in his hair and he was amused when she tried to take charge of the kiss. There was no way he would allow that.

Breaking the kiss, he nudged her off his lap then stood. His cock was as hot and hard as a steel beam in the sun but he ignored his discomfort in the face of things to come.

"Go to my bedroom."

Her mouth opened and he thought for sure she'd object. Instead her gaze dropped to her toes.

"Yes, Master."

He followed her into the house. Her bare feet made little sound on the shiny wood floors. Halfway through the living room, her shirt fell from her hips to end up on the floor. Her perfect ass bounced a little when she walked and he thought he'd come right there.

Entering the bedroom, she started to climb onto the bed when he stopped her.

"You will undress me," he commanded.

Without a word she turned to him and her hands zeroed in on the button at the placket of his jeans. She loosened them, straining over the part which covered his cock. He made no move to help her, enjoying the brush of her fingers over his erection. With his jeans around his ankles, she removed his boxers before having him step out of the clothing.

"Now fold them."

Surprise registered in her eyes and her brow shot up. A slight smile twisted her lips and she did as he bid. Neatly she folded his jeans and boxers, leaving them on the dresser. Turning, she faced him and waited for his next command.

Rachel could hardly stand the build-up of sexual arousal. Etienne stood before her, nude, his body bathed in afternoon sunlight. His cock rose in a thick, long arrow from a dark patch of hair at his groin. He really was magnificent, his beauty spellbinding. How she wished she could paint, capture that wild male essence in canvas or clay.

"Get on the bed."

She did as she was bid. Climbing onto the bed, she moved to the middle to kneel, her eyes down and her hands in her lap. While she might appear to be submissive, it took every ounce of willpower to not throw herself on him and hump his leg like a dog.

Etienne climbed onto the bed and lay down beside her. His erection prodded her in the thigh.

"You will touch me now."

Rachel needed no second request. She lay down beside him, her fingers encircling that heavy cock. Stroking him, every now and then she'd give him a gentle tug and his eyes would widen slightly. Using both hands now, she alternated the stroke, never leaving his cock or balls untouched.

"Spread your legs."

Lying on her side, the best she could do was bending her leg at the knee and pressing her foot behind her other leg. He placed his big hand over her pussy, one finger dipping inside, and her hands jerked in their caresses.

"Sometimes it takes time for a woman to become aroused. A considerate lover always makes sure his woman is properly prepared before fucking her." He slid his fingers into her damp, heated pussy. "I see you're already wet."

"Yes, sir."

"It doesn't take much to turn you on, does it, Rachel?" he whispered.

"No, sir." Her lower lip trembled.

"I think I will taste you, slowly."

She seemed stunned when he released her and her breathing was harsh.

"On your back."

She rolled onto her back and he produced some pillows to place under her hips. The position left her more vulnerable than before. Her hips were about eight inches off the mattress with the weight balanced on her shoulders.

"Now spread your legs wide."

Her gulp was audible when she did as he said.

The hair on her pussy was brown and neatly trimmed. He opened her pussy, first the outer lips, then the inner ones. Her flesh was the color of a rose in bloom. A thick layer of shiny arousal painted her flesh and the aroma was knee weakening.

His mouth covered her, his tongue prodding at her slick warmth. Instead of entering her with his tongue, he danced around her pussy, caressing every inch of her from the clit to the perineum. With each pass her thighs grew tighter and her hips began to dance. He smiled against her pussy, his tongue savoring her hot, sweet taste.

He sucked her clit and her body arched as much as it was able. She was more than ready for him, though he was enjoying teasing her more than fucking her. With one final lick, he moved back and got to his knees.

"I think I'm ready to fuck you now," he said.

He took his cock and directed it to her vagina. Her dark gaze was fixed on his but when he gave a tentative thrust, a shudder rocked her body and he withdrew. The head of his cock was damp with her arousal. He ran his finger over the tip of his cock then tasted it. Her taste mingled with his and his teeth came together with a click.

Slowly he entered her. There was no stopping this time. His cock slid into place and she made to wrap her thighs around him only to unbalance herself.

"No slave, you are only to receive me," he commanded. "You will remain in place and take what I give you." He pressed her legs back into position, spread wide and vulnerable to him.

Once she was settled, he slowly began to fuck her. Each thrust was slow, dreamy, his cock dragging against her skin. It was so delicious, so bone tingling that he tipped his head back and gave a loud, earthy groan. Keeping his pace even, slow, the build up of arousal was like walking through caramel rather than skating over ice.

Rachel moved beneath him, her back arching ever-so slightly and his cock sunk into her pussy that much deeper. A hiss sounded between his teeth and he kept his eyes closed. Never had he experienced such joy in a woman's body as he was with her. The slow buildup to a teeth-jarring release was almost more than he could bear, though he was determined to not race through sex this time around.

He wanted it to last.

The silken in-and-out glide of his cock was brain-numbing and he reached for her plump breasts. Her skin was soft and her nipples hard in his fingers. Giving them a gentle twist, Etienne reveled in the sound of her scream.

Her pussy convulsed around his cock and he gritted his teeth. He grabbed her hips and tried counting backwards from twenty to keep from his release. Slowly she settled and he opened his eyes.

Her curvy body was covered with a light sheen of sweat, her eyes were dilated and held a dreamy look of a satisfied woman. Sunlight played across her body accenting her rose nipples and the pale caramel of her skin.

He thrust gently and her eyes widened.

"Do you feel me," he said.

"Yes, sir."

"We're special together, Rachel." He rolled his hips, his cock sliding inside then out again. "We should be together."

She moaned and her hands caught his. "If we're meant to be together, we'll receive a sign," she panted.

"Like the alligator?"

Rachel frowned and when he thrust again, her expression went into orbit.

"Alligator?" she hissed.

"The one that stopped you on the road."

"Y-yes?"

"I was on my way to New Orleans." His cock slid into her pussy, her flesh clenching around his. "I wasn't supposed to be here."

"I don't understand—"

"I was stopped in Chauvin by a large alligator in the road." He released one of her hands and grabbed her hip.

"Really?" she hissed.

"Really." He began to increase his thrusts. "I tried to get around it, and it wouldn't let me. Damned thing kept moving and blocking me. I had to come back."

Her eyes were slits and her thighs were tight to his hips. "And this was a sign?"

"Wasn't it?"

He launched himself over her, their lips meeting in a wild tangle of heat and emotion. Rachel's hands landed on his spine, her inquisitive fingers grabbed his buttocks in a firm, high grip.

Together they battled, her arms yanking him to her, his thrusts deeper than ever before. It took only two more thrusts for Rachel to reach her release. She wrapped her body around him like sticky tape and her pussy milked him for all she was worth.

Her wild screams of release drove him over the edge. He covered her with his big body, his hips low and tight to hers. Coherent thought was impossible at this point. His body was intent upon mindless orgasm and nothing would stop him from gaining his pleasure.

He threw his head back and howled, his body emptying into hers, his hips spasming and all sense of coordination was gone. Muttering incoherently, he buried his face in her neck, wondering if all his sense had exited his body through his cock.

Chapter Seven

ᏁᎩ

"Do you really think the alligators were a sign?" Rachel sat on his lap in the swing. Even when she was wrapped only in a bed sheet, Etienne made for a comfortable place to sit.

"What do you think?"

"I think we are in the bayou and you can find an alligator about every thirty yards 'round here."

He chuckled. "Ever had one smile at you?"

Rachel froze, the image of her alligator flashed in her mind and the eerie sensation that the creature had been smiling at her.

"Did yours smile at you?"

"It sure looked like it," he said. "Damnedest thing I'd ever seen."

"I'll bet." Her voice was faint.

Her mother was a sensible, levelheaded woman and she'd raised her daughter to be the same. Her grandmother, on the other hand, was very superstitious. In her eyes this would definitely be a sign that someone wanted them together.

"Well, I just don't know what to think about this," she said. "I think I need to chew on it some more."

He grinned and reached for a bottle of water. "You do that. In my book it is a sign and I don't know what else you'd need to change your mind."

"Well, if it is meant to be then it's meant to be—"

The sound of an engine coming at a fast clip had her sitting up.

"Sounds like a boat." Etienne nudged her toward the door. "Get some clothes on."

The sound grew louder and Rachel ran for the door. In his bedroom, she rifled through his dresser until she located a T-shirt that came within two inches of her knees. Outside the engine cut out and she heard Etienne speaking. She ran for the door and almost tripped when the electricity came back on. Every light blazed but that wasn't enough to deter her.

From the window, she peered outside to see who it was. Her father and three brothers had the mud devil and were in the boat in the wash.

"They found her purse and her driver's license," her father yelled to Etienne. "I need your help to search for her."

"John Paul—" Etienne started.

Rachel ran out the door and came to stand by Etienne. The look on her father's face was absolutely priceless.

"Papa!!" she called.

"Rachel?" her father said. "Is that you?"

"Yes, sir." She started down the steps then stopped when their faces changed from relief to anger.

Her father grabbed a shotgun and had it pointed at Etienne before she could draw a breath. "What you got to say for ya'self, boy? You been messin' wid my girl?"

Stunned, Rachel turned toward Etienne. His expression was bemused.

"I told them you weren't here because I didn't want them knowing we'd spent all this time together, alone," he said to her.

"I—"

"Boy," her father roared.

Rachel danced up the steps and placed her body in front of Etienne's.

"Daddy, you cain't just shoot anybody who touches me," she yelled. "Just because we had sex doesn't mean anything."

Behind her, Etienne sighed.

"Now you did it," he muttered.

"Boys, get the rope." Her papa's voice was louder.

Forcing a bright smile on her face, she faced Etienne. "Hey, you're the one who said them damn gators were a sign."

He smiled. "And you said let's wait and see if anything else happened." He nodded toward the boat. Her father now stood in the bow, his shotgun pointed at Etienne. Her younger brother Jimmy held a push pole like a weapon while Matthew walked toward them with a rope and a glint of anger in his eye.

"Don't let them force you into anything," she started.

"Too late. Your brother is coming to kick my ass and the only thing that will save me is your hand in marriage."

She gaped at him. "What?"

"Marry me."

"I…" She looked from her brothers to her father then back to Etienne. "I think I need time—"

"You have about thirty seconds, your brother has a rope and I don't like the look on his face."

"I—"

Etienne's mouth came down on hers and she melted into him.

Dimly she heard her family whoop with delight.

"Damn, Daddy, we're havin' a weddin'!"

Also by Dominique Adair

෨

Blood Law

Holly

Katie

Last Kiss

Party Favors (*anthology*)

R.S.V.P. (*anthology*)

Single White Submissive (*anthology*)

Tied with a Bow (*anthology*)

Writing as J.C. Wilder

෨

Ellora's Cavemen: Tales from the Temple II (*anthology*)

In Moonlight (*anthology*)

Men of SWAT: Tactical Maneuver

Men of SWAT: Tactical Pleasure

Shadow Dwellers 1: One with the Hunger

Shadow Dwellers 2: Retribution

Shadow Dwellers 3: Tempt Not the Cat

Shadow Dwellers 4: Atonement

Shadow Dwellers 5: Sins of the Flesh

Shadow Dwellers 6: Temptation

Things That Go Bump in the Night 2004 (*anthology*)

'Twas the Knight before Christmas

About the Author

ℬ

Dominique Adair is the pen name of award-winning novelist, J.C. Wilder. Adair/Wilder (she chooses her name according to her mood—if she's feeling sassy and brazen, it's Adair—if she's feeling dark and dangerous, it's Wilder) lives just outside of Columbus, OH where she skulks around town plotting her next book and contemplating where to hide the bodies (from her books of course—everyone knows that you can't really hide a body as they always pop up at the worst times).

Dominique welcomes comments from readers. You can find her website and email address on her author bio page at www.ellorascave.com.

Tell Us What You Think

We appreciate hearing reader opinions about our books. You can email us at Comments@EllorasCave.com.

LIFE SENTENCE
Jennifer Dunne

ഔ

Trademarks Acknowledgement

Prologue
Summer, 1967

ℰᴑ

"He's a menace. The officials should bar him from racing."

Giacomo Bravetti turned from the hydroplane race where Rodrigo Valente's boat had just forced its way inside of another craft to gain speed around the turn, their sponsons passing within inches of each other, and smiled at his younger brother. "You're just upset you're not out there with them."

"I should be. If Valente hadn't damaged my hull last week…" Nico's glare could have ignited the motorboat fuel into a fireball, although minor crashes like the one he'd had with Valente were commonplace in the sport. At least one racer was sitting out for repairs at every meet, but Nico had no patience when he was the one with no ride. "Jeffrey's right behind him. But he's too conservative. He could catch him if he opened up the throttle a little more."

Giacomo glanced at Jeffrey Middlemarch's bright yellow motorboat. Its sponsons slapped the water as it rounded the buoy then rose out of the water in the straightaway. Unlike his boat-crazy brother, Giacomo's interest in hydroplane design was academic, the subject just one of the many facets of racing he'd analyzed and mastered to understand his brother's obsession.

He shook his head. "It's riding rough. I don't think he's quite got the new design perfected."

"That's just because he's behind the others, crossing their wakes."

They watched in silence, the thundering roar of the aircraft engines powering the approaching boats making

185

further discussion impossible, even drowning out the amplified voice of the announcer calling the race. Giacomo narrowed his gaze on Jeffrey's boat as a dark green challenger sped alongside it. An American by the name of Michaelson, he had only joined the European circuit this year, but his different style of driving had already caused quite a stir. The yellow boat rocked, losing precious seconds, and the challenger flew past.

The four leaders circled the near turn in a tight pack, the two remaining boats in the heat charging down the straightaway well behind them with no hope of a win.

Valente's bright red boat surged forward as he opened the throttle to full power. At over a hundred miles per hour, the craft was a red blur.

His wake pushed the white boat behind him to the right just as the green boat tried to pass. The American swerved to avoid him and caught the tip of his sponson in the chop. The green boat spun out of control, crashing into the rear of the white boat.

Both boats broke apart, their drivers thrown from the wreckage by the force of the collision. A collective gasp of horror rose from the crowd as thousands of spectators held their breaths, waiting to see if the drivers were all right. The announcer's voice called out the details of the crash in hushed tones. Jeffrey cut his speed and circled wide around the accident.

The driver of the white boat surfaced, clinging to one of his sponsons, and waved at the crowd, signaling that he was not injured. A cheer went up, cut short by the announcer's curt, "There's a body in the water. Michaelson is floating among the wreckage of the *Sweet Liberty* and he's not moving."

Giacomo stiffened, adding his silent prayer to those he knew the crowd around him was saying. Minor crashes were common in the sport and spinouts or flips could easily destroy hundreds of thousands of dollars in equipment. As soon as they could get another boat in the water, the teams would be racing again. But very few men had the courage and skill required to drive a thunderboat, and any serious injury sent shock waves through the racing community.

The accident had taken mere seconds and Jeffrey's boat was just now rounding the debris. Instead of resuming the race and trying to catch Valente, he dove into the water and swam to the unconscious driver, turning him over and holding his head above water. A bright red flare burst in the sky as the officials halted the race.

Giacomo could barely see the two men bobbing amid the waves and scattered debris. A chunk of debris briefly blocked his view and he hoped it hadn't hit them. But Jeffrey managed to keep his hold on the other man until the rescue boats arrived and Michaelson could be loaded into an inflatable stretcher.

The rescue team fastened the stretcher down, their every move described by the announcer. Then one of the rescuers raised his arm, signaling the shore.

"Michaelson has opened his eyes," the announcer reported, and the crowd erupted in cheers.

Giacomo let out his breath in relief and turned to smile at his brother. Nico was cheering and waving like the rest of the crowd.

Jeffrey declined the rescuers' assistance and climbed back into his boat. As he turned his craft to shore, only his left hand was on the wheel. The announcer reported this development, speculating that his right arm might have been injured while he was in the water. If that were true, he wouldn't be able to race in the rematch.

"I've got to get down there," Nico cried, race fever burning in his eyes. "He'll need a substitute driver."

"There's no hurry. It will take at least an hour to clear the course."

Giacomo could have saved his breath. Telling Nico there was no reason to hurry was about as useful as telling a hurricane there was no reason to blow so hard. He lived for speed.

Shaking his head, Giacomo followed his brother more slowly through the crowd, pausing to speak to the business acquaintances who were his reason for attending the race. By the time he reached the Middlemarch pit crew, Nico was already suited up and in Jeffrey's boat.

The announcer reported that Michaelson had been examined at the hospital. X-rays showed he had two cracked ribs but otherwise he would be fine. A second hearty cheer rose from the crowd, drowning out his next words and rendering the five-minute horn barely audible.

Giacomo waved at his brother who returned the salute before starting the boat's engine and motoring toward the starting line. Jeffrey stood beside him, silently watching his boat queuing up for the race.

"Your first heat looked rough," Giacomo said. "Are you sure the new design was tested enough?"

Jeffrey startled, whirling to face him. "I didn't see you there."

The crack of the starter's pistol silenced any further conversation as the four remaining boats opened their throttles and roared down the straightaway. Valente's red boat surged into the lead with Jeffrey's yellow boat at his side. Slowly Nico edged forward, running neck and neck with Valente then beginning to pass him.

They thundered up to the first turn buoy. Giacomo frowned. Valente was on the inside and would gain precious tenths of a second in the turn.

"He's not throttling back enough," Jeffrey muttered beside him.

As Valente slowed for the turn, Nico shot past him. He cut sharply, the yellow boat rocking violently as the sponsons bounced over the waves. The nose dipped, brushing the surface of the water and Giacomo's heart clenched as he realized his brother was losing control of his boat.

The world slowed and sound became a meaningless roar as Giacomo watched helpless. The front of Nico's boat submerged, caught in the water, and the heavy engine thrust the rear of the boat into the air, flipping it over to crash upside down. The sponsons separated and the deck splintered, the boat snapping in two between the cockpit and engine compartment. The heavier engine section quickly sank.

"Come on, Nico," Giacomo whispered. "Get out of the cockpit."

But his brother did not appear.

The rescue boat arrived, divers leaping into the cold water. Long seconds passed as they worked beneath the surface. Then their heads broke the water and they lifted a limp body out of the waves.

"Nico!"

He started forward, intent on rushing to the pier where the rescue boat would dock, but two firm hands held him back.

"Wait, Giacomo. Give them room to work."

He struggled briefly against Jeffrey's hold, unable to break it, then froze as the meaning caught up with his stunned brain. Jeffrey was strong enough to grip both of his arms. He was strong enough to drive his boat.

"You knew. You knew there was something wrong with your boat and you let my brother drive it."

Jeffrey released him, stepping back. "There was nothing wrong with my boat. Nico took the turn too fast."

Giacomo growled but didn't want to waste time debating with him. He turned and ran to the pier, forcing his way through the crowd with a mixture of apologies and curses. The leisurely pace of the rescue boat as it tied up to the dock told the tale but he refused to give up hope until they carried

Nico's lifeless body ashore, the unnatural angle of his head bearing mute testimony to the cause of death.

Tears streamed down Giacomo's cheeks as he fought his way to where the race doctor was declaring Nico officially dead. Grasping his brother's cold hand in his, Giacomo fell to his knees. For the last five years since their parents' deaths, Giacomo had cared for Nico like a father as well as a brother. He'd done his best but he'd failed. Silently, he vowed not to fail his last task for Nico—vengeance.

His brother's funeral was held at their family estate outside of Palermo with Nico's final resting place in the private cemetery overlooking the ocean. Giacomo hoped the view would give his brother's spirit joy. It was the least he could do for him.

Jeffrey had the prudence to stay away, but many other racers came to pay their respects. Nico had been well-liked and his fellow racers mourned his death as a tragic accident.

They didn't know what Giacomo did. After the mourners left, he knelt in the newly turned earth of Nico's grave and swore again that he would see the man responsible brought to justice.

But as days turned into weeks, it seemed he was destined to fail his younger brother in this as well. The officials ruled that the cause of Nico's accident was unsafe speed around the corner, helped by the many witnesses who'd heard Nico's hotheaded declarations that he would beat Valente in their next match, whatever the cost. Giacomo's warnings about the boat's rough riding during the first heat and Jeffrey's feigned injury were dismissed as the rantings of a grieving brother, especially since Jeffrey received his injury saving John Michaelson's life. Yet when Jeffrey announced his plans to build another boat and continue racing, only Giacomo found it suspicious that he was abandoning his last design and building one similar to an older boat. Surely that indicated he knew the design was flawed!

Giacomo tried once more to confront Jeffrey, needing to prove to himself that the man had known of his boat's flawed design during the race when he let Nico drive it, rather than discovering the flaw after he'd had a chance to reflect on the accident. He waylaid him as Jeffrey escorted his wife and young son to a matinee theater performance.

"You go ahead," Jeffrey told his wife. "I'll be there before the curtain goes up. This won't take long."

As soon as she was out of earshot, Giacomo asked, "Tell me the truth, Jeffrey. We both know your boat had a design flaw. But did you know that when you let Nico drive it?"

"I told you, there was nothing wrong with the boat. Nico was just driving too fast." He looked away, his attention on his wife and son who waited on the steps to the theater. "I'm sorry he's dead but there wasn't anything I could have done to prevent his accident."

Giacomo's blood turned as cold as the frigid Atlantic water. Years of high stakes gambling had made him an expert at reading body language. Jeffrey was lying. And he was going to get away with it. "This isn't over."

Jeffrey looked back at him, annoyance compressing his already thin lips to a faint line. "Yes, it is. The investigation is officially closed. The accident was your brother's fault. It doesn't matter what you think happened. The boat's been scrapped and your brother's buried. Put it behind you and move on."

He shouldered past, striding quickly to catch up to his wife and child. They were too far away for Giacomo to hear what Jeffrey said but his wife glanced back, frowning. Giacomo glared at her. Jeffrey was the one in the wrong, not him. Jeffrey was the one who needed to pay for Nico's death. Only then would Giacomo be able to move on.

That night he put his plans in place. He slipped onto Jeffrey's cruiser where it was tied up at the dock, opened the engine compartment and carefully nicked the fuel line, just enough to let gas vapors escape. After making sure that all the doors and windows of the cabin were closed, he slipped back to the dock then walked quickly to where the Bravetti boat was moored. He spent the rest of the sleepless night surrounded by Nico's possessions, his brother's memory reassuring him that he was doing the right thing by destroying Jeffrey's other boat.

The sunlight spearing through the cabin's windows roused him from his dark reflections. Voices drifted on the early morning air as engines coughed and growled, heading out for a full day of fun on the water. Hearing Jeffrey's voice, Giacomo hurried onto the deck.

Jeffrey had thrown open the door of his cruiser then turned back to call further directions to his family. His wife was wearing a blue halter-top, white shorts and a broad-brimmed white hat, a blue and white beach bag over one shoulder. Their son trailed behind her in navy blue swimming trunks and an orange-and-blue-striped polo shirt.

Giacomo's stomach churned, his throat tightening so that his shout of "No!" was barely a squawk. Jumping to the dock, he raced toward Jeffrey's boat. Jeffrey had already disappeared inside the cabin.

"No!" he shouted again. This time his voice carried.

Jeffrey's wife grabbed her son's hand and began hurrying him to their boat, no doubt trying to get the boy away from the madman her husband had warned her about.

He reached the boat just before she did. Ripping her son from her grasp, he threw the boy into the water on the other side of the dock. Grabbing her around the waist, he tried to toss her after her son. She kicked and clawed at his arms.

"What are you—?"

Jeffrey turned the ignition, cutting off her words in a ball of fire as the boat exploded. A wall of heat and sound swept over Giacomo, followed a moment later by pain more intense than any he'd ever experienced. The world went black.

Then everything was silent.

The pain disappeared, replaced by bone-chilling cold. He began to shiver.

Light stabbed his eyes and he blinked. A sudden fog had rolled in, obscuring everything from his sight except the small patch of dock upon which he stood. He couldn't see Jeffrey, his wife or his son.

Giacomo whirled, eyes straining to see into the fog, ears tuned for the sounds of splashing or a child's frightened cries. He circled around to where he'd started and saw a masked man standing before him.

The same height and build as Giacomo, the man was dressed entirely in black. Black leather pants hugged his legs and a loose black shirt fluttered in the faint breeze off the invisible water. Most ominously, a black mask covered the upper half of his face.

"Did you see what happened?" Giacomo asked. "The woman and the boy, are they all right?"

The man lifted his shoulders in a liquid shrug. "That is no longer your concern."

Giacomo took a step backward. The fog moved with him.

"You are, as you've no doubt just realized, well and thoroughly dead."

"Are you the devil?"

The man smiled. "There are some similarities, but no. I am Master Dante. I am here to offer you a choice."

Giacomo shivered and rubbed his arms. The friction did nothing to combat the cold threatening to consume him. He'd killed three people and died before he could confess. He was going to hell.

"You're not going to hell," Master Dante snapped. "At least not yet. You weren't fated to die today. And you died trying to save others' lives."

He rolled his shoulders in another liquid shrug. "That you were saving them from an explosion you caused, well, that makes things difficult. But you have a choice. If you wish, you may serve your penance at the Monastery of Mastery and eventually be restored to complete your fated lifespan. Or you may go directly to hell."

"I'll serve my penance."

"I thought that's what you'd say."

Chapter One
Present Day

ℬ

Two days before her thirty-fifth birthday, Samantha Taylor received the phone call that ended her life, although it hadn't seemed that way at the time.

"Mom needs you. Come home." The voice of her sister Melinda sounded strained but not upset or tearful. Whatever their mother needed couldn't be that serious.

"What are you talking about, Mel? Why didn't Mom call if she needs my help?"

"She was carrying in some groceries, the bag broke and she fell. Thank God, she didn't land on her cell phone. We just got back from the hospital. She cracked her vertebrae."

"Not her hip?" Sam knew that was a potentially deadly injury among the elderly.

"Not her hip. And it's only cracked, not broken. But she's supposed to rest for four weeks. No bending. No lifting. No twisting. No driving."

"She needs someone to stay with her."

"Right. I can stay with her tonight while Bob watches the kids. But—"

"No problem. My new job with Central High doesn't start for another two months. I can easily come down and stay with her for a month." She took a deep breath. "How's she taking it?"

"I think she was more upset about seeing a doctor who used to work with Dad than she was about the injury. It's been almost a year since he died but she still cries when she thinks no one is watching. Since she was so upset, they gave her

195

really strong painkillers and she's sleeping now. She'll probably sleep straight through the night. The fun will begin tomorrow when it starts sinking in how much of her usual routine she can't do."

"I'll pack tonight and hit the road first thing tomorrow morning. Expect me in the late afternoon, around three or four o'clock, depending on how bad the I-75 traffic is."

"Thanks, Sam. You're a lifesaver."

"She and Dad were there for me after my divorce, letting me stay with them rent-free then dipping into their retirement savings to send me back to school for my Education degree. A month of playing nurse for her is the least I can do."

But when Sam arrived the next afternoon, a month's worth of clothing, books and knitting piled in cartons in the back of her car giving her an unpleasant sense of déjà vu, she quickly realized that there was much more she could do to repay her mother.

The two-story colonial had always gleamed beneath her mother's touch, as clean as one of her father's operating rooms. She didn't notice the change when she relieved Mel and received a whispered status so as not to wake their napping mother. Then Sam carried the first pile of clothes into her old bedroom.

Dust visibly coated everything and not a light layer either. Balancing her box on one hip, she dug a tattered tissue out of her jeans pocket to wipe off the surface of her desk. She put the box on the newly dusted desktop then looked at the tissue. It was black. She'd have to give the room a thorough dusting and vacuuming before she brought the rest of her things in.

It looked as if her mother hadn't dusted since Sam's last visit home at Christmas. The holiday had been just a few months after her father's sudden death and everyone was still in shock. They'd tried so hard to act happy for Mel's kids, it had been painful. She'd hurried back to finish her final year of school, leaving early to escape the strained atmosphere of the house where everything reminded her of her missing father.

Curious, she looked in on the shared bathroom. Mold stained the corners of the walls and discolored the shower curtain. Dirt gathered in the nooks and crevices beneath the fixtures, and the once pristine grout was gray and cracked. The neglect wasn't limited to Sam's room. That knowledge both relieved and disturbed her.

Mel's room and the master bedroom were not obviously dirty. But now that Sam knew what to look for, she could see cobwebs stretching between the curtains and the windows, and lines of dust crusting the folds of the curtains.

The first floor, where her mother rested in her father's old recliner in front of the forty-two-inch plasma television that had been his last big purchase, was marginally cleaner than upstairs. But even there, dust gathered around the bases of furniture and darkened lamp bulbs. Unread mail, magazines and newspapers covered the dining room table and cobwebs skirted the kitchen cabinets.

In fact, the only room that seemed up to her mother's former standards was the foyer, which anyone coming to pick her up would see, with the unforgiving Florida sun streaming through the open door to highlight any dust or spider webs.

The house had obviously not been cleaned in months. Quietly opening the cupboard under the sink, Sam dug out waterproof gloves, cleaning solution, a bucket and a rag. She'd start in the kitchen.

Half an hour later she'd emptied the black water in the bucket three times until it remained a dingy gray and the kitchen was as clean as she could make it. She had no idea what the sticky stuff on top of the refrigerator had been but felt much better knowing it was no longer anywhere near the food.

As she was rinsing out the rag her mother called from the den, "Melinda? Are you making tea?"

She dropped the rag into the sink and hurried into the den. "It's Sam, Mom. I was just tidying up the kitchen."

Her mother frowned, her once-smooth forehead creasing in newly etched lines. "Samantha? When did you arrive?"

"I got in about half an hour ago. You were resting and I didn't want to wake you." Sam leaned down and kissed her mother's cheek. "Mel called and told me what happened. I came down to take care of you."

A happy light sparked in her mother's eyes, quickly hidden when she glanced away. "I'm sorry I didn't have a chance to prepare your room. I didn't know you were coming."

"Mom! You cracked your vertebrae. I didn't expect you to clean when you're supposed to be resting."

The frown returned. "When your father was alive, I wouldn't have needed to do anything besides change the sheets. Keeping up with the housework has just been beyond me lately though."

"Don't worry about it, Mom. I'm here to help. You tell me what needs to be done and I'll do it."

Her mother smiled, relaxing back into the recliner, a brief spasm of pain crossing her face as her back twinged. "How long are you staying?"

"As long as you need me. I've got two months before school starts."

But as days turned into weeks, it became clear that two months would not be sufficient. Her mother had lost interest in everything. She was forced to abandon her gardens and her morning swims due to her injuries. But she also stopped reading, ignored fashion magazines and sale circulars, and couldn't even sustain her interest for the length of a movie on television. If Sam didn't put out different clothes for her, she'd wear the same jogging suit every day.

Sam's new life as a high school math teacher was over before it had even begun. She resigned from her job, canceled the lease on her apartment and moved back home to care for her mother. A part-time work-at-home job proofreading math books and standardized tests gave her a little bit of income. It was a far cry from the independent existence she'd envisioned for herself when she'd gone back to school for her teaching certification, but the warm glow of satisfaction that filled her with each of her mother's grateful smiles was nearly enough to make up for the lost opportunity.

Caring for her mother kept Sam almost too busy to think about what might have been. But in those odd moments of time between tasks, she occasionally spared a thought for her dreams of independence and accomplishment. The thoughts were quickly dismissed with a stern reminder that she'd had her chance to do something with her life and wasted it. Second chances were earned and she obviously hadn't done enough to deserve one. Each time the selfish thoughts occurred, she firmed her resolve to earn a second chance by being the best, most helpful daughter she could be, doing whatever it took to help her mother recover.

Yet it seemed that the longer she helped her mother, the less she could do right for her. She tried to tell herself that her mother was cranky and upset because of her long, enforced inactivity, but in her heart, she knew the failing was hers. Over and over she vowed to do better, to do more. Time after time she failed to measure up to her mother's needs and expectations.

Her mother was at the doctor's office now, followed by a visit to the physical therapist. Sam had two glorious hours all to herself and hadn't hesitated about how to spend them. As soon as she'd dropped her mother off, she'd driven to the used book store, looking for escapist fiction to temporarily transport her out of her life.

Her tote bag was already bulging with over a dozen romances, exciting stories of women taking control of their lives and going after what they wanted the way she wished she could. Romance heroines rarely had sick parents who needed constant care. Although if she found a book featuring one, she'd pick it up in an instant.

Having combed the romance shelves, she moved to her other love, fantasy. There wasn't as much turnover in this section of the store so she located the new books quickly.

A heavy leather-bound volume caught her eye. Most of the books in the store were paperbacks but occasionally someone cleaning out an estate would bring in hardbacks and fancy leather-bound editions. This looked old enough to have been on some collector's shelves for decades. In faded gold print on the spine was printed, *To Serve Man*, and in smaller type, "M. Dante".

She smiled, reminded of the classic *Twilight Zone* episode, and pulled the book from the shelf. The pages fell open to a pen and ink illustration of a naked woman, her hands tied behind her back, kneeling in front of a masked man who held her hair in one fist and a whip in the other. She appeared to be giving him fellatio.

Sam's eyes bugged out. "What kind of book is this?"

She flipped through the pages, finding illustration after illustration of how exactly the beautifully muscled man should be served. His cock was thrust variously between the woman's bound breasts, into her mouth, into her vagina and into her anus while the woman knelt, crouched on all fours or was bound to the wall or bed.

The pen and ink sketches were beautifully rendered, every straining muscle and fervent expression as clear as if the book's pages were windows into a strange black and white world. She expected the man's features to be twisted into the self-satisfied smirk her ex-husband had worn every time events confirmed his position at the center of his own universe. But she didn't recognize the man's expression as one she'd ever seen.

After a brief struggle, Sam dismissed the puzzle as unimportant. Instead, she was transfixed by the expression of bliss the artist had drawn on the woman's face. On page after page whenever her face could be seen, she appeared nearly transported by rapture. As if the heady ecstasy could be transmitted through the paper upon which it was drawn, Sam found her own breath growing shallow, her nipples tightening and her pussy heating.

Lightly she traced her finger over the woman's spread thighs, stretched nearly into a full split as she sank onto the reclining man's cock. Sam's own thighs burned imagining being spread that wide. Her ass muscles tightened and her pussy dripped hot lubricant into her panties. Her lips were spread as wide open as the woman's in the picture, ready to claim the man's thick cock for herself.

She wriggled uncomfortably, trying to rub her clit against the seam of her jeans and get some relief. Her breasts tingled, the nipples tight and hard, and her lungs labored to draw breath.

For the first time in weeks she felt truly alive. She had to have this book.

Stuffing it into her tote, she hurried up to the counter. The clerk rang up the romances without comment then paused when she saw the leather tome.

"*To Serve Man*. I don't remember seeing this one come in." She reached for the cover to flip it open.

"It's a cookbook," Sam blurted. "Get it? To serve man?"

"Oh." The clerk pushed the book unopened into the pile with the romances. "I just do the fiction sections. That'll be nineteen dollars and fifty-six cents."

Sam's hands barely trembled as she counted out the money then scooped her books back into her tote. Her blood sang with a heady mixture of daring and dread. She'd die if anyone saw the contents of this book. And she could hardly wait to get home and read it in private. Carefully she stowed the tote in the trunk of her mother's car, braced in the corner of one of the empty cardboard boxes kept there to prevent bags of groceries from sliding around.

It took three tries before she could force herself to close the trunk lid. The book seemed to be calling to her, begging her to read it immediately. Locking it away caused a physical wrench in her chest and she had to fight not to pop the trunk and retrieve it. Instead she hurried around to the driver's seat and drove off to pick her mother up at the physical therapist's.

She arrived just as the session was ending. The therapist praised her mother's progress and reminded her to continue exercising. Sam shook her head, anticipating her mother's response.

"I try. But it's so hard. It's too hot to go walking during the day and the pain keeps me up during the night so I'm too tired to go out first thing in the morning. And you know what the traffic is like in the evening. It's not safe to walk on the roads."

"Well, make an effort. Every little bit helps."

They left the therapist's office, her mother leaning on Sam's arm. Instead of going to where the car was parked, they walked to the luncheonette in the same plaza.

Somehow Sam made it through the soup and sandwiches, listening to her mother's health complaints and what history suggested was a highly selective recitation of what the doctor had said, even while her mind played over and over again the images she'd seen in the book. Fortunately her part of the conversation consisted mostly of nodding her head and saying, "Mm-hmm."

By the time the waiter delivered their check Sam could barely breathe, her chest was so tight. Her breasts ached, the nipples hard and painfully sensitive, the light press of her elasticized bra nearly enough to make her come. Her panties were soaked through, her pussy hot and wet and begging for that gorgeous man's long, thick cock to be buried deep inside her. She'd almost rested her water glass in her lap in a desperate attempt to cool herself down before she realized how the condensation would stain her jeans. So she fidgeted and counted to ten in base 2 through base 8 and tried desperately not to let what she was thinking show on her face.

As she counted out the money for their meal, her mother said, "Here I've been running on and on. How about you? Did you enjoy your trip to the bookstore?"

Sam's cheeks heated. Her mother had no idea — and she had to keep it that way! "I got a whole bunch of books this time. Romance and fantasy mostly. I can hardly wait to start them."

They left the restaurant, her mother making the drive home an interminable hell as she adjusted and readjusted her seat, all the while complaining about the speed at which Sam drove as well as every pothole in the road, which were all well and good for healthy people, but she was injured and couldn't be shaken around like a sack of potatoes. Sam's efforts to modulate her driving to suit her mother warred with her need to race home as quickly as possible. She breathed a soft sigh of relief as she finally pulled into the driveway, throwing the car into park and counting to ten before slowly unclenching her fingers from the wheel.

"Come on, Mom. I'll put the pillows on the love seat for you and you can have a little rest."

Her mother opened her own door and unclipped her seat belt then sat waiting until Sam circled around to hand her out of the car. Slowly they walked to the house, her mother leaning heavily on Sam's arm.

The smell of citrus-scented cleaner greeted them as they stepped inside the gleaming foyer. But it was no longer the only clean room in the house. In the past four months every cobweb and dust speck had been eradicated.

Sam positioned her mother's pillows on the love seat then helped her mother stretch out for a rest, covering her with a light cotton throw knitted in an airy feather and flame pattern.

"You relax too, Sam." Her mother's eyes drifted closed. "Read one of your new books. I know how much you enjoy reading."

"I'll be in the workshop. But I'll have my cell phone. If you need me when you wake up, just call."

She made sure her mother's phone was within easy reach then paused in the doorway in case she had any last requests before Sam left. Today was a good day. No pillows needed adjusting. Her mother did not discover any sudden needs for water or tea.

Sam tiptoed carefully from the room.

She grabbed her bag of books out of the trunk then hurried up the stairs to the finished room above the detached garage. It had been her father's haven when she'd been growing up, someplace he could go to escape the estrogen-laden atmosphere of a house filled with a wife and two daughters. Even their dogs had been girls, their mother insisting that she wasn't going to clean up after a male dog who wanted to mark his territory.

Fishing poles were lined neatly in racks against one dark-paneled wall, ranging from short and stiff to long and whippy for different conditions and types of fish. Hand-tied lures studded canvas-covered boards, organized according to some system that had been known only to her father. A worktable sat beneath the boards, the bench pushed under it. The hooks, strings and bits of feather and fur used to craft the lures were stowed neatly in boxes under the bench.

Her mother had sold his boat shortly after his death, blaming it for the swamp sickness he'd caught while helping with hurricane rescue and relief efforts. That illness had rapidly escalated to the pneumonia that killed him. But she couldn't bear to get rid of the fishing gear that had meant so much to him.

Sam dusted the rods, reels and lures occasionally, if only because the workshop was her space now and she wanted it to be clean. The only other reminder of her father's hobby was the small black vise mounted on the end of the table. The rest of the table had been given over to her escape hobbies — piles of books and skeins and balls of yarn.

She cleared a space on the table and set her newest bag of books down. Taking the heavy, leather-bound volume with her, she crossed to the beat-up brown recliner that faced an old portable color TV. It was so old it still had independent dials for adjusting UHF and VHF stations.

Unzipping her jeans, she pushed them and her wet panties down around her ankles. Rather than sitting in the recliner, she straddled one of the arms, pressing the rough leather against her swollen pussy.

She moaned, her head dropping back to rest against the back of the recliner. The pressure felt so good. But it wasn't enough.

Slowly she began rocking back and forth, rolling her spread lips against the leather padding, pressing the recliner's arm deeper between her lips. But no matter how hard she rocked, it couldn't go as deep as she wanted. It couldn't slide inside her.

She whimpered and reached between her legs. Two fingers slid inside her with no resistance, she was so wide open and ready. Her inner muscles clenched around her fingers and she stroked the hot, wet walls of her vagina, her fingers quickly growing sticky with her body's lubricant.

It still wasn't enough. Struggling one-handed, she opened the book. It fell open on a picture of the woman seated at the end of what looked like a padded sawhorse, her legs spread wide and tied to the supports while her body bowed backward to where her arms were tied to the supports at the other end.

The man held her by the hips and thrust his cock deep into her open pussy as she screamed in ecstasy.

Sam scooted to the very edge of the recliner's arm and arched her back, mimicking the woman's posture as best she could. As the angle of her hips changed, her fingers slid deeper inside. She pumped her fingers back and forth, imagining the man's hard, commanding cock was thrusting deep with every stroke. Her thumb teased her clit, sliding across the sensitive flesh at the end of each stroke, pressing as hard as she imagined the root of his cock would crush against her as he thrust deep inside her.

An agonized whimper built deep in her throat and her hand moved faster, harder.

"Please," she begged her imaginary lover. "Please."

With a final thrust of her fingers, she came, the spasms lifting her hips and slapping her ass against the leather recliner again and again. She moaned, lost in the waves of heat and pulsing thunder that swept over and through her body with every beat of her heart.

When her heartbeat finally slowed to normal, she opened her eyes. She was draped half naked across the recliner. The book had fallen to the floor, leaves spread and spine up.

Her limp and passion-wrung muscles didn't want to obey her but eventually she turned to her side and reached for the book with one flailing arm. Her fingertips brushed across the leather cover, trailing a line of wet fluid across the gilt title.

"Damn!" She'd reached for the book with the hand she'd been pleasuring herself with. She hoped the leather didn't stain.

The gilt sparkled in the late afternoon sunlight where her juices crossed it. Then a faint steam rose from the leather as the rest of her trail evaporated, leaving the cover looking the way it had when she'd picked it up in the bookstore.

Sam's eyes widened. Not quite the way it had been. The gilt lettering had been worn and faded in places when she found it. Now it glittered as if it had been newly made.

And steam was still rising from the leather in faint wisps, pooling around the book and drifting toward the legs of the recliner. She jerked up her panties and jeans, pulling her legs away from the strange phenomenon, and huddled on the recliner's seat.

A quick glance over one arm confirmed that the strange mist had spread across the floor while she'd been pulling up her pants. There wasn't any way out without going through it and she was reluctant to let the vapors touch her if she could avoid them. She was trapped on the recliner.

The fog coalesced before her, rising in a column over the spot where the book had been, now invisible in the swirling mist. The scent of the ocean drifted past her, borne on a faint breeze. The wind strengthened, ripping fluttering plumes of vapor from the column of fog, thinning it just enough to show a glimpse of black at its heart.

Sam held her breath.

The mist rippled, bulging outward. The wind caught it and tore it to tatters. A man stood before her, shirtless, his strong hands on his hips, black leather pants molded to his legs. A wide belt hung low on his hips, a black leather riding crop dangling from one side and a multi-tailed black leather flogger from the other. A thick silver bracelet encircled his left wrist, etched with delicate and flowing scrollwork that both matched and contrasted with the masculine power of the black tribal tattoo on the back of his right hand.

Her startled gaze lifted to his face. Black hair curled past his shoulders, softening a face that was otherwise dominated by dark unforgiving eyes, strong jaw and patrician nose. A face she had seen only minutes past in the illustrations from her book.

"I am Master Giacomo," he said, his English bearing a heavy Italian accent. "You used the book to summon me. Now you will serve me."

Chapter Two

ဢ

"What do you mean, I summoned you?" Sam demanded. "And I sure as hell am not 'serving' you!"

Giacomo frowned, the aristocratic planes of his face stiffening in hauteur. "As the book explains—"

Heat washed her cheeks. "Oh."

"Oh?"

"Well, I didn't actually *read* the book."

They both glanced at the floor beneath his booted feet. The book was gone.

His eyes widened slightly, his mouth softening. Even his posture shifted, becoming more relaxed and less rigid. Without the veneer of arrogance his natural beauty was clearly visible, reawakening the heat deep within Sam that her earlier touches had only placated, not satisfied.

He studied her as intently as she studied him. "But you performed the summoning ritual. You intoned your request for a master and repeated it exactly so there could be no mistake. Then you anointed the cover of the book with the fluids of your arousal. How could you have done that without reading the instructions?"

"I didn't."

He shrugged, his broad shoulders rippling and his bare chest flexing. "Yet I am here."

The sight of those sculpted chest muscles momentarily distracted her. She hadn't realized it was humanly possible to have such magnificent muscle definition without having a bodybuilder's overdeveloped physique. Then again, odds were pretty good that her mystery guest was not exactly human.

Years of reading fantasy novels allowed her to face this possibility without falling into a gibbering terror. Yet she also knew that magical and otherworldly visitors were never good things, no matter how hot they looked. She needed to get rid of him. Fast.

Clearly she couldn't overpower him and she sensed asking nicely would get her nowhere. Her only choice appeared to be negotiating with him. The fantasy novels she was relying upon for guidance in this unfamiliar situation suggested that the negotiations would not go smoothly or have the consequences she expected. But she had to try. Starting with his claim that she'd summoned him.

Sam thought back to what she'd been doing before his arrival. She hadn't said anything on purpose, certainly hadn't *intoned* anything. But had she called out in the heat of passion?

"Please," she whispered. "I said, 'Please'. That was enough to summon you?"

Giacomo shrugged again. "Apparently. For, I repeat, I am here."

"Yes, you are." She sighed. "What am I supposed to do with you?"

He smiled, a devilish light sparking in the depths of his dark brown eyes.

"Besides that!"

Another shrug. "I am here in answer to your request. I will stay until you are pleased. *Thoroughly* pleased. The sooner you allow me to begin mastering you, the sooner you will experience transcendent pleasure."

She thought again of the illustrated woman's rapturous expression, a thread of longing curling within her. She squelched it. The risk was too great, no matter what reward beckoned.

"That's not happening any time soon, no matter what kind of sex genie you are."

He frowned, his expression returning to the cold arrogance he'd first shown. "I am a man, not a demon or djinn."

"Right. A man who steps out of the mist into the middle of my workroom. Nothing out of the ordinary about that."

"I did not say I was ordinary, merely that I was human." He smiled slowly, lids veiling molten chocolate eyes. "You will find little ordinary about me when you let me master you."

Sam blinked. "That's the second time you've said that, that I have to give you permission to master me."

"But of course."

"Well, I'm not going to so you can just go back to wherever you came from."

"I cannot. It is forbidden." His eyes grew shadowed, his physical presence diminishing in some indefinable way as he drew deeper within his own thoughts. "There can be no failure."

Her heart trembled, aching to soothe his obvious distress. She always wanted to fix things, to make people feel better. That's why she was here after all. She could help her mother. But her need to fix things hadn't worked with her ex-husband and she wouldn't allow herself to fall into the same trap now.

"I'm not letting you use me just to get back to wherever you came from. You'll never have my permission to master me. You're on your own."

"Use you?" Giacomo stiffened in outrage. "I promise you transcendent pleasure and you think I want merely to *use* you? I have trained night and day for years without rest, all so that when I was summoned, I could wring every drop of pleasure from a woman's body. From your body. And you call this *using* you."

Sam licked her suddenly dry lips, her body clenching at the barely restrained passion vibrating in his low voice. God, what would it be like to have that passion turned on her, to have this gorgeous specimen of manhood focusing his single-minded intensity on the needs of her body? On being pleased instead of always on pleasing others?

But his words were as much a lie as any man's. He would gain her agreement by promising her pleasure then once she was under his spell, he'd care only about his own satisfaction. She wasn't falling into that trap a second time, no matter how attractively it was packaged.

He smiled seductively. "You want me, I can tell. Your breathing is fast and sharp, your face is flushed and your nipples strain against your blouse like two ripe olive pits, begging to be squeezed."

"Maybe I do."

Triumph gleamed in his eyes, cut off by her next words.

"But I won't be your or anyone's slave, so it doesn't matter."

"Are you certain? You anointed the book with the juices of your passion. You found the images stimulating. Why are you so unwilling to experience the pleasure I can give you?"

"Because it will cost too much."

Again, he stiffened. "Are you calling me a *berdascia*?"

She didn't recognize the word but his tone left no question of meaning. She shook her head, instinctively reaching out to comfort his hurt before realizing what she was doing and snatching back her hand. He didn't need any encouragement from her.

"I didn't mean I thought you wanted money to make love to me. I meant the emotional cost of opening up, of giving myself to someone who is only going to disappear."

Comprehension dawned in his eyes and he nodded. "Ah, *certamente*. You thought I would return to the half world after I gave you pleasure and denying yourself was the only way to keep me beside you. But so long as I am your master, I will stay here to pleasure you."

She shook her head, denying him, even as the urgency of his fervent plea vibrated low and deep within her, making her ache to accept his offer.

Her pussy pulsed, throbbing with each slow beat of hot blood filling her desire. Warm lubricant slid over her lips, pooling in her still-wet panties.

Giacomo sniffed, his aquiline nose flaring. "Even now your body hungers for my touch, to know the ecstasy of submitting to my will. Why do you resist?"

"I can't let you in," she whispered. "I was married. It nearly destroyed me. I can't go through that again."

He tipped his head, considering. "Then you will not let me into your body. I will not touch you."

Sam straightened, a sense of imminent loss driving her from her curled position on the recliner to her knees, reaching out to stop him before he left.

He smiled. "You say you do not want my hand, but your body betrays you."

"I do want you—your hand, your mouth, your cock. All of you, inside me, again and again. I admit that. But it's never going to happen."

He nodded, accepting her terms. "But I can still give you pleasure. If I can not touch you, you will touch yourself while I watch and tell you what to do."

A wave of cold washed over her, followed by a wave of blazing heat. Touch herself while he watched? The idea was shocking, outrageous…and deeply erotic. But really, it wasn't that different from pleasuring herself while she looked at the book for inspiration, was it?

The heat coiling low in her body told her it was very different. It was the same in the most important way though. She'd be in control. She wouldn't be trading her hard-won independence for a brief physical gratification. She could stop at any time if she didn't like what he was telling her to do.

Her muscles trembled, her nipples tightening with eager anticipation. She could stop but she knew she wouldn't. Doing what others wanted was too deeply ingrained in her. Once she let him tell her what to do, he could tell her to do anything, no matter how outrageous and she would comply. She felt both ashamed of her weakness and at the same time liberated. If she did something to please him, she wouldn't have to feel guilty or selfish when it pleased her too. She just had to make sure she didn't sacrifice her own pleasure for his.

She licked her lips. "What would you want me to do?"

He smiled and took a half step backward as if, now that she was close to giving in, he didn't want to do anything she might perceive as threatening.

"Take off your blouse. Let me see your breasts."

Before good sense could stop her, Sam jerked her T-shirt over her head. His gaze locked on her swollen breasts, the nipples thrust against the thin cotton of her bra. Her breath grew shallow, her breasts swaying with her rapid inhaling and exhaling. She could feel the heat of his gaze on her flesh, a soft pink flush coloring her skin. Her nipples tightened even more, becoming hard pebbles that tingled with the need to be freed from the restraint of her bra, free to be touched and tasted.

"Now the brassiere," he instructed.

She reached behind herself to pop the hooks, the motion further straining her sensitive nipples against the cotton.

The bra snapped open, freeing her breasts. She gasped at the sudden sense of release. Tension began building in her pussy, hot and eager for a different kind of release.

If she'd been pleasuring herself, she'd have one hand inside her panties already, following up the feeling with some long, hard stroking. That she couldn't touch herself there, constrained by her agreement to follow Giacomo's commands, only increased the trembling need between her legs.

She snatched her bra away and tossed it to the floor, exposing her breasts in all their swollen, hard-nippled glory.

Giacomo breathed deeply, as if he could inhale her arousal. Judging from how wet her panties were, he probably could.

"You are beautiful. Ripe and red, like two pomegranate seeds atop the velvet skin of twin peaches. If I were touching you, I would taste you now, taking each of your nipples into my mouth. Licking. Sucking. Scraping your sensitive flesh with my teeth."

Sam moaned, arching her back to offer her breasts to him. She wanted his mouth on her, to feel the sweetness of his tongue and teeth caressing and possessing her. She wanted him, but feared him more.

Giacomo sighed, deeply and theatrically. "Alas, I am not touching you. So you must put your fingers in your mouth, two fingers, and lick them then swirl your wet fingers around your nipples."

She put her fingers in her mouth, slipping them over her lip and swirling her tongue around them, sucking and drawing her fingers deeper into her mouth as if it were his cock between her lips. She slicked her fingers in and out twice then put her wet fingers on her nipple and squeezed.

Her fingers were hot and wet, just like his mouth and tongue would be. Sam put her head back and moaned. With one finger to either side of the nipple, she rotated her hand.

"Harder," Giacomo ordered. "And do the other one."

Sam whimpered softly, squeezing her nipple hard enough to spangle her vision with stars. Her pussy pulsed with need. She sucked her other fingers, one fast thrust into her mouth, then grabbed her other nipple and twisted.

She rose onto her knees, hips tilted forward and head back, a low groan torn from her throat.

"Undo your slacks. Take them off and your panties as well."

She considered ignoring the low growl of his voice. Her fingers felt so good on her nipples. Another few sharp tugs and twists should send her over the edge.

"Stop! Take your hands away from your breasts."

She opened her eyes to see him glaring at her, his fists planted on his hips. She'd failed to please him. A tremor of fear rippled through her, dousing her arousal, and she dutifully dropped her hands.

Realizing what she'd done, she tilted her chin up and squeezed her nipples again, although it didn't feel anywhere close to as good as it had a moment ago. This wasn't supposed to be about pleasing him. It was about pleasing her and she'd better start remembering that.

"No. I like touching my breasts."

His gaze dipped to her nipples, peeking out between her damp fingers. A hint of a smile softened his stern features.

"As I like seeing you touch them. But how can I prove to you that following my commands will bring you pleasure unless you do as I tell you?"

She blinked. Right. That's why he was ordering her around. For a moment, he'd sounded like—

"I forgot."

"Obeying my orders was bringing you pleasure then?"

Sam's face heated, recalling the abandon with which she'd touched herself. "I'm sure you could see that for yourself."

"I want to hear you say it."

"Yes, obeying you was giving me pleasure."

A hot thrill went through her at the words, once again tightening her nipples and spiking low and hard in her pussy. This time when she squeezed her nipples, she felt the throb of swollen flesh between her legs.

Sam groaned. That's why it hadn't felt as good before. Touching herself wasn't what was turning her on. Touching herself for him was doing it.

So much for her much-vaulted independence.

She cupped her breasts in her palms, her nipples peeking between her fingers, and squeezed lightly. She gasped, her thighs trembling as arousal pulsed hot and hard in her pussy.

"Is this what you like?" she whispered.

"Your obedience is what I like. Take your hands away from your breasts and remove your slacks."

This time Sam obeyed without hesitation. She shoved her pants and panties down to her knees then sat back in the recliner to kick them and her shoes off. She was completely naked, except for her socks.

Unbidden, memories overwhelmed her. Of countless hours at the gym, trying to transform the wide hips she'd developed at puberty into the fashionably straight silhouette her ex-husband wanted. Of his disapproving glance and her efforts to find clothing to minimize her figure flaws that never satisfied him.

She realized she was holding her breath and released it in a huff.

"*Donna bella*," Giacomo whispered. "*Molto bella. Più bella.*"

Bella. That meant pretty, didn't it? He thought she was pretty?

Sam breathed deeply, relaxing beneath his heated gaze.

"Now, *mia bella*, recline the chair."

He waited while she struggled with the ancient mechanism, bracing her hands against the recliner's arms, kicking off from the floor and leaning back with all her weight. It popped loudly and fell backward, the footrest rising with an audible *sproing*.

"Lean back," he ordered. "Put your knees over the armrests and let me see your pussy hot and wet, pulsing with eagerness."

Sam eagerly complied, whimpering as the cooler air of the room wafted across her steaming flesh.

"Spread your lips. Feel how wet you are. How hot."

Her fingers slid over her throbbing flesh, slick with her juices. Even that light pressure was enough to make her arch her hips and moan.

"You may not move," he warned her.

A disappointed whine broke from her lips but she obediently stilled her hips. An inadvertent tremble rippled through her thigh and ass muscles but that didn't count since it was outside her conscious control. "I will not move."

"Good."

His praise stroked her like warm velvet and she wanted to wriggle with the pleasure. Instead she remained motionless, the heat of her swollen pussy radiating against her fingers.

"Very good. Slide the fingers of one hand into your slit and push one finger all the way inside you."

Her right hand dipped between her folds, the fingers splaying in the wet heat as her middle finger thrust deep into her vagina. She was so hungry for him she barely touched her flesh.

"Are you tight?" he asked.

"No," she whispered. "I'm wide open."

"Use two fingers."

She slipped her middle finger out, brushing across the sensitive entrance, then thrust her middle and ring fingers back inside. They slid down her wet walls but teased her rather than filled her. She moaned in frustration.

"Are you tight?" he asked again.

"Not too tight to move."

"Use three fingers."

Sam's eyes flew open and she stared up at him. His dark gaze was fixed on her spread pussy, his nostrils flaring as he inhaled the scent of her arousal. She could see the strength of his own arousal straining against his leather pants.

"Three?" she whispered. "I've never—"

"Three." His gaze shifted to her face. "Do not question my orders again."

Something dark and deadly lurked beneath the passion glazing his eyes and the sudden spike of fear only added to her desire. She felt her pussy expanding, heat rising in waves with every rapid beat of her heart.

She pulled her two fingers out, joined her index finger to them and pushed all three into her throbbing vagina. They almost didn't fit, the walls of her channel forcing her fingers into a tight triangle even as her fingers stretched her opening wider than it had ever stretched before.

She moaned, shivers of delight cascading through her body as her inner muscles clenched and released over and over, trying to accustom themselves to the invasion.

"Dip your other fingers into your juices and paint your nipples."

Releasing her folds, now held spread open by the palm of her hand, she stroked her other fingers across her wet clit. A lightning bolt of pleasure seared through her, making her hips spasm and her shoulders bow backward as a hoarse cry ripped from her throat.

"I did not give you permission to touch yourself there!" he snapped.

Sam blinked, his furious expression transmuting her pleasure into pulse-pounding terror. "I'm sorry! Forgive me!"

Her knees tightened against the arms of the recliner but she could neither close her legs nor rise to a less vulnerable position.

"I warned you what would happen if you did not follow orders. Now you must be punished." A hint of a smile played around his lips and his dark eyes filled with smoldering heat. However he planned to punish her, he was looking forward to it.

She trembled, each shiver rocking her against her fingers, which were still buried deep inside her. Slowly, her fear transformed to desire until she panted with frustrated need.

Giacomo stepped forward, holding out a six-inch-long tapered steel weight that must have been tucked into the back of his belt or a back pocket. Or maybe he'd magicked it into existence. The black angles of his tattoo reflected in the polished steel surface, giving it a hint of savagery.

"Take it. And place it inside you instead of your fingers."

Hesitantly, Sam reached out and took the weight from him. It was cold against her fingers, hard and unyielding. Her throat closed, her lungs struggling for breath as she imagined the alien invasion of her most private parts.

"I'm waiting," Giacomo cautioned.

She nodded. Taking a deep gulp of air, she held her breath as she slid her fingers free and placed the narrow end of the weight against her opening.

"The other way. This is a punishment after all."

Silently Sam reversed the weight. The narrow end was only a half-inch wide, barely wider than her finger. The wide end, on the other hand, was huge. Over an inch wide, maybe even an inch and a half. Wider than all three of her fingers together and that wide all the way around. She could never take something so big inside her.

But she had no choice. She had disobeyed, moving when she'd promised she would not. She deserved whatever pain her punishment brought her.

Her total subjugation to Giacomo's will made her pussy pulse hot and wet, opening eagerly to take her punishment.

Slowly, hesitantly, she placed the bulbous end of the weight against her flexing muscles. Her pussy spasmed, trying to pull the slick steel deeper inside—to the hungry emptiness aching to be filled. But it was too big. She couldn't stretch that far.

Tears leaked from her eyes. She wanted to obey him, she did! But her body failed her, as worthless as her ex-husband had claimed.

"I can't!"

"You can. Put the heel of your hand against the end and press between the contractions."

Sam gasped. "You make it sound like labor."

His low chuckle rasped across her taut nipples, vibrating into her rib cage, as if his face were buried between her breasts. "If a woman can give birth to a nine-pound baby, a one-pound weight shouldn't be any problem."

"If I were giving birth, I'd be high on drugs by now." But she dutifully pressed her palm against the end of the weight and when the next spasm ended, she shoved the steel past the ridge of muscle.

She gasped, spirals of pleasure shuddering through her as every nerve was stimulated. A low, hoarse groan ripped from her throat.

"Now, for your punishment. Ten strokes."

She focused her blurry vision on the whips at his belt but he made no move to detach either. "Ten strokes?"

"Pull the weight almost out then push it deep inside, ten times. You are not allowed to come until after the final stroke."

Sam nodded and pulled on the weight. It slid along the tight walls of her channel, prompting another breathy moan before she shoved it deep inside again with a cry.

"One."

Oh God, he was counting the strokes, like a captain overseeing a sailor's whipping. Her muscles tightened around the weight, trying to hold it, contain it, but she obediently slid it to the very edge before thrusting it back inside. Another sharp cry burst from her lips.

"Two."

Her vision filled with gray, starbursts of light obscuring the rest of her sight. Sound dimmed, lost behind the roaring tide of the blood in her ears. The weight rose and fell again.

"Three."

She'd never make it to ten. The punishment was going to kill her. But, God, what a way to go! She moved faster, pulling and pushing.

"Four. And you must bring it all the way to the end for the strokes to count."

She whimpered. How many strokes had he refused to count? Carefully, spreading her legs as wide as possible so that he could see she was obeying him, she brought the weight to the very edge of her vagina and let it hang there a moment, supported only by her tight ring of muscle. Then she shoved it back where she needed it to be.

"Five."

Again, she let the weight hang, this time rotating it so that it caressed the opening to her pussy. Moaning deeply, she thrust it inside.

"Six."

She lost the ability for anything more creative, simply pulling the weight until it stretched her muscles then forcing it back up her channel as hard and fast as she could.

"Seven. Eight."

Her legs trembled, her ass bouncing on the old recliner cushion in a puddle of her fluids. Her nipples were so tight she thought her breasts might be trying to turn themselves inside out. And every breath was a struggle to drag oxygen past the shards of glass filling her lungs.

"Nine."

She wanted to come. She needed to come. Her muscles clenched the weight, refusing to release it, begging her to stroke it faster, deeper and harder until she got what she needed. The fingers of her other hand twitched, wanting to grab her clit and rub it hard until she split in two from the release.

But she did none of those things. She pulled the weight exactly as far out as Giacomo had told her to then pushed it back in.

"Ten. Good girl. You've been punished enough. Now you may have your reward."

"Oh yes, please."

"Take the weight out."

Sam tugged the heavy steel all the way out of her body. It stretched the sensitive ring of muscle at her entrance, pressing hard against her nerves as it slid free and triggered an explosion.

She screamed, bouncing and trembling uncontrollably as wave after wave of ecstasy tore through her helpless body, the ripples flowing out and back, crashing against the later ripples to form new and exquisite wave patterns of pleasure. Long after she lost her voice, long after exhaustion claimed her limp body, pleasure still pooled and flowed through her veins.

When she finally opened her eyes, the room was noticeably dimmer than it had been but Giacomo was still standing before her, hands on hips, an arrogant smirk on his lips.

Sam tried to speak, resulting in only a hoarse croak. Licking her lips and swallowing, she tried again.

"I've changed my mind. I give you permission to master me."

Chapter Three

೪೨

Giacomo's swollen cock pressed hard against the tight leather of his pants. The woman who had summoned him lay sprawled in the recliner, eyes closed and arms splayed limply where they'd fallen, her legs spread to reveal her wet and glistening pussy. The scent of sex filled the room.

She had admitted she wanted his mastery. She had given him permission to master her. Now all he had to do was bring her to transcendent pleasure as she served him and his curse would be broken. He could resume his life.

A brief sliver of guilt stabbed his conscience but he ruthlessly pushed it away with the ease of long practice. If he, who had killed in the name of revenge, had been offered an option to continue his life simply because he had died before his time, no doubt Jeffrey's blameless wife and son had been granted similar clemency. If they had even died. It was possible that he'd managed to save them from the blast. Master Dante had refused to tell him their fate and Giacomo had quickly learned obedience at the end of his lash.

The first few times Master Dante had come for him, Giacomo had asked questions—what had happened to Jeffrey's family, what had happened to his family's holdings, how long would he be there? Master Dante would answer only that the world of the living was no longer his concern then strike unerringly with his whip for maximum pain and damage. The session would only end when Giacomo was dead, allowing him a brief moment of respite before his body was once again recreated as it had been the morning of his first death, with the addition of a black tattoo on his hand that marked him as an initiate of the Monastery of Mastery.

Locked naked in his dark stone cell, Giacomo could do nothing but remember the tortures he had already endured and dread the tortures yet to come until Master Dante came for him again. Because of the way Jeffrey had been killed, Giacomo had his skin flayed off then the underlying flesh burnt with hot irons, or sometimes his skin was burned before being flayed away. Occasionally, his bloodied body would be dunked into a tank of brine or a rag would be stuffed down his throat to keep it open and saltwater poured in until he drowned. Beyond the physical pain of those tortures, he feared they indicated he was also paying for the deaths of Jeffrey's wife and son.

When the heavy iron door of his cell swung open, silhouetting Master Dante in the light of the hallway, Giacomo couldn't help himself. He began to tremble, tears filling his eyes as he cringed into the farthest corner of his cell. If he still ate and drank, no doubt he'd have soiled himself in terror.

The black figure of justice asked the same question each time. "Do you willingly accept the penance for your sin?"

Giacomo had only to refuse and his torment would end. But it would be replaced by an eternal torment, with no hope of ever ending. So each time, he answered, "I do." First speaking then whispering, then finally mouthing the words when his terrified throat permitted no sound to escape.

When Master Dante said instead, "Your penance is completed. Now you begin your training," Giacomo had gaped at him in incomprehension. He'd thought at first it was a particularly cruel form of torture, but Master Dante did not change his mind and return him to the torture chamber. Instead, after fastening the silver bracelet inscribed with the terms of his sentence around Giacomo's wrist, he led Giacomo to the main area of the monastery where he met the other initiates learning to become Masters.

The rules of the monastery dictated that they could not speak of what they'd done to end up there or what price they had paid for their sins, but it was permissible to relate the date of their death and news of the world. The other men had surrounded Giacomo, eager for a source of new information, in return teaching him what he needed to survive Master Dante's more advanced lessons.

Noticing that he was absentmindedly fingering the leather tails of his flogger, he snatched his hand away, clasping his wrists behind his back. Feet spread, he lifted his head and puffed out his chest in Dominance Position #4.

"As I said, I am Master Giacomo. Now you will give me your name."

The woman blinked sex-sated brown eyes and blushed. "Oh God, you never even knew my name. It's Sam. Samantha, I mean. Samantha Taylor."

He nodded. "Sam. You are—"

A high-pitched, piercing melody echoed through the room, the short pattern of notes repeating twice as he glanced about, trying to find where the noise was coming from. Sam dove for her purse and fished out a glowing blue plastic device little larger than a matchbook. She flipped it open, silencing the annoying chirping. Her eyes widened.

"Shit! Look at the time. I've got to get dinner started."

She threw the device into her purse then quickly gathered her clothing. Shaking each piece free of dust with a loud snap, she dressed rapidly. Giacomo was adrift in confusion but knew he had to recover control of the situation quickly.

"Stop," he ordered.

Sam paused, her fingers clenched in the hem of her T-shirt she was tugging down. The scent of her arousal increased, her nipples poking against the thin cotton covering them. After just one session her body was already primed to associate obeying him with sexual ecstasy.

"I did not give you permission to dress."

"You don't understand. That was my cell phone alarm. If I don't start dinner soon, my mom might come looking for me."

He raised an eyebrow. Sam was a fully adult woman, the signs of aging clear in her naked body. Her breasts were not the sagging, loose breasts of an older woman but neither could they be mistaken for the newly budded breasts of a girl. He'd expected that she lived on her own in this small studio apartment. He hated being wrong. Being wrong meant the lash, meant pain and suffering, meant barely endurable agony.

"You live with your parents?" He tried to make his voice nonjudgmental but by her stiffening spine and raised chin, had not succeeded.

"My father is dead. I'm staying with my mother to care for her. She can't look after herself. You have a problem with that?"

Her words kindled an eager excitement within him. She was already acting as a slave. He only needed to transfer her devotion from her mother to himself and Sam would be his completely.

Reaching out, he grasped her jaw in his hand.

"You will speak to me with proper respect and call me Master."

Her eyes dilated and she licked her lips. He felt her jaw flex as she swallowed.

"Yes, Master," she whispered.

"In the future, you will ask me for permission to clothe yourself or to leave my presence."

"Yes, Master. May I go now?"

He frowned. She was following his orders but her earlier arousal was no longer evident. He'd thought she was a submissive type 3, the kind who needed to be reassured that the man dominating her was more powerful than her in all ways, who would struggle and protest only so that he could defeat her and force her to his will. Yet if that were so, she should be growing excited at the thought of a future battle of wills.

Still, that was a puzzle he could work out later. He didn't want to cause trouble for her by keeping her longer than necessary.

"You may go. Return tonight, after all around you are in bed for the night. And bring me a dinner."

He released her chin and she nodded briskly, her gaze falling to the floor. "Yes, Master."

He nodded. "Go now."

She turned and ran from the room, snatching up her purse as she passed it. The door slammed, her shoes tapped rapidly down the wooden stairs then he heard the faint crunch and rustle of her footsteps against a shifting surface. Pebbles? Shells?

He shook his head, dismissing the question as unimportant. First he needed to determine exactly when and where he was. Then he could worry about such minor details.

There was no way to tell time in the monastery, every agony stretching out for an eternity with no artificial intervals of mealtimes or sleep breaks to interrupt their lessons. He didn't know how many years had passed since his death, but from what he'd seen in his quick glances as the mist of mastery cleared, the world had seemed little changed.

Obviously, he'd been wrong. That glowing plastic device she'd pulled from her purse was like nothing he'd ever seen before. Considerably more time had passed than he'd first suspected.

He examined the contents of the room he'd mistaken for a studio apartment. The television was recognizably a television, although smaller and lacking a wooden cabinet to protect it. The recliner was larger and operated more smoothly but otherwise seemed much as he remembered them. He had no familiarity with the sport of fishing to judge if the rods and reels along the wall were contemporary but the books and knitting supplies seemed perfectly ordinary. Even Sam's clothing, jeans and a T-shirt, had been a common outfit for young American women in his time.

Stalking over to the television, he studied the buttons for a moment before switching it on. He was going to keep making stupid mistakes until he understood the world in which he now found himself, and mistakes were inevitably paid for in blood and pain. It was time to start learning.

*   *   *   *   *

Sam tiptoed past the den, peeking in to check on her still-sleeping mother. Letting her breath out in a relieved sigh, she hurried into the kitchen and began preparations for dinner.

Nothing too complicated. The way her arms were still trembling, she didn't trust herself to chop vegetables without taking off a finger. And browning meat would probably end up with the meat either burned or splattered across the stove. Basic boiled pasta was about the limit of her culinary skill tonight.

She bent down to pull the four-quart pot out from the back of the cabinet where her mother kept it and her jeans tugged against her swollen pussy. Clenching the countertop above her head, she bit her lip to stifle a moan of pleasure.

Her breasts throbbed, the nipples longing to be tweaked and pulled at Giacomo's direction. Panting softly, she rocked her hips, flexing against the taut seam of her jeans. She was still wet and needy. She could hardly wait until tonight when she could see him again. Just knowing he was in the workshop waiting for her kept her body humming in a constant state of readiness as she boiled the pasta, heated a jar of sauce and microwaved a frozen loaf of garlic bread.

The buzz of the microwave woke her mother or perhaps the cloud of garlic-butter-scented steam released when she opened the door did it. But whatever the cause, by the time Sam had everything turned out into serving bowls and on the table, her mother was already entering the kitchen.

Falling into her Good Daughter role with ease, Sam's body high faded beneath the weight of her responsibilities as she helped her mother sit down, filled her plate and poured her water. She expertly sliced the garlic bread in thick diagonal slices, stuffing one in her mouth before setting the basket beside her mother's plate.

"Did you have a good time reading, dear?"

Sam colored and pointed at her mouth full of garlic bread. Saved by Emily Post.

Her mother tsked. "How many times have I told you not to put the whole slice in your mouth at once? Break it into ladylike pieces first."

Sam grunted a noise her mother took for assent.

Dodging the landmine of how Sam had spent her afternoon, her mother launched into a detailed planning session for the next day. She had an appointment with her hair stylist at 11:45 and didn't want to be late. After her cut, color and set, they would have lunch and if she was up to it, shop for Melinda's youngest boy's birthday present. She preferred shopping at the Gray Goose children's store but the cramped, crowded store would be beyond her capability now. They'd have to drive outside of town to shop at the Toys "R" Us where the store offered electric shopping carts for their patrons.

Sam dutifully nodded her agreement and the rest of the meal was spent discussing what kind of toy Toby would enjoy the most that still met with his parents' approval.

She cleaned up, wrapping the leftovers to be reheated for Master Giacomo while her mother rambled on about Toby's upcoming birthday and other birthday parties of her children and grandchildren.

They retired to the den where her mother watched a prime-time drama on television while Sam knitted. As her needles slid rhythmically in and out of the growing swath of fabric, she felt her pulse and breathing steadying and stabling, her normal demeanor returning. The last of the evening's tensions drained away, released from her body and bound into her knitting.

When the show was over, Sam helped her mother upstairs. Her mother didn't actually need any help to climb the stairs but she felt nervous about the possibility of a fall so Sam had to walk behind her, gripping the banisters tightly so she could catch her mother in the case of a misstep.

It took another hour before her mother finished getting ready for bed, changing into one of her delicate lace peignoir sets, washing up then applying her nightly regime of creams and lotions. The pile of vitamins, supplements and prescription medications was a recent and grudging addition to the routine.

Sam finished her own routine in half the time, changing into lightweight boxer shorts in a blue and yellow monkey print and a yellow tank top with a blue monkey appliqué. For the first time, she wished she had nightwear that made her feel delicate and ladylike like her mother instead of the cool and comfortable shorts set. What would Master Giacomo think of her clothing choices?

Sam frowned. She was doing it again, defining herself by a man's opinion. If Master Giacomo didn't like her nightwear, would she buy something else he liked better? Would she change her hair color or style? Take on new mannerisms he found more pleasing?

She'd done all that and more for her ex-husband. She'd allowed him to transform her into his view of the perfect wife, an extension of his will in every way until there was nothing left of *her*. The slightest evidence of his displeasure had been enough to send her into a crushing depression for days, because if she wasn't his ideal wife, she was nothing.

She was never going to be that person again.

It had taken a lot of hard work to recover her identity. No matter how hot the sex with Master Giacomo was, it wasn't worth losing herself. Nothing was.

She sighed. She'd thought she was strong enough to be able to take her pleasure from their encounters without giving in to him entirely. Apparently, she wasn't. She'd have to tell him that she was taking back her permission for him to master her, that she'd granted it by mistake during the aftermath of passion and her good sense had since reasserted itself.

Of course it would be nice if she could tell him of her resolution after they had sex. Her skin heated at the thought of the things she'd seen in the book, things Master Giacomo might order her to do. But judging from this afternoon, when she'd been so carried away just from stroking herself while he watched, if she allowed him to master her tonight, she'd lose all resistance and be unable to tell him of her decision.

No, it would be better for everyone if she never saw him again.

She threw back the sheet and spread on her bed then clicked the ceiling fan down to its lowest setting. Her fingers closed around the chain controlling the light, ready to plunge the room into darkness and crawl into bed.

Master Giacomo had asked her to bring him dinner. He'd be waiting for her.

Sam's heart stuttered with a familiar mix of fear and desperation. He needed her. She couldn't disappoint him.

She gnawed on her lower lip, considering. She had to bring him dinner. She'd promised him, and if she didn't feed him, he'd starve. There were no restaurants within walking distance and she doubted her mystical visitor could drive. She certainly wouldn't trust him with her mother's car!

No, she had to take his dinner out to him. She couldn't live with herself if she didn't. But she didn't have to stay for any…entertainment afterward. She'd drop off his meal, explain that they weren't having any further contact and suit actions to words by coming home and going to bed immediately. She wouldn't have anything to do with him after that. If she refused to acknowledge him, to feed him or help him in any way, eventually he'd have to leave.

Her mind decided, she jerked off the light then sprawled on the bed in the sluggishly moving air. She'd just lay here waiting until her mother's light went out.

Lying in bed in the darkened room, she wondered what Master Giacomo was doing. Was he preparing some decadent and sensual surprise for her, in keeping with his admonition that he was here only for her? Or had she faded out of his consciousness as soon as she was out of his sight, not thought of again until hunger roused him?

Her former husband had been an expert at telling her what she wanted to hear, to make her believe he loved and adored her. Except love wasn't supposed to put you through the emotional wringer that he had. It had taken a long time before she understood she needed to pay attention not just to his words but to his actions as well.

Love was not demanding, demeaning or belittling. It did not make you helpless and dependent.

She'd taken far too long to figure out the truth. But she wouldn't forget the lesson that had cost so much to learn.

Reassured that she was not falling back into bad habits, she allowed herself to rest in the darkened room, waiting for the house to become dark and quiet. Breathing deeply and slowly, she let her mind drift, remembering her first sight of Master Giacomo.

The black leather of his pants clinging to his muscled legs like a second skin. Dew from the strange mist beading his chest, begging her to capture each drop with her tongue. His expression, at first so stern, yet when he relaxed, revealing a banked heat and a hint of humor.

Her body tightened, muscles tensing deep within her as a slow pulse began to throb between her legs.

She wouldn't submit to him. She couldn't. But oh, if she did…if she did…

Her breath turned shallow, her breasts tightening and tingling in rhythm with the pulse between her legs. Unbidden, she recalled an image from the book.

She imagined kneeling naked before Master Giacomo, her ankles crossed behind her and her knees spread so that the cool night air whispered across her hot pussy with a teasing touch. Her wrists were bound behind her back, tilting back her head and thrusting her breasts proudly upward.

The soft silk of his cock brushed back and forth across her lips, gently coaxing them open. Her tongue touched his firm head, swirling around his slit.

Master Giacomo groaned deep in his throat and thrust both hands into her hair, gripping her skull and holding her prisoner to his strength.

Sam whimpered, suddenly aware of the complete and total vulnerability of her position.

"Open your mouth, Sam. Open wide."

Trembling, she obeyed. Gripping her skull tightly in his strong fingers, Master Giacomo thrust his cock past her lips, filling her mouth with hot male flesh, stroking deep into the back of her throat.

Mercilessly, he tilted her head back even farther, opening her throat so that he could push farther still. His musky thatch of hair covered her nose, filling her senses with the scent of his arousal.

He pulled back, the heavy head of his cock resting just within her lips. Sam whimpered again, swallowing frantically, trying to draw him back inside her mouth.

His fingers gently massaged her scalp. "Good girl. You want this, don't you?"

She couldn't speak with his cock in her mouth, could only nod her head in short, emphatic arcs. Just to make sure she got her point across, she licked the head of his cock, her tongue sweeping up and down his slit.

Master Giacomo groaned, his fingers tightening briefly.

"Yes, you want this. You want me filling you hard and deep until you're drowning in my cum. Don't you?"

Hot tears slid out the corners of Sam's eyes, tracking down her cheeks to her ears. Yes. God help her, yes. That's exactly what she wanted.

To be his toy, his tool, his plaything. To give up everything in order to create one perfect moment of bliss.

She must have nodded or whimpered or otherwise indicated her agreement because suddenly he was thrusting into her mouth hard and fast, over and over again.

Sam struggled to relax her throat and take him deep, to let herself go limp and not fight him despite her body's natural choke response. Then she felt his rhythm pounding in her blood.

She breathed in time with his thrusts, drawing musky air through her nose as he withdrew, exhaling against his skin with his grunting surge forward. Her head spun from lack of oxygen as she breathed the same moist air she'd just exhaled.

He filled her mouth and throat, and her pussy wept with loneliness. Hot and aching, it throbbed with need.

Her breasts brushed against his thighs, the hairs on his legs teasing her budded nipples. She leaned into him, crushing her breasts against his flexing muscles.

Hot fluid ran down the inside of her spread thighs and splashed against the carpeting under her knees. Her pussy pulsed and throbbed, clenching the empty air. And still his cock strained to fill her mouth and throat, swelling thicker and longer.

There was nothing but him. His cock deep in her throat, his fingers gripping her skull, his musky thatch burying her nose. He groaned again, his fingers digging painfully into her scalp.

And then he was coming, hot salty fluid shooting down her throat. She swallowed over and over again, and it wasn't enough. Cum spilled out her open mouth, dribbling hot and sticky onto her breasts. She sucked harder, desperate not to spill any more, terrified *that she might displease him. With mouth and tongue she milked his limp cock, draining the last of his seed as he groaned with pleasure.*

He slipped out of her mouth and she cried at the loss. Then realized she could speak now.

"Did I please you, Master? Did I do well?"

"Oh yes, my pet. You did very well." He chuckled softly, his fingers rubbing slow circles in her hair. "And for that, you deserve a reward."

The steel weight was suddenly in his hand. Then he dropped to one knee and pressed the ball of the weight between her legs.

The cold steel touched her hot pussy and Sam trembled with uncontrollable need.

"Please, Master! Please! Don't torture me!"

He laughed darkly. "Not now at any rate."

Then he thrust the weight inside her, filling her pussy the way his cock had filled her mouth. Sam gasped, her senses completely overwhelmed, and shattered.

He sat on the floor, her trembling body cradled in his lap, and murmured soothing nonsense to her. Or maybe it wasn't nonsense, but it was Italian, so it made no sense to her. She didn't need to know what he was saying. All she needed to know was that she was his and she had pleased him.

Her heavy eyelids drifted open, confusing her when she saw the rotating blades of her ceiling fan in the dim light filtering through her windows. She was not in the workshop with Master Giacomo. She had fallen asleep while waiting and had the most delicious dream.

Her breasts ached slightly as if she had been pinching and twisting the nipples in her sleep. And her monkey-patterned boxer shorts were unpleasantly damp. It had been one hell of a dream.

Recalling Master Giacomo's total possession of her, her body tightened with eagerness to turn her dream to a reality. Sighing, Sam got out of bed. Silently easing her dresser drawer open, she reached for a fresh pair of shorts then changed into them.

He could never know how deeply he affected her. Because she'd learned her lesson. She was never again becoming merely an extension to a man's ego.

She gave her hair a quick brushing and checked her moon-washed reflection in the mirror. Her eyes were still too big, too soft, but she blamed that on the lack of light. Once she got to the workshop, there'd be no sign of her weakness.

He'd believe her when she told him she'd changed her mind and wanted nothing more to do with him.

He had to.

Chapter Four

ℬ

Sam tiptoed through the silent house down to the kitchen. Silently she took the pasta and bread from the refrigerator. She pressed the minimum number of buttons on the microwave to reheat them, holding her breath after each beep and opened the door before the buzzer could sound.

She loaded a tray with a dinner plate, cutlery, serving bowl, bread and water glass. Her gaze stole to the floral arrangement in the middle of the kitchen table. A few gaillardia blooms would not be missed from the centerpiece and would make the simple pasta dinner more appealing.

Damn it, no. She was not going out of her way to please Giacomo. She'd take over their leftover dinner because she'd promised him, but that was all he was getting.

Back straight and head high, she carried the tray through the darkened yard, the crushed shell path to the garage gleaming white in the moonlight. Flickering blue light painted the curtains of the workshop, beckoning her onward like a flame calling a moth.

As she climbed the stairs, she heard the low voice of a television announcer dispassionately reporting the latest financial news. She expected to find Master Giacomo sprawled in the lounger, feet up, as he watched the television. Instead, when she pushed open the workshop door and stepped inside, she saw him hunched over in the recliner, elbows on his knees as he leaned toward the screen.

His head snapped around at the sound of the door closing behind her. If she'd thought her eyes were too wide before, they were nothing compared to his. White showed all around the iris and his olive skin had turned sallow and pale.

Instinct overrode all her good intentions. She placed the tray on the nearest flat surface and ran to him, kneeling on the carpet so she could take his cold hands in hers.

"What is it? What's wrong?"

She glanced at the image on the television but news of a bank merger in Hong Kong could not be causing this distress.

His fingers tightened around hers, the pressure stopping just short of pain.

"So much has changed. My world, it is gone." His voice broke and he swallowed convulsively. "There is nothing to return to. I am in hell after all."

He closed his eyes and bent his head but she doubted he was praying. His throat worked as he swallowed rapidly and she guessed he was fighting back tears.

Silently she rose to her feet. Still holding his hands, she circled around to the front of the recliner. He opened his eyes, gazing at her with dark brown orbs sheened with moisture. At least they were no longer ringed with white.

"What are you doing?" he demanded.

This was a bad idea. She was supposed to tell him that she wanted nothing more to do with him. But he was in pain and she could ease his distress. She was as helpless to resist as if she were caught in one of the deadly riptides off the coast. She knew how to survive a riptide—go with the current and wait for it ebb before fighting toward the shore. The same advice applied here. Rather than struggle not to help him, in fact to actively hurt him, she would go with the flow of her emotions and help him recover from his pain. Then she'd tell him she'd changed her mind, once the emotional current had subsided.

She climbed onto the recliner, kneeling astride his lap. Her pussy tingled with anticipation as she spread her legs, but no leather-clad bulge rose up to meet her. Sex was the farthest thing from his mind at the moment. Sam was a little disappointed but mostly relieved. He would be able to accept her comfort without confusing it with other things, and make it easier for her to break away later.

She slipped her fingers from his grasp. Reaching up, she glided them between the thick strands of his hair.

"What does it look like I'm doing?"

Before he could answer, she bent her head and sealed his mouth with a kiss. He hesitated for a terrifying moment, an eternity when she feared her gesture would not be accepted, that her efforts to comfort would be met with scorn and derision.

Then his mouth opened, taking control of the kiss. He sucked gently on her lower lip, his tongue caressing the sensitive skin. A moment later, she felt a cool draft against her back, as he lifted her pajama top. Then his warm hands were sliding up her spine, beneath the thin cotton, and she sighed into his mouth.

Gently he pressed her body closer until the swell of her breasts bumped his chin. He lifted his mouth from her lips, muttered something dark and urgent in Italian, and bent his head to take one cotton-covered nipple into his mouth.

Sam moaned, her eyes closing and head tipping back as she lifted her breasts to him, offering him more. Her fingers flexed, gripping his thick hair. Her brain urged her to push him away, to stop this before it went any further and tell him of her resolution. Her body begged her to pull him closer, to fuse his hot mouth to her breast and drown in the waves of sensation emanating from his skilled lips and tongue.

In the end, she did neither.

He lifted his head but only to transfer his attention to her other breast. The air upon the damp cotton of her shirt chilled the nipple he'd abandoned, beading it to a hard point. When he lifted his head from her second breast and blew lightly across the wet tip, Sam felt the pleasure down to her core.

His fingers trailed up her sides, pressing just hard enough not to tickle, eliciting shivers of delight instead. Beneath her shirt, his thumbs caressed her wet nipples, stroking back and forth in a seemingly random pattern of fast and slow touches that quickly drove her mad. She stopped trying to anticipate his touches and sank into the feeling.

Her sleep shorts grew damp, hot and humid like a summer night and she rolled her hips, seeking relief. She bumped up against the solid iron of his cock stretching the front of his leather pants in a hard ridge.

Sam moaned, rubbing against him. His answering groan seemed torn from the depths of his soul.

"Take your hands from my hair," he whispered, the English words husky and heavily accented. When she reluctantly complied, he added, "Now put your hands behind your back."

She smiled as she obeyed. He'd frightened her with his first demand, making her think he did not enjoy her touch. Now the rush of fear was fading, transmuting to a desire that throbbed between her legs. She needed him. She needed him to take her hard and fast and screaming his name in desperate passion. But he wasn't going to, not until he was ready, and nothing she did could hurry him.

Her helplessness added yet another thrill zinging through her bloodstream. When he stripped off her shirt and pulled it halfway down her arms, effectively binding them behind her, she laughed from the sheer bubbling joy.

"Why do you laugh?"

"You've caught me completely and I'm helpless."

His brow furrowed. "This makes you laugh?"

"I was already helpless to stop you. Now I'm helpless to urge you onward too."

"Ah." He nodded sagely. "But you can speak."

She blinked in surprise. That's right. Just because he'd been muttering in Italian as he kissed and caressed her didn't mean he'd forgotten how to understand English.

He used her moment of inattention to smooth his hands down to her waist, trailing rivulets of pleasure from his fingertips, and a teasing hint of coolness where his silver bracelet brushed against her hot skin. Then, one hand supporting her ass and his arm wrapped securely around her waist, he stood up.

Sam squeaked, instinctively trying to put her arms around his neck for balance, only to find herself hobbled by her shirt and unable to.

"Do not worry, *mia tesora*," he whispered, his cheek pressed to hers and his warm breath caressing her ear. "I will not let you fall."

Turning, he placed her on the edge of the recliner's seat, pulling off her boxer shorts as he did so, then knelt on the carpeting before her. He caressed her hips and thighs before trailing his hands down to her knees. With one quick motion he lifted her legs, spreading them wide, and hooked her knees over the arms of the recliner. Sam's hips tilted back and she splayed her bound hands behind herself to catch her weight.

Her pussy was spread wide open before Master Giacomo and he was staring hungrily at it. She tried to close her legs but his hands still rested on her spread thighs and in her current position, she lacked the muscle strength to dislodge them. Her pussy heated, throbbing in time to the rapidly escalating beat of her heart and she felt the moisture welling up within her.

He breathed deeply, savoring the scent of her arousal. His eyelids drifted partially closed and he smiled softly.

"A treasure indeed. And you are all mine. Mine to look at."

His hot gaze traveled up her body, lingering at her swollen breasts with their tight, wet nipples before reaching her mouth and finally, her eyes. Her skin flushed in anticipation beneath his frank admiration, her nipples tightening even further and her lips suddenly felt parched. She darted her tongue out, the quick movement capturing his gaze and he followed the wet path trailing across her lips.

Bracing his hands against her thighs, he rose up and leaned forward, sweeping his tongue across her lips. Her mouth opened on a breathy sigh.

"Mine to taste."

He looked deeply into her eyes, whether searching for an answer or to ensure she understood his meaning, she had no idea. She just wanted him to kiss and lick her lips again. Mutely she tilted her chin up, lifting her lips to him.

He smiled but returned to his position on the floor. Then he leaned forward and blew softly across her damp pussy.

Sam shivered and moaned with pleasure.

"*All* mine," he insisted. Then his tongue plunged between her wet folds.

Dimly she was aware of his hands on her thighs, stroking lightly across her skin or holding her still when she bucked against his mouth. But her focus was on that glorious, heavenly mouth. He licked and nibbled his way along her folds, paying attention to the sensitive skin that was so often ignored, all the while her clit throbbed with growing urgency.

Then he was between her folds at last, stroking his tongue around and across her clit. Sam gasped and tried to buck, only to be pinned in place by his grip on her thighs. She felt the warm rush of her juices, excited at her helplessness.

Master Giacomo chuckled softly and began lapping up her eager flow. She lost all sense of time and place, surrendering herself to the flickering caress of his tongue. Short and quick, long and deep, and gentle, sweeping circles, he knew just how to bathe her pussy to keep her balanced on the knife-edge of arousal without sending her over the edge.

"Master. Master, oh please, Master. Please. Oh Master."

She moaned his name in a ceaseless litany of begging, the sounds without meaning in the sensual haze through which she drifted.

He lifted his mouth away and she cried out in loss and frustration, her bound hands unable to reach for him.

"No, Master, please, don't go, don't leave me like this, please."

His fingers tightened on her thighs, piercing the fog of her arousal with a hint of pain.

"Do you think to give me orders?" he snapped.

Her pussy clenched, her knees pulling against the recliner's armrests in a futile attempt to protect herself from his anger.

"No, Master. No. I didn't know what I was saying. Please don't be mad at me."

He stroked his thumbs over her inner thighs, circling gently, soothing her distress. "I am not mad, *mia tesora*. But I am your master. You are mine to do with as I will. To look at. To taste. To take."

He lifted his hands and she heard the rustle of leather against leather. She tried to open her eyes and see what was going on but they didn't seem to be working. Then his hands were on her thighs again, sliding down to her hips and holding her steady. With a single deep thrust, his hard, thick cock entered and filled her.

Sam gasped, her muscles clenching and trembling. He gave her no time to get used to his presence within her however, before he was moving, thrusting in and out in time to his words.

"You are *mine*. Mine to *taste*. Mine to *take*."

Then faster, harder, "Mine…to…make…come!"

The last thrust was the deepest yet and Sam cried out as she climaxed, her entire body shaking, deep shudders rippling through her, tearing her apart in agonized ecstasy. It went on forever. There had never been anything but his cock inside her, filling her with unbearable pleasure, and there would never be anything else. Until at last it was too much for her body to bear and she drifted free, lost on a tide of pure bliss.

She came slowly to awareness, conscious first of warmth and deep, drugging contentment. Then of her body positioned at an unexpected angle and pressure against her side, lifting and lowering her ever so slightly.

Sensations resolved into sense and she found herself naked, cradled in Master Giacomo's lap and leaning against his reclined chest. She rose and fell with his breathing.

The warmth she'd sensed came only partly from being pressed against his shirtless chest, one of his arms wrapped loosely around her waist to keep her from falling. He'd found the old afghan she'd made when she was first learning to knit as a child, an awful thing of red, white and blue acrylic kept for sentimental value but banished to the workshop so company could not see it. The ratty old thing was tucked carefully around her, even wrapping her feet where they dangled over the arm of the recliner. It was ugly but it was warm.

He'd turned off the television and the overhead light, leaving the workshop in darkness. She wondered if he'd dozed off but as soon as she lifted her head to look, he tightened his hold and lifted his free hand to caress the side of her face.

He'd been sitting in the dark, watching her sleep. She wasn't sure if she should feel charmed by his attentiveness or vaguely disturbed.

"How long was I out for?"

His brow creased briefly until he worked out the meaning of the idiom. Then he shrugged. "I have no watch."

Sam shifted restlessly, beginning to feel the ache of overuse between her legs. She smiled, remembering the feel of his mouth driving her to distraction until his cock slid inside —

She stiffened.

"What is wrong, *mia tesora*?"

"Did you use a condom? You know, protection, so I don't get pregnant?"

He shook his head. "No, but there is no cause for worry."

"Why, because you'll take care of me if I do?" She'd heard that line before, from her ex-husband. That hadn't been why she'd married him but in retrospect, she realized it should have clued her in to his true nature, that his immediate comfort and convenience meant more than the possibility of a life-altering event for her.

Master Giacomo merely shrugged. "It is a function of life and thus denied me."

She blinked. "You mean, you shoot blanks?"

Again his brow furrowed but this time the expression didn't clear. "Shoot blanks?"

"Yeah. Blanks. Duds. Your sperm don't swim."

His expression froze into the haughty glare she remembered from their first meeting. "They are Olympic-class swimmers."

Before she could reply, he sighed, his arrogance deflating. "But now they do not swim. My body is as it was moments before my death and it will remain unchanged until my life is restored. I do not eat. I do not sleep. I do not bleed. And I do not find sexual release."

"Wait a minute, your death? And what do you mean you don't eat? You told me to bring you dinner."

A dull red flush stained his cheeks and he glanced away. "I wanted to taste food again, even if I could not eat it. It was delicious. Thank you."

"You're welcome. But what's this about you being dead? You seem pretty alive to me."

"No. I died in 1967, in a…boating accident. But it was not my time to die so an arrangement was made. When the terms are fulfilled, I will resume my life." His eyes clouded with the same pain she'd seen earlier. "*A* life, rather. Not mine. Mine ended. I had been told but I did not truly understand."

Sam longed to comfort him but didn't know how. And she was having some trouble adjusting to his revelations herself. She'd just made love to someone who'd died before she was born. How freaky was that?

He traced patterns on her skin with one fingertip. "I am trapped in this half-life until I give you the pleasure you requested when you invoked me. Tomorrow your training begins in earnest. We will begin at dawn."

She shivered, imagining a day devoted to carnal exploration. If it were anything like what he'd done to her tonight before they finished, she'd be the one who was dead.

"I'm sorry. I can't do that." She pressed her index finger lightly against his scowling lips, silencing his unvoiced objection. "You're trapped by magic but I'm trapped too. By bonds of duty and devotion. I have to take care of my mother. That means tomorrow driving her to her hairdresser's, to lunch and to go shopping for a toy."

There was something else on her agenda too. Something about Master Giacomo. She struggled to remember, but could recall only that it was important.

He pulled her fingertip into his mouth and nibbled lightly on the pad of her finger. Sam moaned softly, her body instantly heating, and stopped trying to think. Tomorrow could take care of itself.

He licked and nibbled his way up her finger, to the palm of her hand. She sighed with pleasure as he swept his tongue along the sensitive paths of nerve endings she'd never known she had. Then he moved his attentions to the inside of her wrist. Licking, kissing and nibbling, his featherlight touches made her writhe in ecstasy.

"Is there no one else to care for her?" he whispered against her flushed skin.

Care for who? Oh right. Her mother. "In an emergency, my sister. But she has her own family. I can't call her just to spend the day with you."

"What of cousins?" His lips nibbled a trail up to the inside of her elbow.

"They live in Virginia and Texas. They're out of the picture."

He sighed dramatically, his breath steaming her inner elbow and turning her blood to lava. "If you must, you must. But I cannot spend the day watching television. It will drive me mad."

"I've often felt the same way." She smiled, thrilled to be able to offer him what she considered a luxurious treat. "I can drop you off at the library while Mom's having her hair done then pick you up when our errands are done. You can read books, magazines, newspapers—I'll even give you my library card so you can use the public terminals to surf the Internet."

Sam straightened up and twisted to face him, needing to see his reaction. "You can find anything on the Internet. I'm sure someone, somewhere, has digitized all the news since 1967. You can find out—"

She stopped, suddenly realizing she might have overstepped her bounds. Emily Post never wrote an article detailing the proper way to discuss the circumstances of someone's death with him.

Master Giacomo's already dark brown eyes seemed to darken even further until they were nearly black. He smiled, a predatory expression of teeth that had nothing to do with pleasure and that chilled her to her marrow. Instinctively she pulled away, only to be brought up short by the arm of the recliner behind her.

"Yes," he whispered. "Finally, I will know."

Chapter Five

ဢ

Sam slept late the next morning and had to listen to her mother's constant lectures and recriminations as she snatched a quick breakfast of instant oatmeal and coffee and dressed in a feminine blouse and skirt set of pastel peach, aqua and coral flowers, suitable for being seen around town in, and strappy sandals. She wasn't dressing in her frilliest clothes to impress Master Giacomo. She just didn't want to embarrass her mother if they met any of her friends while they were running their errands.

Even as she told herself that, she didn't believe it. Maybe because when she'd glanced in the mirror, her first thought had been to wonder if he'd find her desirable in this outfit.

Despite her mother's dire warnings, they arrived at the beauty salon with fifteen minutes to spare. She pulled into the handicapped space by the door and circled around the car to help her mother out.

Her mother leaned heavily on her arm until they entered the salon. Because they were early, the stylist was still working on her last appointment. One of her mother's former friends from the garden club was under the dryer.

Normally Sam would seat her mother on the first chair beside the door, take care of checking her in for her appointment then wait until the stylist came to walk her into the back of the salon. This morning however, her mother pushed her arm away and stepped toward the receptionist.

"Mom, shouldn't you—?"

"I'm not an invalid, Sam. I can take care of myself. You go to the library and I'll meet you for lunch."

Sam forced herself to smile for the interested eyes she felt upon her, even though her mother's curt dismissal and rejection of Sam's help made her feel sick to her stomach. Emily Post frowned upon causing scenes in hair salons. And a proper lady always did what was mandated by good manners.

"All right, Mom. Enjoy yourself. I'll be back at one."

She leaned over to give her mother an air kiss then stalked out to the car, back straight and chin high. If her mother didn't want her help, fine. She knew someone who did.

Her pussy warmed and her blood turned thick and slow remembering how much Master Giacomo wanted her. Too bad she had to drive all the way back home to pick him up before going to the library. There wasn't any time to delay.

Although if he wanted to, it would serve her mother right if Sam were late. Especially since it now appeared her mother didn't need Sam's help nearly as much as she claimed. As Sam had secretly suspected, her mother used her weakness as a way to keep Sam nearby. But Master Giacomo really did need her.

She'd remembered what had been so important last night after she was back in her own room and her blood had finally cooled so that she could think again. She'd meant to tell Master Giacomo she was no longer going to submit to him. But things had changed.

He wasn't just any old magically appearing, half-naked stud. No, he was cursed, trapped in a half-life between life and death. And she was the only one with the power to free him. By submitting to him and letting him give her pleasure beyond her wildest imagination.

It was a combination too perfect to resist. She'd had sex so good it transported her into another dimension and she didn't have to feel at all guilty because she was doing it to help him.

Of course she did feel guilty. She felt guilty that she wasn't giving her mother the time and attention she deserved.

She felt guilty that she was using Master Giacomo's situation for her own pleasure without being able to please him in return. She even felt guilty that she'd somehow summoned him without reading the book and so was completely unprepared for the situation.

But what she didn't feel guilty about was submitting to a man as her Master. Not when that man was Master Giacomo.

Smiling, she pulled the car into the garage. Her steps light on the stairs, she ran up to the workshop.

Master Giacomo was just turning away from the window that overlooked the driveway. He was no longer bare-chested and wearing leather pants. Instead, he wore sharply creased khaki trousers and a lightweight linen shirt whose olive green tone looked fabulous with his Mediterranean coloring and carried a navy blue blazer slung negligently over one shoulder. His loafers were woven leather in an odd shade of greenish-brown that managed to complement both the khaki pants and olive shirt.

Her ex-husband had been obsessed with appearances. So she knew Master Giacomo was wearing extremely expensive designer clothing. He wore it well. But where did he get it?

"We go to the library now, yes?"

She smiled. "Yes. But what are you wearing? Where did it come from?"

"I do not wish to be expelled from the library for indecency."

Sam grinned, imagining his reaction when he saw some of the likely library patrons. It was too late in the year for beach bunnies to be prancing about in their string bikinis, but a multiply pierced teen in torn low-riders would no doubt raise his eyebrows.

He frowned, his posture stiffening and the warmth fading from his eyes. "The clothes do not matter. I am still your Master. On your knees!"

She glanced at her watch. "We don't have time—"

"On. Your. *Knees*!"

Sam dropped to her knees before him, eyes wide and her breath rapid. And damn it, already hot and wet for him. "Yes, Master. I'm sorry, Master."

He glanced down at her, his nostrils flaring as he inhaled the scent of her arousal. He smiled, his stance softening slightly and the front of his khakis bulged outward with his growing erection.

"Unbutton your blouse," he ordered.

With no hesitation, Sam obeyed, her fingers fumbling the tiny pearl buttons of her top. When the sides of the blouse hung free, she lifted her gaze to his, eager for his next command.

"Lift your breasts out of your bra."

Trembling, she cupped her breast, her fingers brushing her nipple and sending lightning bolts of electricity skittering through her body. She caught her breath, feeling the heat throbbing between her legs. Carefully, she eased her breast up and over the shelf of the bra. Then she did the same for the other.

The elastic of the bra supported her breasts from beneath, lifting and stretching them while the shoulder straps pushed them together toward the center of her chest.

Master Giacomo sighed deeply. "Beautiful. So red. So ripe. And mine for the taking."

He reached out and lightly squeezed one nipple. Sam arched her back, eyes shut and moaning in delight. Sticky wetness drenched her panties and she clenched her thighs together, but that only emphasized the throbbing pulse between her legs.

Softly he traced the edges of her breasts where the bra straps were beginning to cut into them. "What can I do with these?"

"Anything you desire, Master."

Even as she said the words, Sam knew they were the truth. Despite her protestations, she had no resistance where he was concerned. She was his willing slave.

She heard the rasp of a zipper and opened her eyes to see him taking his cock out of his pants. It was already hard and thick, the golden olive skin stained like wine with his arousal. Sam's gaze locked onto it as his fingers wrapped around the shaft, pumping his fist up and down his length until he was fully engorged.

She licked her lips, swallowing nervously as she recalled her dream. He was so big, she wasn't sure she could take him without choking. But if that's what he wanted from her…

He chuckled. "No, my pet. That's not what I want from you. This is."

Clasping her breasts in his large hands, he pushed them even closer together until they spilled upward in a fountain of flesh. Then he stepped forward and thrust his cock between them.

She gasped, the hot shaft forcing a path between her compressed breasts until he was buried to the hilt. Then he began to massage her breasts, his fingers and palms rocking, pushing and pulling. He never touched her aching nipples, only the sides of her breasts, massaging his cock through the medium of her flesh.

Sam whimpered, a broken cry of distress. He couldn't have made her position any clearer. If he brought her body to unbearable ecstasy, that was because it was what he wanted to do. And if he used her body for his own pleasure, with no thought for hers, that was also because it was what he wanted to do. He could take her in any way he wanted. And so long as she was his slave, she had no say in the matter.

Her pussy pulsed and throbbed in time to his rough massage. She wanted him, ached to have him inside her, filling her, thrusting in and out to the pounding beat of her heart.

"Put your hands on mine," he whispered in a hoarse voice.

She placed her trembling hands over his, feeling the flex of his muscles as he rubbed and tugged on her breasts, rolling them up and down the length of his cock.

"Now squeeze your breasts, just like I was doing."

He took his hands away and she continued the rhythm he'd established. Not touching her painfully tight nipples. Not trying to increase the pressure to find some relief for herself. Just rolling herself up and down his length, his low groans telling her when she'd done it correctly and his silence a dreadful warning to do better the next time.

His fingers slid into her hair, tipping her head back so that she looked up at his face.

"*Madre del Dio*, that feels good. What would you say if I came right now, spurting all over your chest and stomach?"

She shivered, trembling at his words and more turned-on than she could believe. She wanted him to lose control, to bathe her in his cum. In this strange dynamic of powerlessness, it would be the ultimate power.

Swallowing twice before she could force words through her too-tight throat, she whispered, "I would say, 'Thank you, Master'."

He groaned, fists tightening painfully in her hair. Then a mighty shudder racked his body and he cried out in agony.

His limp cock slipped from between her breasts. It was completely dry.

Sam threw herself to the floor before him, hugging his khaki-clad legs and kissing his loafers. "I'm sorry, Master! I didn't mean to hurt you!"

"Stop that. You didn't hurt me." He pulled her free of his legs and nudged her into a somewhat more upright position.

She blinked back the tears that threatened to spill. "But I heard you cry out. As if you were being tortured."

"No. I've been tortured. That wasn't it." He lifted her to her feet and pressed a gentle kiss first to her forehead and then to her lips. "You did nothing wrong. I told you, until I give you your ultimate pleasure, I can not find sexual release."

"But, Master—"

He pressed one finger to her lips, silencing her. "No. You did nothing wrong. Pain is very close to pleasure, as you know. It is enough."

He tucked his limp cock back inside his pants, hiding it behind the closed zipper. Picking up his blazer, which had fallen to the floor, he snapped it sharply, ridding it of any dust or bits of yarn that had adhered to the weave.

Sam bit her lip, watching him. It wasn't enough. It wasn't enough for her and it couldn't be enough for him. But if that's what he needed to tell himself, who was she to argue? She'd been doing nothing but lying to herself in the name of ego preservation since she met him. But no more. It was time for her to admit her true nature.

She was a submissive and probably a slave. Her body came alive at the thought of being a man's pawn, his pet, his plaything. Her problem before now was that she'd chosen the wrong men.

Men like her ex-husband, who were controlling, macho tough guys. But unlike Master Giacomo, he wouldn't have been concerned with her feelings, certainly not enough to tell her twice that she'd done nothing wrong. And he'd have been more likely to yell at her to shut up than to give her an explanation. He would have found a way to turn the situation into a pity party for himself while Master Giacomo accepted his situation and acted forcefully to change it for the better.

Master Giacomo smiled gently down at her. "Do up your blouse. We shall hurry to the library."

She scrambled to her feet, quickly buttoned her blouse, dusted off her skirt then tugged both blouse and skirt into their proper positions. She glanced at her watch. They weren't late, yet. But they weren't going to be early either.

Cutting down the side roads less likely to be congested, she hurried to the sweeping structure of tinted glass and steel that was the city's library. She tried telling Master Giacomo everything he'd need to know in order to use the library terminals to access the Internet but he was more interested in playing with the automatic door locks, automatic windows and dashboard controls than in listening to her.

"I'm trying to help you. Pay attention," she snapped.

He turned to look at her, one eyebrow raised. "I am not ignoring you, *mia tesora*. But you explain too much. You have given me your card. I will go inside and ask the librarian for assistance. That is all I need to know."

"But you need to know how to swipe the library card and type in the password—"

"No. You forget how much has changed in the years I have been away. I had secretaries who did all my typing for me. So I will need far more help than you can give me to find all the necessary keys and demonstrate a *click* and *double-click*."

"I suppose I could go in with you and show you."

"I delayed you once already. There is no need to make you late when it is the librarian's job to assist patrons."

She pulled into the parking lot, stopping in the loading area in front of the main doors and cut the engine. "Really, I don't mind."

"I do." He brushed her cheek with his fingertips then unclasped his seat belt and opened his door. "It is important for you to be needed, to be allowed to help others. But your desire to help overwhelms your self-preservation. As your Master, it is my job to prioritize for you when your emotions render you unable to think clearly. You have a prior obligation. I will be here when you return."

He got out of the car, closing the door on any possible protest then walked into the library without a backward glance. She frowned, cranky and out of sorts. Objectively she knew he was doing the right thing. Her mother was relying on Sam to pick her up after her hair appointment, to take her to lunch and to take her shopping for Toby's toy. Master Giacomo would be fine on his own for a few hours.

Sam threw the car into drive and punched the accelerator, looping around the lot and back onto the road with total disregard for the lot's striping. Master Giacomo was right. He didn't really need her, not for this. He could find out the details of what had happened to his family and friends after his death without her.

But she wanted him to need her for more than just technical assistance. Whatever he found would likely shock him, much as his first exposure to a modern news broadcast had. She'd helped him cope with that and she wanted him to turn to her for help now.

Stopped at a light, Sam beat her forehead against the steering wheel. Stupid, stupid, stupid! She was falling for him.

It was easy to see why. He was gorgeous, intelligent and single-mindedly devoted to giving her the ultimate orgasm. He pushed all of her buttons with his dominant strength and control wedded to the incontrovertible need that arose from his strange condition.

She pulled forward at the green light, her teeth clenched and her fingers white on the wheel. He needed her, all right. For sex. To get his life back. But he didn't need *her*. Anyone who summoned him from the book would have done equally well.

Her breasts ached from the unfamiliar use he'd just put them to. And he had used them, used her, to prove a point. She was his willing slave. Whatever he asked of her, she would do. Whatever he wanted, she would give.

But she feared that what he wanted most was his freedom. Once he'd given her the ultimate sexual pleasure and his life was restored to him, he would have no more need of her. He might even view her as a distasteful reminder of his former weakness, his own slavery to the mystic power that had stolen him away to the half-life he'd existed in since 1967, and be in even more of a hurry to leave her.

Somehow she managed to make it to the beauty salon before her mother was finished. It helped that the stylist was running late. But when her mother tottered to the waiting room on the stylist's arm, Sam was seated in one of the plastic and vinyl chairs, leafing through a style magazine.

"…after sitting for so long. You understand," her mother was telling the stylist.

"Of course, Mrs. Taylor. Don't you worry about it."

Sam hopped up and took her accustomed place at her mother's side. As expected, her mother transferred her grip from the stylist's arm to Sam's.

The physical therapist insisted that there was nothing wrong with her mother's legs and spine that exercise and attention to balance couldn't cure. Her initial fracture had healed cleanly and completely. But the blow to her mother's confidence hadn't. She should be able to walk, garden and drive with no assistance. Instead she relied upon Sam to help her with everything. Given how badly she'd let the house deteriorate after the death of Sam's father, Sam was afraid to leave her alone to fend for herself.

Sam waited patiently while her mother counted out the money for the stylist. Both Master Giacomo and her mother needed her, but for the wrong reasons. Master Giacomo needed her because she'd been the submissive who read the book who called him back to the world of the living. Her mother needed her because the bonds of family ensured she would care for her and the lack of a family of her own meant she could care for her 24/7.

They needed her because of what she was. Not because of who she was.

The situation sucked.

Still dwelling on the unfairness of it all, Sam escorted her mother to the deli where they routinely ate lunch after visiting the salon. As they both sat picking at their sandwiches, Sam realized her mother wasn't prattling on about the latest gossip as usual.

"Mom? Is something wrong?" She dropped her sandwich to the plate. "Did tipping back in the chair hurt your back?"

Her mother smiled reassuringly. "No. I'm just tired."

"Oh." That was good. Except, her mother wasn't the sort who got quiet when she grew tired. She got louder, a lot louder. And her complaints grew both strident and irrational.

So something was wrong. But what?

"Did you have a nice chat with Mrs. Peterson?"

Her mother's lips pressed together. "Eve Peterson is about to become Mrs. Jerome Watkins."

Sam blinked. "That's what, her fourth husband?"

"Fifth."

Five husbands and only one divorce. She was either the unluckiest woman alive or a very successful black widow.

"Where does she find all these men?"

"She found Jerome Watkins at the center."

"The *senior* center?" She'd have thought Mrs. Peterson would rather die than admit she was old enough to get a membership there. Much like her mother.

Her mother nodded. "Apparently, they have a new manager. It's not all arts and crafts while you wait to die anymore. They've started a lecture series, an investment club and other things."

"Do you want to swing by after we get Toby's gift? They probably have fliers printed up with all their events on them."

"Actually, I'm feeling rather tired. Why don't you just bring me home? You can get the gift and pick up the fliers."

Sam frowned. "Are you sure?"

Her mother nodded but refused to meet Sam's eyes. She wasn't tired, she was guilty.

"What else did Mrs. Peterson say, Mom?"

"Her granddaughter Rebecca is having a birthday next week. She was looking for a specific plastic slide, shaped like a medieval castle and Toys 'R' Us had one in stock. She was going out with Jerome to pick it up this afternoon."

"And you don't want to run into her?"

Her mother flushed. "Not looking like an old cripple, I don't."

Right. The electric shopping carts. The whole reason they'd planned on going there instead of to the Gray Goose.

"Not a problem. I'll take you home then go back out and pick up Toby's gift."

Her mother nodded then bit into her sandwich, her appetite apparently restored by the news she wouldn't accidentally run into Eve Peterson a second time in the same day.

Sam took a huge bite of her own sandwich, hiding her grin behind a wall of turkey, lettuce and bread. She hoped she did run into Mrs. Peterson. Because she intended on stopping at the library first and getting Master Giacomo. And the only thing better than strolling about town with a charming hunk was having a notorious gossip see them together.

If he was going to be gone soon, she needed to make sure people saw her with him before he disappeared.

Chapter Six

ಲಾ

Sam pulled open the library door and strode inside, trusting that the foyer would be empty of obstacles as her eyes adjusted to the dimmer, book-friendly light. Her sandals slapped against the terra cotta tile as she hurried across the foyer and through the second set of doors into the main stacks.

She glanced quickly to her left, her eyes drawn to the primary-colored foam seating groups for the children's area and the low, round tables and chairs behind them. Turning to the right, she passed the shelves of new books and periodicals and spotted the ring of computers on their tall tables. Two college-aged young men stood in front of terminals, no doubt making quick search queries before diving back into the stacks. An elderly woman in an electric scooter was using the accessible terminal mounted at a lower height.

Sam's heart plummeted. Master Giacomo wasn't here! Where could he have gone?

One of the patrons doing a search cleared his computer screen and turned away, allowing her to see across the top of his computer. A dark head of hair was bent over the computer on the other side of the ring.

It was him. Her blood grew heavy, making her hyper-aware of the pulse in her neck and throbbing through her pussy, and her chest tightened, making it hard to breathe. She felt so light she practically danced around the computer ring to join him. Or maybe she was just feeling lightheaded. Whatever it was, she could hardly contain her eagerness to see him again.

The screen upon which he was focused so intently was for Coral Isle, an assisted living facility on the coast. He was copying down the driving directions.

"You can print that screen out, you know. You don't have to copy it."

He snapped upright, twisting to face her. His eyes glowed with pleasure as he smiled and held out his hands. She eagerly clasped his fingers in hers, reveling in his heat and strength.

"*Mia tesora*, you're early. Did you find your nephew's gift so quickly?"

"No. Mom felt tired and wanted to go home so I thought I'd come by and see if you wanted to go shopping with me."

Sam bit her lip and glanced down, only now realizing what a foolish request that was. She'd been so fixated on seeing him again and spending more time with him, she'd forgotten his purpose in coming to the library. He was looking up information on his remaining family. That was far more important than shopping.

"Did you find a relative? Someone staying at Coral Isle?"

"No. This is not for me, it is for you."

"For me?" She frowned. Coral Isle was one of the premier facilities in the area with a residents-only golf course and private beach as well as a small marina for family members who came to visit by yacht. She didn't know anyone staying at Coral Isle.

"For your mother. To free you from your obligation to care for her."

That would teach her to speak in hyperbole. "I was exaggerating. I don't really feel trapped. I just meant, I couldn't get out of taking her places today since I'd already promised."

He didn't look convinced.

"Besides, do you have any idea how much a place like that costs? It's a fortune."

He shrugged. "It is taken care of."

He nodded toward a platinum credit card lying on the table beside the keyboard. The scenic background picture was a black monstrosity of a medieval monastery, crouched and lurking among broken shards of a bleak mountainside. Raised gold letters spelled out Giacomo Bravetti, and that the card had been issued just this month. If Sam had to guess, she'd have bet that the card had been issued just this morning, from the same magical source as his change of clothing. God only knew what sort of fairy gold was backing the line of credit.

She stilled, her hands turning to ice in his grasp. "What do you mean, it's taken care of?"

"I mean that I already gave them a deposit of the first month's rent, to hold the suite for her."

"You. Rented. An. Apartment. For. My. Mother." It was an effort to force each word through numb lips, impossible to draw breath to speak with frozen lungs.

"It was necessary, to convince them of my interest. All of the reviews said that this was the best facility in this county. I knew you would want only the best for your mother."

"What is *best* for my mother is staying in her own home with her own family to care for her!" She let her voice's pitch and emphasis convey her anger, keeping the volume soft in deference to the other library patrons. Even so, the elderly woman in the scooter was now watching them instead of her terminal.

Master Giacomo's eyes darkened, his eyebrows lowering and his fingers tightened on Sam's. "You will not even consider it? After all I went through to get it for you?"

Oh God. She didn't even want to consider how someone who had some seriously spooky ties to the spirit realm knew that there was an opening at a nursing home. She prayed he hadn't pulled any metaphysical strings to *make* an opening. But he wasn't entirely human. She had to remember that. He was dangerous for more than just the obvious reasons.

"What did you do?" she whispered.

He relaxed on his stool, a confident smile teasing his lips as he stroked the back of her hands with his thumbs. "I've spent hours on this computer looking at facility reviews, comparing features and benefits then selecting Coral Isle and making a reservation."

"Hours."

"Yes. Since the librarian showed me how to use the computer."

"So you didn't look up anything about your family. Your…accident." She glanced at their audience. The old woman was still eavesdropping.

"According to the librarian, the newspapers from 1967 are not online and are on something called microfiche."

"You didn't have to read the entire newspaper! An Italian obituary wouldn't have been carried in a Florida newspaper anyway. But there are genealogical records online. As well as news stories."

He pulled his hands from hers and stood up, glaring. "I did not have time to search those things. I was finding this for you."

"Liar." She stabbed a finger at the screen. "You found this for you. So I'd have time for you. And you'd have time to get what you want from me."

"But it is what you—"

"Liar, liar, liar! You're lying to me and you're lying to yourself. You spent all that time on this because you were too chicken to look up what you came here to find out."

He drew himself up to his full height, his face an icy mask of fury. Her heart clenched and she feared she'd gone too far. Was he familiar with the idiom of calling someone a chicken? Had she insulted his manhood and his machismo?

"I'm sorry. That was uncalled for."

He closed his eyes briefly, inhaling deeply, then letting his breath out on a shaky sigh. When he opened his eyes, he was no longer glaring.

"No. You were right. I was hiding from the truth."

Sam stared at him in dumb fascination. She was right? She insulted him and she was right?

This was something completely outside the realm of her experience. She knew that all men did not react like her ex-husband, screaming and shouting as they demeaned and belittled the person responsible for making them uncomfortable. She had after all dealt with plenty of men while getting her degree and doing her student teaching. But the most common reaction she'd seen was denial, ranging from angry to merely insistent and sometimes walking away from the argument. In the heat of the moment, they seemed as a gender to default to the need to win the argument first and only later considering what had been said during the argument when they had a chance to cool off.

"Sam?" Master Giacomo waved his hand in front of her eyes and she blinked rapidly.

"I'm sorry. You surprised me."

He smiled again, a boyish grin — if the boy had just been caught putting a frog where frogs were not supposed to be.

"As did you. We are neither of us at our best when surprised, *sì*?"

"*Sì*," she agreed, and caught herself before apologizing a third time.

A quick glance to the side showed that the old woman had no interest in watching them make up after their fight and had returned her attention to her computer.

He heaved another deep sigh and Sam realized this was his technique to keep himself calm and rational, the way she counted to ten in all the different bases. "I have spent years wondering and worrying about what happened that day. The one who saved me refused to say anything about it."

"You mean you have amnesia? You can't remember the accident?"

"No. I remember it clearly. But I was not alone. I don't know what happened to the others." He shook his head and his hand closed about hers. "I need to know. But...you were right. I am afraid of what I may find."

She wove her fingers through his, clasping his hand securely and giving it a reassuring squeeze. "Then we'll find it together."

He nodded and stepped away from the tall stool in front of the computer, leaving the keyboard open for her. She pushed the stool away, preferring to stand in front of the computer. Master Giacomo stood behind her, his arms wrapped loosely around her waist and his jaw brushing her hair as he looked over her shoulder at the screen. She smiled, relaxing into his embrace, and called up her favorite search engine.

"What name are we looking for?"

"Jeffrey Middlemarch." He spelled both names for her. "1967."

"And what kind of accident was it?"

"The fuel line leaked and the yacht's engine exploded."

She quickly keyed in search terms, using the Boolean operators to find any combination of his name, the terms boat, ship, yacht or engine, and any word starting with the letters "explo".

The first hit was an About Us page for the Middlemarch burn clinic in England. It had been endowed with funds by Reginald Middlemarch, a British earl, in memory of his youngest son, who died in the explosion of his yacht in 1967.

"But what of his family?" Master Giacomo whispered. "Did they survive or not?"

"His family?"

"His wife and young son. I did not know their names."

His arms tightened around her waist and his deep breathing blew furrows through her hair. This is what he was afraid of learning the truth of.

She thought for a moment then searched within the results for a combination of wife or mother, and son or father. If she got too many hits or too few, she could reshape the query.

Five pages popped up. The first was an article on automotive designer Jason Middlemarch, for a sports car enthusiasts' magazine. She called it up.

She skimmed the article, key phrases catching her eye…a unique merger of safety and speed…father, a power boat designer…his death in the explosion…burned his mother and forever changed young Jason's life.

Master Giacomo rested his forehead on her shoulder. "*Rendiamo grazie a Dio.* They lived."

His arms quivered slightly where he held her and his breathing hitched unsteadily. She waited patiently while he restored his composure.

"Do you want me to print out the entire article?"

"*Grazie.*"

She sent the article to the library's printer and clicked back to her original search. Then hesitated, her fingers poised over the keyboard. "Is there anything else you want to look up?"

"*Scusilo?*"

"Do you want to see if there's anything about you?"

He thought for a long time then nodded, his hair brushing up and down her cheek. "*Sì, per favore.*"

She typed over Jeffrey's name with Giacomo then stopped. "'Is the name on your credit card correct?"

"*Sì*, Bravetti."

The search engine promptly displayed two articles. The first was from a corporate report on the history of the company. *After both Bravetti sons were killed in boating accidents mere weeks apart, Nico in a wreck during a power boat race and Giacomo in an explosion, control of the company passed to their father's brother Antonio.* The second was an article on a fan website devoted to European power boating history titled "A Sad End to 1967".

She opened the document.

Scrolling down, she skimmed the description of the various races throughout 1967, changes in engine placement and materials until she reached an account from one of the witnesses of the race that had killed Master Giacomo's brother.

"Nico," he whispered, his voice a breath away from a sob.

Sam rested her free hand on top of his, giving him her silent comfort while she continued to scroll down with the other hand, reading the web site's summary of subsequent events.

Although the investigation ruled the accident that killed Nico Bravetti was a tragedy caused by unsafe speed and his determination to best Rodrigo Valente, his brother Giacomo insisted that the new Middlemarch design had been partially to blame. Ironically, he was most likely attempting to confront Middlemarch with his suspicions when they were both killed, the result of a faulty hose in the engine compartment of Middlemarch's yacht. Bravetti's yacht was tied up just a few slips down and Middlemarch's son Jason recalls seeing him running down the dock when he heard them arrive. Although neither Jason nor Pauline Middlemarch remembered the explosion that killed Jeffrey and Giacomo, they survived because they were in the water when the fireball swept over them. Jason's arms bore bruises in the size and shape of a man's hands, so investigators speculated that Bravetti's final act, rather than diving into the water himself, had been to throw both Jason and Pauline to safety. Middlemarch, aboard the yacht when it blew, was killed instantly.

"Oh God. How horrible!" she whispered.

He reached past her and closed the browser window. Operating on autopilot, Sam finished logging out, returning to the library's main screen.

That's how he'd died. He'd spent the decades since then wondering if his sacrifice had been in vain, if his heroic efforts to save Jason and Pauline Middlemarch had been successful. She couldn't imagine what it must be like to give your life for something and not know if it was worth it. No wonder he'd been scared of what he might find.

"Come on. Let's pick up the printout of Jason's article. Then I can take you home."

Master Giacomo nodded silently. He followed her as she picked up and paid for her printout then out to the car.

Once they were seated inside and belted in, rather than put the key in the ignition and start the engine, she twisted to face him. "I'm sorry about your brother."

"Nico was a good man. Many people came to his funeral." He took another of his deep, sighing breaths then stiffened his shoulders and turned to look her in the eye. "Jeffrey knew his design was flawed and he let Nico drive his boat in the second heat with no warning. He bragged to me that it didn't matter, because nobody would ever be able to prove it."

She felt the blood draining out of her face, leaving her cold and frozen. "What are you saying?"

"The fault in his engine hose was a small puncture that let the gas vapors escape. I know because I put it there."

She just stared at him, unable to find words. Her lover, her Master, the man she was falling in love with, was a murderer.

"I don't know what I was thinking. I don't think I intended to kill him, although I wouldn't have been terribly upset if he'd died, betrayed by an unreliable boat the way my brother had been. He'd murdered my only remaining immediate family. And no one would believe me when I tried to tell them."

"Temporary insanity."

He nodded. "Yes. But Jeffrey was the only one I blamed, not his wife, not his son. They were innocent. I was on the dock that morning so that I could witness my vengeance for Nico. I tried to stop them from boarding the boat, getting away from it before the explosion. She thought I was mad. I probably was. I threw the boy into the water but she struggled."

"You saved their lives at the cost of your own."

"That is why I was given a second chance, not because I saved them, but because I'd willingly died in the attempt." He closed his eyes and shuddered. "Do not ask me to describe my penance but be assured, I suffered fully for my crime."

She remembered his flat statement that he'd been tortured. At the time, she thought he'd meant it figuratively.

"How long?" she whispered.

"Time has no meaning there. There is no day, no night, only an endless sliver of eternity. But the first new man to arrive after my penance ended died on January 17th, 1989."

Twenty years. He'd been tortured nonstop for over twenty years. She couldn't imagine how he had endured with any shred of sanity intact.

"Why are you telling me all this?"

He gazed directly into her eyes. "I need you to understand. I made a mistake back then. Taking vengeance into my own hands, yes, but also believing that because I knew best, I had the right to act on my knowledge."

He reached out and clasped her frigid hands in his. The warmth of his fingers slowly thawed her frozen skin.

"I made the same mistake earlier today. Knowing of a solution and having the means to implement that solution does not give me the right to make it so. The decision rests with you and your mother. You offered me your submission, a gift that I treasure, but that is not the same as handing over control of your entire life. *Perdonilo*. Forgive me."

"You're saying…you're sorry?"

"More than that." Moisture shone in dark brown eyes. "I sincerely repent my actions and will do my best never to make the same mistake again. I can offer information and guidance but I can not make decisions about your life for you."

"Even if you're certain I'm making a mistake?" she whispered. "Doing something stupid and foolish?"

"If that is true, I will tell you so and try to convince you to take another course of action. But it is your mistake to make." He smiled softly. "We are not discussing your mother's care any longer, are we?"

"No. Not really. She's staying at home and I'm looking after her, like always. Maybe if you've got so much money to throw around, I could look at getting some help so I can take time off occasionally. But she's finally starting to show an interest in getting a life again. It was only a little thing and she backed off immediately, but compared to what she's been like these past few months, it's a huge step. So she might not need as much help anyway."

"Then of what are we speaking?"

Sam bit her lip. But after what he'd just confessed to, how could she feel nervous about her admission?

"I was married. My ex-husband said he loved me and wanted only the best for me, but that meant the clothes I chose were never good enough, I didn't work hard enough at my exercise program, I ate the wrong foods, et cetera. I started doubting that I could make any decisions at all. I realized what was happening, left him and started over again. That's why I didn't want to submit to you. I was afraid you'd swallow me up, the same way he had."

Master Giacomo snorted. "Such pathetic attempts at mastery are the mark of a weak man who must weaken a woman in order to best her. I do not wish you to be weak, *mia tesora*. It was your strength I relied upon when I faced the answer to what happened to Jeffrey's family. And your compassion to listen to the entire tale before judging me."

271

Sam pressed the heel of her palm against her breastbone. Her chest felt on fire, as if an explosion had torn through her heart and lungs, engulfing her in a fireball no less deadly than the one that had killed Giacomo. She couldn't breathe. She gasped for air but her throat was too tight to give any relief.

"Sam? What is wrong, *mia tesora*? Do you need a doctor?"

She heard the rising panic in his voice. If she'd had the breath for it, she would have laughed. Wrong? Nothing was wrong. Something was very, very right.

"You value me," she whispered.

He stared at her, as if he could no longer understand English, so she repeated herself.

"You value me."

"But of course! Why else would I call you *mia tesora*, my treasure, if I did not?"

"No. I mean, you value *me*. The person I am." The tightness in her chest eased and she took a deep breath, her first truly free breath since her divorce.

"Yes, I—" Master Giacomo stopped, clutching his right hand as if it pained him. His eyes grew wide, staring at the unblemished skin. With a sharp crack, his silver bracelet broke in two, the halves falling into his lap. He blinked twice then laughed. "This? *This* is your ultimate pleasure?"

"What are you—? You're free!"

"*Sì, mia tesora.* My life is my own again."

Sam nodded. She'd known she couldn't keep him forever. And he'd given her a gift far greater than any she'd expected. The least she could do was let him go with a brave smile.

"What are you going to do with yourself?"

"I plan to devote myself to bringing you pleasure, in all the ways possible." He smiled. "If that is all right with you?"

Her answering grin split her face. "That's more than all right with me, it's the answer to all my dreams."

Unsnapping her seat belt, she knelt awkwardly on the floor space in front of the center console and laid her head in his lap, her wrists crossed behind her back.

"You are my Master and I am your willing slave."

He rested his hand on her head, stroking her hair. "You are my treasure, bending to my will but never breaking, growing only stronger in my care."

Gently, he placed a finger beneath her chin and tipped her head up. He leaned down and pressed a kiss to her forehead then to the tip of her nose before finally claiming her lips.

An eternity later, Sam swam up from the depths of delight in which she'd been drowning and blinked his beloved features back into focus. A sudden thought made her gasp in realization.

"*Mia tesora?*"

"We've decided where my mother is going to stay. But where are you going to live, Master?"

He smiled wickedly. "I think perhaps you should introduce me to your mother."

Also by Jennifer Dunne

ဢ

Hearts of Steel (*anthology*)

Hot Spell (*anthology*)

Luck of the Irish (*anthology*)

Party Favors (*anthology*)

R.S.V.P. (*anthology*)

Santa's Helpers

Sex Magic

Single White Submissive (*anthology*)

Tied with a Bow (*anthology*)

About the Author

෨

Jennifer Dunne is the author of over a dozen novels and novellas spanning the genres of fantasy, science fiction, and romance. (She's either a unique individual who is difficult to categorize, or easily bored—you decide.) Beyond that, there's no point describing her hobbies or activities, since they'll have changed by the time you read this. (Score one for "easily bored") She lives in upstate New York, where she happily plays the lead role in her very own love story, thankfully with fewer explosions, occult happenings, and dire situations than in her fiction. Although, there was that one time…

Jennifer welcomes comments from readers. You can find her website and email address on her author bio page at www.ellorascave.com.

Tell Us What You Think

We appreciate hearing reader opinions about our books. You can email us at Comments@EllorasCave.com.

Why an electronic book?

We live in the Information Age — an exciting time in the history of human civilization, in which technology rules supreme and continues to progress in leaps and bounds every minute of every day. For a multitude of reasons, more and more avid literary fans are opting to purchase e-books instead of paper books. The question from those not yet initiated into the world of electronic reading is simply: *Why?*

1. ***Price.*** An electronic title at Ellora's Cave Publishing and Cerridwen Press runs anywhere from 40% to 75% less than the cover price of the exact same title in paperback format. Why? Basic mathematics and cost. It is less expensive to publish an e-book (no paper and printing, no warehousing and shipping) than it is to publish a paperback, so the savings are passed along to the consumer.

2. ***Space.*** Running out of room in your house for your books? That is one worry you will never have with electronic books. For a low one-time cost, you can purchase a handheld device specifically designed for e-reading. Many e-readers have large, convenient screens for viewing. Better yet, hundreds of titles can be stored within your new library — on a single microchip. There are a variety of e-readers from different manufacturers. You can also read e-books on your PC or laptop computer. (Please note that Ellora's Cave does not endorse any specific brands.

You can check our websites at www.ellorascave.com or www.cerridwenpress.com for information we make available to new consumers.)

3. *Mobility.* Because your new e-library consists of only a microchip within a small, easily transportable e-reader, your entire cache of books can be taken with you wherever you go.

4. *Personal Viewing Preferences.* Are the words you are currently reading too small? Too large? Too... ANNOYING? Paperback books cannot be modified according to personal preferences, but e-books can.

5. *Instant Gratification.* Is it the middle of the night and all the bookstores near you are closed? Are you tired of waiting days, sometimes weeks, for bookstores to ship the novels you bought? Ellora's Cave Publishing sells instantaneous downloads twenty-four hours a day, seven days a week, every day of the year. Our webstore is never closed. Our e-book delivery system is 100% automated, meaning your order is filled as soon as you pay for it.

Those are a few of the top reasons why electronic books are replacing paperbacks for many avid readers.

As always, Ellora's Cave and Cerridwen Press welcome your questions and comments. We invite you to email us at Comments@ellorascave.com or write to us directly at Ellora's Cave Publishing Inc., 1056 Home Avenue, Akron, OH 44310-3502.

COMING TO A BOOKSTORE NEAR YOU!

ELLORA'S CAVE

Bestselling Authors Tour

erridwen, the Celtic Goddess of wisdom, was the muse who brought inspiration to storytellers and those in the creative arts. Cerridwen Press encompasses the best and most innovative stories in all genres of today's fiction. Visit our site and discover the newest titles by talented authors who still get inspired - much like the ancient storytellers did, once upon a time.

Discover for yourself why readers can't get enough
of the multiple award-winning publisher
Ellora's Cave.

Whether you prefer e-books or paperbacks,
be sure to visit EC on the web at
www.ellorascave.com

for an erotic reading experience that will leave you
breathless.